Jamie stood by the desk, his hand on the lamp. "You aren't afraid of me, are you?"

Susan considered the question. It was the first time it had occurred to her that she might have reasons to be afraid; but the accumulated facts suddenly washed over her and took her breath away. The coincidental meeting, the discovery of the old man's body, the interest of this stranger in her affairs. . . . And now her presence alone and unprotected, in his room when they should have been reporting a murder.

"No," she said, with perfect truth. "Should I be? What do you have in mind?"

Also by Elizabeth Peters
published by Tor Books

THE CAMELOT CAPER
THE DEAD SEA CIPHER
DIE FOR LOVE
JACKAL'S HEAD
LION IN THE VALLEY
THE MUMMY CASE
STREET OF THE FIVE MOONS
SUMMER OF THE DRAGON
TROJAN GOLD

ELIZABETH PETERS

LEGEND IN GREEN VELVET

TOR

A TOM DOHERTY ASSOCIATES BOOK
NEW YORK

LEGEND IN GREEN VELVET
Copyright © 1976 by Elizabeth Peters

A TOR Book
Published by Tom Doherty Associates, Inc.
49 West 24 Street
New York, NY 10010

ISBN: 0-812-50750-9   Can. ISBN: 0-812-50751-7

First Tor edition: March 1989

Printed in the United States of America

0 9 8 7 6 5 4 3 2 1

To Mother
best friend, severest critic,
fellow traveller, and all-round inspiration

Foreword

With the exception of certain historical personages, all the characters in this book are wholly fictitious and bear no resemblance to any persons living or dead. A similar statement might be made in regard to many of the places described in these pages; for the Central Highlands are no longer isolated from the world of tourism and industry. A gothic villain could not pursue the heroine far without being run down by a truck, or tripped up by a pack of officious Boy Scouts. I feel no need to apologize for this minor departure from vulgar reality in a tale, and a literary form, which is inherently fantastic. Nor, I feel sure, need I apologize to Scottish readers for an occasional note of levity. Contrary to the opinion of the ignorant, no one has a finer sense of humor than a Scot; and I should know, because I am a quarter Scot myself.

Chapter 1

The gravestones were black.

Jetty crosses, ebon urns and tablets, sable angels folding sable wings over somber stones. . . . A Devil's graveyard; a cemetery of Satanists.

In actual fact Susan did not find the sight at all sinister. In the mellow summer sunshine, nestled cozily among emerald grass, the black stones had a certain bizarre charm. As Susan looked down on the cemetery she felt not a single premonitory shiver. Which only goes to prove that premonitions, like history, are more or less bunk.

She had an excellent view from one of the bridges that arch superbly over the gorge separating the lower section of Edinburgh from the high ridge of the old city. Edinburgh is three different cities: the drab, sprawling suburbs of the recent past; the elegant, formal squares of the eighteenth-century town; and, dominating the skyline, the tangled closes and wynds of the ancient capital. From the heights of Castle Rock, more than four hundred feet above sea level, the old streets slant down toward the foot of Arthur's Seat; and the mile-long slopes are crowded with buildings whose turreted, gabled, and towered roofs form a skyline unsurpassed in any city of the world.

Susan had fallen in love with it that morning, when she came out of the station after the all-night train ride from London. The weather had been fine; the stone battlements of Edinburgh Castle were outlined against a translucent sky, and the tall old houses reached up out of lavender shadows like elderly aristocrats stretching toward the warmth of the sun. Susan was staring bemusedly out the taxi window when the driver's sour voice shattered her reverie.

"Aye, aye, gawk awa'," he remarked disagreeably. "Rich, spoiled Americans, wasting guid siller on pleasure and paying nae heed to the struggles of an oppressed people. . . ."

"I've come here to work," Susan said, with perfect good humor; it would take more than a grumpy taxi driver to destroy her mood on such a morning, and the man's accent delighted her. "I'm an archaeology student, and I expect to spend the summer on my hands and knees, digging. And living in a leaky tent. At least I assume it will leak. I'm not getting paid, either. I saved the plane fare by baby-sitting and doing housework last summer. Who's oppressing you?"

It was tantamount to removing a plug. The tirade continued all the way down Princes Street. When they turned into the neatly squared-off streets in the "new" city, Susan interrupted. She suspected that the lecture would have continued indefinitely if she had not.

"You're a Scottish Nationalist," she said, pleased. "How fascinating!"

"Fascinating!" The driver's voice expressed ineffable scorn; no one in the world can express it better than a Scot. "Five meelion souls writhing in the mailed fist o' Sassenach oppression, and ye call it—"

"We broke away from the Sassenachs ourselves," Susan reminded him. "What are you mad at me for? I don't know much about the subject—at least I didn't, until a few minutes ago—but you ought to expect an American to be sympathetic about home rule."

The driver was silent for a moment, maneuvering the car through a crowded intersection.

"Aye, weel," he said thoughtfully. "That's true. Nae doot I've been a wee bit unfair. But ye'd be better off studying some moder-r-rn history, instead of delving in the past."

"But it's Scottish history we're digging up," Susan said. "Macbeth and Duncan—the Picts—Robert the Bruce. . . . Aren't you proud of your history?"

It was an unfortunate question, for it started another lecture that lasted until they drew up in front of the small, unpretentious hotel Susan had selected to fit her limited budget. The driver was in a better mood by then, however; he gave Susan a meager smile as he turned to open the door for her, and when she offered him a tip, he waved it away.

"A wor-r-king pairson should not be extravagant," he announced. "Keep yer siller, lass. And apply yer mind to serious matters."

Eight hours later, leaning on the parapet of the bridge, Susan smiled as she remembered the conversation. It had been an engaging introduction to Edinburgh; and the ensuing time had confirmed her affection for the city and its inhabitants. She had stopped in the hotel only long enough to unpack. The streets drew her, and she had been walking ever since, with a short stop for lunch. Her legs ached from the unaccustomed climbing.

Like most tourists, she had headed first of all for the old city and the Royal Mile; but, unlike the majority of visitors, she knew all the famous landmarks and the stories connected with them. She had been infatuated with Scotland for as long as she could remember. It

was one of those unaccountable attractions, for to the
best of her knowledge she had not a drop of Scottish
blood in her veins. She liked to think of herself as a
reasonable romantic, who could enjoy the legends and
traditions without believing in their reality; and she told
herself firmly that it was not some mystical theory of
déjà vu, but rather prolonged study, that made every
view seem familiar to her doting eyes. From the Castle,
through Lawnmarket, the High Street and Canongate,
the thoroughfare called the Royal Mile slopes down to
Holyroodhouse, the palace that has housed so many of
Scotland's ill-fated kings—and her most ill-fated queen.
Mary, Queen of Scots, the femme fatale of royalty—
how many men had died for her legendary charm? Rizzio, her favorite, stabbed to death under her very
eyes—and one of the murderers Mary's own husband,
Darnley. . . . Darnley himself, the victim of one of history's most mysterious unsolved crimes. . . . Bothwell,
Mary's third husband, probably the murderer of her
second husband, dying mad in a Danish prison. . . .
And the young men who had conspired to rescue Mary
from her prison, and who had perished horribly under
the ax and on the rack.

Mary's was not the only ghost that haunted Holyroodhouse. Prince Charles Edward, the Bonnie Prince
Charlie of romance, had danced at the palace in the
days of his short-lived triumph, before the Stuart cause
died forever in the bloody shambles of Culloden. His
would be one of the brighter spirits to roam Holyroodhouse; the cause had burned high with hope at that time,
and the fatal Stuart charm had run strongly in Charles
Edward. Tall and handsome, crowned with ruddy-gold
hair, he must have been a gallant figure in the kilt and
plaid he wore to please his Highland supporters.

Satisfied, but not surfeited, with her day of romance,
Susan stared dreamily down at the black graveyards of
Edinburgh and wondered why they were that color.

Smoke and smog and soot? Probably. But the problem was purely academic. She was much more interested in the prospect of tea. No wonder the British needed that extra meal; they deserved it, if they habitually walked as far as she had walked that day.

Finding a teashop was not as easy as she had expected. It was Sunday, and many stores were closed. Susan was finally driven back to Princes Street, and the lounge of one of the hotels. She felt out of place in its quiet respectability; apparently few of the younger, student types took tea in such dull surroundings. Hers were the only jeans to be seen, and her scuffed sneakers looked shabbier than ever. She put them under the chair, pushed her brown hair back from her face, and surreptitiously studied the other guests. For the most part they were well dressed and elderly. A few of the men were wearing the kilt, which delighted Susan's romantic soul. She was not inclined to linger, though; summoning the waiter, she paid her bill, with a silent groan at its size, and escaped into the crowds of Princes Street. This would be her last visit to a big hotel; she couldn't afford the prices, even if she had enjoyed the stuffy atmosphere.

In this northern summer, daylight lingered late. A few souvenir shops were still open; tourists, frustrated at their inability to spend money elsewhere, crowded the counters buying cheap dolls dressed in kilts and bonnets, tartan placemats, tartan coasters, tartan scarves. Susan passed them by. She had no money for souvenirs, even if she had been attracted by the omnipresent and often inappropriate tartan. She was lucky to be here at all.

As she walked along, savoring the view of the battlemented old city and the long green park that stretched at its foot, she gloated, again on her luck. If her history prof hadn't happened to know Dr. Campbell. . . . If her grades hadn't been so good. . . . If she hadn't spent all those evenings baby-sitting her professor's wretched brats. . . . The professor's recommendation had been sufficient. Campbell had accepted her services for the summer. Of course, she told herself, with what she fondly believed to be adult cynicism—why shouldn't Campbell accept them? She was trained and able, and she was working almost for free. A cot in a leaky tent and a few meals, that was all Campbell had to offer. Everything else was on her, and summers spent scrubbing other peoples' floors and amusing their spoiled children had produced barely enough money for a cheap excursion fare. The most expensive part of the trip was the week she had planned to spend in Edinburgh before the dig officially began. It was pure extravagance, but she had to have it; Scotland had always fascinated her, she had been in love with the legend for years. If she counted her pennies carefully, there would be enough money for a few cheap bus tours. The lovely ruined abbeys, Scott's home, Carlisle. . . . And no more posh teas in expensive hotels, Susan told herself sternly.

The weather was so lovely, and the light so good, that she decided to sit on a bench in the park and read for a while. The stuffy little room in her hotel held no charms; it was just a place to sleep in, and she recalled the single overhead bulb pessimistically. Why didn't hotels furnish decent reading lamps? Presumably because most people didn't read. But what else were they supposed to do in a hotel, especially on a Sunday evening in Edinburgh, where the Sabbath was properly observed?

The park, a mile-long stretch of greenery, lay at the foot of the ridge on which the old city had been built. Susan found a bench and opened her book. It was Professor Campbell's *magnum opus* on Scottish prehistory, in a convenient Penguin edition. She had bought it in London, and meant to know it by heart by the time she met Campbell.

She was unable to concentrate on brochs and vitrified forts for long, however; the changing light on the castle ramparts and the stream of people passing by were too fascinating. Carrying the book, she strolled down the path toward the Royal Scottish Academy. As she drew near she heard voices, raised in impassioned speech, and saw several small groups of people collecting around the orators. Apparently the open space beside the Academy was an unofficial forum for aggrieved citizens, like Chicago's "Bughouse Square" and London's Hyde Park. Only one of the speakers had succeeded in attracting a crowd of any size; it was large enough to conceal him from Susan's meager sixty-two inches of height. Intrigued by this evidence of popularity and by the broad grins on the faces of the people on the fringes of the audience, Susan made her way through the onlookers until she could see the speaker. Then she stopped, frozen by a chill the black gravestones of Edinburgh had failed to produce. The orator was a tall, elderly man, with shaggy hair and an unkempt gray beard. To Susan he was more than that. He was a ghost that had haunted her adolescent dreams.

Shadows of the historic dead had companioned Susan's childhood, not replacing normal friendships, but adding a rich and secret dimension to life. It had to be secret; the other kids would have laughed at her if they had suspected the extent of her preoccupation with the past, and Susan couldn't risk that, for mockery would have destroyed the fragile ghosts. She ran and swam and rode her bike as energetically as her friends, but her daydreams were peopled with shadowy warriors and princes. In high school, while her girl friends were swooning over football players and TV heroes, she hid in the heather with Bonnie Prince Charlie, and allowed him to kiss her hand before he left her forever. In junior high, when the other girls had crushes on teachers and Scout leaders, she had wept over the tragedy of Mary

Stuart, and hated Mary's enemy, the fierce Calvinist
preacher John Knox. An old woodcut had given her a
picture of the man—hard, fanatical eyes, jutting nose,
long, stringy beard. Knox was a bigot. Mary was gay
and frivolous—Catholic—and female. Any one of these
would have sufficed to damn her in Knox's eyes, and he
had not been reticent about expressing his opinions.

As she grew older and wiser, Susan came to feel that
Mary had perhaps been more sinning than sinned
against, less romantic than slightly stupid; but she had
never forgotten her dislike of Knox—who had been in
his grave for hundreds of years, and who would have
been supremely contemptuous of Susan's opinion in any
case. Susan had dreamed about him when she was thir-
teen—dreamed that she was cowering under the thun-
dering denunciations Knox hurled at poor Mary. One
night she had wakened, howling with terror, and her
mother had forbidden history books for a week.

And there, by the Royal Scottish Academy was Knox
himself, his eyes blazing with self-righteous hatred,
his voice hurling forth anathemas in the thick Scottish
burr Susan had always attributed to the nightmare
figure.

The impression lasted only for a second. The orator
didn't really look like the old woodcut of Knox; he had
a long beard and wild eyes, but there the resemblance
ended. On closer inspection he was rather pathetic. His
kilt was threadbare, the once brilliant colors faded. The
long beard was gray, and the man's face was lean. He
looked hungry.

Susan found the speech hard to follow, it was so bur-
dened with rolling r's, but she gathered that the patri-
arch was discoursing on politics rather than religion.
"Another Nationalist," she thought, obscurely relieved.

The woman standing next to Susan said something to

her escort, and they both laughed. Then the woman turned to Susan.

"Auld Tammas is one of the sights of Edinburgh," she said, with the casual friendliness Susan had found to be characteristic of the city. "There's nae harm in him."

Susan realized that her initial start had been observed.

"Sure, I understand," she said, smiling. "Poor old guy. He's a Nationalist, isn't he?"

The woman chuckled.

"No, no, the S.N.P. is too respectable for auld Tammas. He talks about bloody revolution and a regiment storming Buckingham Palace! Poor auld daft body, he wouldna hurt a fly."

She didn't bother to lower her voice. The orator's bearded face turned in her direction. Then Tammas stopped speaking. His eyes bulged.

Susan looked again at her neighbor. She was a plump, middle-aged housewife; there was nothing in her appearance, or in that of her lean, sandy-haired husband, to explain Tammas's reaction.

The woman cupped her hands around her mouth.

"Speak up, Tammas," she called. "Let's hear about the King o'er the Water, and the bonnie White Rose!"

But Tammas was finished. When Susan looked in his direction she saw that he had disappeared.

The disappointed crowd started to disperse. The friendly woman gave Susan a wink and a grin as she took her husband's arm and walked away. Susan decided she might as well go back to the hotel. It was a long walk, and she was no longer in the mood for oratory.

She had gone scarcely a block when something caught at her purse, which was slung over her shoulder on a long strap. Making an instinctive grab at it, she dropped her book, and then let out a yelp of surprise. Towering over her was the lean form of auld Tammas.

"Hush, lassie," he whispered, scowling hideously. "Have ye nae wits?"

His hand was in her purse.

Susan tugged at the strap. She was not frightened; there were a number of people close by, and the episode seemed ludicrous rather than alarming. Tammas stepped back, withdrawing his hand. He shook his head disapprovingly.

"Weemen! They're nae suited for serious business. I've said it again and again, but they willna heed me."

And with this sentiment, which might have come from the great Knox himself, he turned on his heel and strode away.

As Susan stood gaping after him, a boy in faded jeans touched her arm. He looked about twenty, and his accents were those of a native.

"It's only auld daft Tammas, miss. He wouldna hurt a fly. Here's your wee buik. . . ."

Susan took her copy of Campbell's masterpiece. She was getting tired of hearing about the harmlessness of auld Tammas.

"He might not hurt a fly, but he scared me half to death," she snapped. "He was trying to pick my pocket. My purse, I mean."

Her companion shook his head, smiling tolerantly.

"Not auld Tammas. But if you're frightened, I could walk wi' you to wherever you might be going."

With some difficulty Susan discouraged the young man and walked on. She hadn't seen Tammas take anything from her purse, but he might be more skilled at Fagin's trade than he seemed. There was no point in trying to check now; the purse was crammed full, and the only way she could be sure nothing was missing was to turn it out onto the floor, which she did as soon as she got back to her room.

The pile of debris that emerged was amazing. For the past two days she had been adding to the collection; but it didn't take her long to find that the important objects were still there. Apparently Tammas had not palmed so much as a penny.

Relieved, Susan sat back on her heels and began to sort through the pile in the hope of eliminating some of it. She had accumulated a lot of miscellaneous papers—pamphlets, receipts, notes, addresses. She sorted them, meaning to copy the pertinent data into the notebook she had bought for the purpose—which was, for some reason, never accessible when she needed it. It took some time for her to discover that, although nothing had been taken from her purse, something had been added.

It was a note, written on ordinary lined paper, but the penmanship was quite unlike her own hasty scrawl, or the casual writing on the other papers. It was an exquisitely precise, old-fashioned hand; and the words were just as extraordinary.

> The bird, the beste, the fisch eke in the see
> They lyve in fredome everich in his kynd;
> And I a man, and lakkith libertee.

Susan turned the paper over. The back was blank. When she looked at the verse again, it was still there; somehow she had half expected to find she had imagined it.

She recognized the lines, of course. Her years of absorption in the romances of Scotland had not been wasted, and this was one of the most romantic of all the legends. The plaintive prisoner's lament had been written by a king—James I of Scotland, held captive by the English through most of his childhood. The "King's Quair," written in captivity, was a love poem as well as a lament. Peering pensively from his barred window, James had seen a lady walking in the garden:

> And therewith kest I doun my eye ageyne,
> Quhare as I sawe, walking under the tour,
> Full secretly new cummyn hir to pleyne,
> The fairest or the freschest yong floure
> That ever I sawe, me thoght, before that houre.

The fair young flower was Joan Beaufort, a niece of the English king, and when James was released he brought her home to Scotland with him as his bride. At least, so the legend ran.

But what on earth had prompted auld daft Tammas to give her this fragment of poetry?

She hadn't the slightest doubt that it came from Tammas. No one else was crazy enough to do such a thing. It wouldn't have surprised her to find that Tammas was in the habit of pressing tracts or political pamphlets on unwilling recipients; what surprised her was the nature of the extract. Was this the old man's way of indicating respectful admiration? It was a love poem, in part. . . .

The idea was obscurely embarrassing. It was also ridiculous. Tammas would have quoted the pertinent part of the poem, instead of the lines that mourned a prisoner's lack of freedom.

Smiling sourly, Susan added the scrap of paper to the articles she meant to keep, though not in her overcrowded purse. It would make an amusing souvenir—an example of harmless Scottish daftness. Perhaps auld Tammas did this to many visitors. She would never know what had inspired the contribution—a fancied resemblance, perhaps? Maybe she looked like Tammas's long-lost love, a brown-haired lassie with wide-set blue eyes and a turned-up nose. . . . Susan let her imagination run riot.

II

Auld Tammas wasn't the only inhabitant of Edinburgh to feel an interest in a brown-haired lassie with wide-set blue eyes, but the others did not express their sentiments in archaic poetry. Susan wondered how the Scots had acquired their reputation for aloofness. Edinburgh was one of the friendliest cities she had ever visited. Perhaps "friendly" was too cool a word for some of the suggestions she received; but she fended them off with the ease of long practice, rejecting the pressing invitations of tourists as she ignored the hopeful smiles of the local lads. The real world would claim her soon enough, when she reported for hard labor at the dig; in the meantime she found ample companionship in the shadows that walked with her through the old streets: Graham of Claverhouse, the gallant Montrose, Burns, Stevenson, and Scott—and, swaggering in kilt and laces and bottle-green velvet, Bonnie Prince Charlie himself. So what if the Bonnie Prince had died a fat, dissipated drunkard? So what if the clansmen who had sacrificed their lives and fortunes for his cause were not chivalrous gentlemen in kilts, but unwashed, illiterate cattle rustlers? The legend of the laughing, fair-haired prince and his gallant Highlanders was immortal.

Even the bitter ending of the legend had its melancholy glamour. It had ended far to the north, on the bloody field of Culloden, and in the lonely glens where the prince had wandered for months before escaping to Skye disguised as the servant maid of the dauntless Flora MacDonald. There was a price on his head; but it was never claimed, although the impoverished Scots who hid the royal fugitive might have won immunity as well as gold for betraying him. Susan wondered if he had ever felt remorse for the slaughtered clansmen of Culloden, for the ravaged glens and burned houses that

marked the trail of English victory. Remorse was not a
royal weakness; but maybe that was why Charles Edward drank so much in later years—to blot out the gray
faces of the dead.

Her preoccupation with history didn't prevent Susan
from enjoying human contacts. She struck up conversations with shopkeepers and chambermaids, and debated Nationalist aspirations with the night clerk at the
hotel. He was a shy, gawky boy with a terrible case of
acne, who would not have interested Susan even if she
had not been involved with her royal ghosts, but she
was too kind to reject his stammering attentions altogether. She discussed her sightseeing plans with him,
and got some good advice on bus tours. Although she
was drawn to the northern glens and the battlefields
where her heroes had played out their dramas, she decided to postpone Culloden and Killiecrankie until after
she had gone north. They could be reached more conveniently from the dig. The time in Edinburgh was short
enough as it was and could be more productively spent
in exploring the border regions.

On Thursday, having signed up for a bus trip to Carlisle and Gretna Green, Susan arrived early at the terminal off St. Andrew's Square. The bus had not yet
come, but there were a few other early birds waiting in
the bay designated as Tour Number Twenty. Susan
joined the queue and leaned against the rail, reading
her brochure. Lunch at Lockerbie, tea at Hawick. . . .
Fifteen minutes at Gretna Green, the goal of so many
eloping English couples in the eighteenth century; forty-
five minutes at Carlisle, the old border capital. People
eat and drink too much, Susan thought contemptuously.
She would have forsaken tea for another hour at Carlisle.

At nine forty the bus arrived; at nine forty-five on
the dot the doors opened, and the driver began to col-

lect the tickets. There were not many passengers. Apparently this was one of the less popular tours.

Susan found a window seat and watched the other tourists trickle onto the bus with more than casual interest. Like most romantics, she believed firmly in the mysterious machinations of fate. The wheel of fortune, in its seemingly random spin, was about to turn up a seat mate for her; and that chance acquaintance might be . . . anyone. A fumbling boor or a crashing bore; a lifelong friend or a lover; a mysterious stranger evading the villains of the Black Stone, a spy carrying the plans of the secret Naval Treaty, a Scottish chief descended from the MacDonald of MacDonald. . . .

Or a man like the one who was now coming down the aisle.

Tall, dark, handsome; his strong, bronzed throat bared by the open collar of his shirt; the muscles on his brawny arms standing out like steel bands. . . .

Susan took a firm grip on herself. He was probably a used-car salesman. Or an accountant. Mysterious strangers, if they existed at all, did not look like mysterious strangers. They looked like accountants, or used-car salesmen.

The sleek black head turned, and the dark eyes looked straight into hers. The corners of the long, straight mouth quirked in a faint, enigmatic smile.

"Is this seat taken?" inquired the stranger.

"No," said Susan. "Uh—you aren't by any chance a used-car salesman, are you?"

"Sorry." Settling himself, the stranger gave her a surprised look. "Are you in the market?"

"Oh, no . . ."

The stranger threw his jacket over the back of the unoccupied seat in front, leaned back, folded his arms, and studied Susan thoughtfully. His regard was intense. Susan's eyes fell.

"Don't tell me," he said. "Let me guess. Your father

is a used-car salesman, so you instinctively trust the breed. Or was your ex-boyfriend a used-car salesman? You instinctively mistrust—"

"No, no."

"Is No all you can say?"

"No . . ." Susan bit her lip. Her companion grinned, showing even white teeth.

"Let's start again," he suggested. "The name is Ed Jackson. I'm thirty-two years old, six feet one inch tall, and I weigh one hundred and ninety. I drink and smoke and. . . . But since I'm leaving Edinburgh tonight, you won't be unduly inconvenienced by my various sins. I'm kind to my mother, and I'm not such bad company when you get to know me; so why don't you relax? My intentions are necessarily honorable; I picked you because you're a pretty girl, and a fellow-American, and— I hope *you* aren't a used-car salesman?"

"No," Susan said.

Her companion's smile broadened, and Susan laughed.

"I'm an archaeology student," she said. "And a history buff."

"Oh, yeah? I chose well, then. I'm an ignorant tourist, myself; you can tell me all about Scotland."

"Don't get me started," Susan warned.

"I'll bet you're putting me on." Jackson's dark eyes looked into hers. "You're too young and pretty to be an expert on anything as dry as history."

"Ask me anything. And skip the flattery, if you don't mind."

"Okay," Jackson smiled. "How about this Bonnie Prince Charlie character? I keep hearing about him. Who was he, and what's his claim to fame?"

Susan studied him thoughtfully. His smile was very attractive—and very confident. She decided to give him both barrels. He had it coming, after that corny compliment.

"His grandfather was James the Second," she began, "King of England and Scotland. James was a Catholic, and the English didn't want a Catholic dynasty, so they kicked him out. It was a nice, bloodless revolution; James fled with his family, and the English invited William and Mary to come over and rule them. Mary was James's daughter by an earlier marriage; but she had married a Protestant, you see—a Dutch prince, William of Orange. When their line ran out, it was succeeded by the Hanoverian kings, from Germany. They were distant connections of the British royal house, and, most important, they were Protestants too. But some people believed that the Stuarts, who were in exile in Europe, were still the rightful rulers. James the Second had a son, James the Third, popularly known as the Old Pretender. *His* son, the Young Pretender, was Prince Charles Edward—Bonnie Prince Charlie.

"In 1715, James the Third came over to Scotland and tried to raise a rebellion against the Hanoverian kings. Some of the clans rose, but the rebellion failed, and James went scuttling back to France. So, in 1745, Charles Edward tried. His father was still alive, but he was too old to do any fighting. Charles Edward was young and handsome and very charming; he raised his standard in the Highlands, and a lot of the clans joined him. They didn't like the English much anyway. They were independent characters, hard to discipline, and there was a lot of rivalry among the different clans. But at the beginning they were united by their loyalty to Prince Charles. They were absolutely sensational fighters; when they charged, screaming in Gaelic and waving their huge, two-handed claymores, seasoned troops broke and fled.

"So, the rebellion went well at first. The Castle at Edinburgh held out against Charles, but he occupied the city and prepared for an invasion of England. He had only six thousand men. He was counting on the English people rising to support him, you see. They didn't. They didn't trust the Scots, and they were perfectly satisfied with their dull German rulers.

"Finding no help from the English, Charles's army turned back. He didn't want to. They say he wept, in angry frustration, when his council insisted. And, in the long run, he was probably right, and they were wrong. Things couldn't have gone any worse than they did in that disastrous retreat. The army began to disintegrate. The chiefs bickered among themselves. And the English army was in hot pursuit.

"The final battle was at a place called Culloden. The Scots were cut to pieces. The English army massacred the survivors and then spread out through the northern glens, hanging and burning. For the next few months Charles was a fugitive, hidden by his loyal supporters. Finally he escaped to the island of Skye, where he was fairly safe, but he soon realized that he had no chance of raising another army. English retaliation had been brutally effective. So Charles finally left for France. He died years later, a drunken, disappointed old man. And Scotland was ruined. The clan system was destroyed. It was a criminal offense to wear a kilt, or the clan tartan. But the romantic legend survived the Stuart cause; and people remember the gallant, handsome prince, not the tired old failure."

Jackson shook his head admiringly.

"You win, honey. You really do know it cold. And you tell it very well."

Susan had heard that line before, but this time it really sounded like more than a line. Not only did Ed Jackson let her talk, he asked intelligent questions and made meaningful comments. Like most women, Susan was unaccustomed to the dizzying pleasure of lecturing to an appreciative audience. It went to her head like Scotch. By the time they reached Penicuik, she had decided Ed was a wonderful guy. AT Moffat (ten-min-

ute rest stop), she was regretting his imminent departure from Scotland; and as they strolled the streets of
Lockerbie after lunch, she made no objection when he
put his arm around her.

"I'm glad you were on this tour," he said, tracing
the curve of her waist with experienced fingers. "It's a
bummer otherwise. Why did you sign up for this one?"

"I told you, I'm a history buff. I've always been crazy
about Scotland."

"A good-looking chick like you shouldn't waste her
time on history."

"I suppose most chicks love that old line," Susan
said coolly.

Jackson laughed and tightened his arm.

"Don't stiffen up like that. I was kidding you. I admire women with brains. Go ahead, dazzle me with
data. Sing me songs of old Scotland. Quote from
Burns."

"I'm not wild about Burns," Susan admitted. "And
I only sing when I'm full of beer."

Jackson took her chin in his lean brown fingers and
turned her face up to his.

"Come on, Sue, don't hold a grudge. Smile. You
have a cute smile. I'll quote you some poetry. I had to
learn a poem once, in school. 'Scots, wha hae wi' Wallace bled. . . .' If I knew who Wallace was, and why
he bled, and what 'wha hae' means, I could render it
with more feeling."

His smile was irresistible. Susan relaxed, and felt the
hard muscles of his arm tighten in response.

"Go ahead," he said coaxingly. "Lecture me. From
you I love it."

"You deserve a lecture," Susan said. " 'Wha hae'
means 'who have,' and don't tell me you didn't know
it. Wallace was the leader of the rebellion against England in the late fourteenth century. He was finally
caught and executed, horribly—hanged, drawn and

quartered, with all the frills—but his example and his martyrdom inspired the Scots to deep on fighting, and he was succeeded by Robert the Bruce, who finally won. There, that wasn't so bad, was it?''

"You are admirably succinct," said Jackson. "I wish my English lit prof had been that easy to follow."

They turned back toward the bus stop.

"You were an English major?" Susan asked.

"How can you ask, after I've just demonstrated my ignorance? I might have liked it, though, if I'd had a good teacher. I kind of like poetry when I'm in the right mood."

"And are you in the right mood?"

"Oh, definitely."

"Naughty, naughty," said Susan, sliding away from his exploring hands. "The bus driver is watching us. Come on, we're the last ones."

To put him in his place, she quoted poetry at him all the way to Carlisle. He listened with apparent meekness, but every now and then a spark flared in the dark eyes that were focused so intently on her moving lips. The light might have been one of amusement, for Susan didn't spare him; she gave him Burns at his broadest Scots, and bombarded him with the archaic accents of Henryson and Dunbar.

> Pray we thairfoir, quhill we are in this lyfe,
> For four thingis; the first, fra sin remufe;
> The secund is fra all weir and stryfe;
> The third is perfite cheritie and lufe. . . .

"What a beautiful thought," said Jackson.

Hawick was the tea stop. Jackson refused tea. He stood by, fidgeting, while Susan ate a few cookies. Then he suggested a walk.

"We've got less than half an hour," she protested breathlessly as he pulled her along.

"That's long enough," said Jackson.

She had a good idea what he meant; her suspicions were confirmed when he led her into a little local park and sought out the shelter of a clump of bushes.

Susan's protests were admittedly perfunctory. She was afraid of missing the bus, but that was her only fear. Ed Jackson wasn't the type to force his attentions on an unwilling partner. He didn't have to; women probably lined up outside his door.

This bland assumption received a rude shock when Jackson caught her in a bruising embrace and bent her head back over his arm. The kiss had no redeeming qualities. It hurt. The man's strength was terrifying, and Susan received an impression of controlled rage that frightened her even more.

After a brief but hectic interlude Jackson released her so suddenly that she staggered. He dropped to his knees and began gathering up the contents of her purse, which were scattered on the ground.

"I'm sorry," he muttered. "Women don't usually have quite that effect on me. . . . Sit down, Susan. There's a bench over there. I'll get your things."

Walking unsteadily, Susan made her way to the designated bench. Numbly she watched Jackson crawl around in search of her possessions. She could feel bruises coming up on her arms and body.

Finally he joined her, his face averted, and offered her the purse with a silent, placatory gesture. Susan took it and located her compact. Her makeup was definitely in need of repair; but for a few seconds she simply stared into the mirror, making no move to restore the damage.

She saw a familiar face—the rosy complexion rather paler than usual, the blue eyes very wide under the curving dark brows. The generous lips were parted, showing the uneven front tooth that she had chipped falling off her bike at the age of ten. Her nose was shiny. There was a blackhead on her chin.

Was this the face of a woman who drove men mad? The face that might have launched a thousand ships and burned the topless towers of Ilium?

"Hell, no," said Susan regretfully.

Jackson turned.

"What did you say?"

"Nothing."

"Are you angry?"

"No," Susan said absently. She applied fresh lipstick.

"Sue, I don't know how to apologize."

"It's okay." Susan stood up. "We'll have to run."

They were not the last ones to board the bus after all. The episode had taken less time than Susan would have believed possible.

Ashkirk, Selkirk, Stow. . . . Jackson was silent except for brief comments on the scenery. Eskbank and Gilmerton passed on schedule. They were due in Edinburgh at eight thirty, and it was only a few minutes after that when the bus pulled into its slot in the depot.

"How about some supper?" Jackson asked tentatively.

"No, thanks."

"You *are* angry."

"No. Just tired."

"My train doesn't leave till midnight. . . ."

"You'll have to entertain yourself," Susan said firmly. "Really, Ed, I'm not mad, but—what's the point? You're leaving, we'll never see each other again. I'm not the twenty-four-hour-type girl."

"Okay. No hard feelings?"

They shook hands, somewhat absurdly, at the entrance to the bus depot. Susan went off at a brisk walk; she did not look back. She knew Jackson was standing still, staring after her.

As she trudged the long blocks to her hotel, she wondered what idiotic instinct had made her reject Jackson's offer. A long, boring evening stretched ahead of her. So the guy had made a pass at her. It had happened before, and she knew how to handle it. He was good company, when he wasn't playing caveman. Why hadn't she accepted his invitation to dinner?

Mumbling discontentedly, Susan reached her hotel. The shabby, dim lobby had never looked less inviting. The hotel had no dining room. She wouldn't even be able to get a cup of coffee. She stamped up the stairs. Her room was on the third floor and naturally there was no lift. She opened the door—and stood transfixed on the threshold.

The room was a shambles. The bedclothes were in a tumbled heap on the floor. Her suitcase was open; the contents had been spilled out onto the carpet. Every drawer in the dresser hung open.

At first Susan was too stunned even to swear. That facility soon returned, and she let out a string of profanity that would have surprised her mother back home in Illinois. She stormed back down the stairs and burst into the lobby. It was deserted except for the clerk and another man, who turned to stare at her as she ran in.

"What are you doing here?" Susan demanded furiously. "How dare you follow me?" Without giving Jackson time to answer, she turned on the desk clerk. "I've been robbed! Somebody broke into my room! Get the police! Get the manager!"

The clerk's face flamed. Appalled at the transformation of his former friend into a screaming shrew, he gaped at her, his mouth ajar. It was Jackson who intervened.

"Calm down, Sue. What are you telling about?"

"My room is all torn up," said Susan, and burst into tears.

"Now, now," said Jackson, patting her on the back.

"But," said the clerk, recovering his voice, "this is serious. Do you mean to say—"

"We'd better have a look," Jackson interrupted.

Susan's tears were tears of rage. She gulped and regained control of herself.

"I left everything just the way I found it," she said.

"I canna leave the desk," said the clerk agitatedly. "This is ter-r-rible! I canna believe—"

Susan couldn't have gotten through the next ten minutes without Jackson. He extracted the clerk from the fancied security of the desk, located the manager—a grim-faced lady of indeterminate age—and swept the entire cavalcade up the stairs. The manager muttered all the way about hysterical lassies; but the sight of Susan's disheveled room silenced her. It seemed to infuriate Jackson; his face took on an expression that made Susan glad he wasn't angry with her.

"See what is missing," he said tightly.

"Not till the police come," Susan said.

The manager cleared her throat.

"You wouldna consider—"

"I want the police! You're supposed to report crimes," Susan exclaimed. "What's the matter with everybody? Don't you believe in obeying the law?"

The manager sighed. "No doubt you're right," she said.

The police were commendably swift, but there was a small gathering of spectators at the door of the room by the time a young constable made his appearance. He surveyed the room in a bored fashion and asked Susan what was missing.

Susan was calmer by then; she rather regretted her impulsive demand for the law.

"Nothing, really," she said apologetically. "I had my traveler's checks and my passport with me. I don't have any jewelry except my wristwatch—"

"Nothing missing," said the constable, making a note.

"Just a piece of paper," said Susan.

"Paper? A banknote, was it?"

"No. Just a—well, actually, it was a poem. Part of a poem."

Susan never knew what inspired her to make this unnecessary admission. If she had not been tired and upset, she would have known better. The expressions on the faces of her auditors warned her that she had made an error; and, as is so often the case, her attempts to clarify the situation only made matters worse.

"Four lines of a poem, written by James the First," she explained. "The 'King's Quair.' He wrote it when he was a prisoner in England—"

"Sue!" Jackson reached for her. Susan stepped back; her bruises still ached.

Jackson turned toward the constable. "She's upset," he explained, in a confidential, man-to-man tone.

"I'm upset, all right," Susan said loudly. "But I'm not *that* upset. You asked me what was missing and I told you. It's the only thing that's missing. It doesn't mean anything, I know that, but you asked me—"

They were all looking at her as if she had lost her mind. The manager's face wore a grim smile. Susan knew exactly what the woman was thinking, and resented it. But—she realized, with a stab of horror—there was no way of proving she hadn't done the damage herself. No one knew her; no one would stand up and swear that she wasn't that sort of person—a neurotic sensation seeker, possibly trying to extract damages from the hotel.

"I told you nothing valuable had been taken," she cried, turning from one strange face to the next. "If I were trying to pull something crooked, I could claim I'd been robbed, right? It was just a scrap of paper! That crazy old man gave it to me—the one who makes speeches outside the Academy Sunday evenings. Tammas, they call him. Maybe he wanted his poem back. Maybe—''

The constable closed his notebook.

The gesture was final. Susan felt as if the prison doors had been slammed.

''Now just a minute,'' Jackson said. ''Somebody got in here and searched her room; what's so funny about that? Edinburgh has its share of thieves, like any other city. The guy was unlucky. He didn't find anything worth stealing, so he got mad and messed the place up. Just an ordinary sneak thief. I suggest you try to figure out how he got in here, so you can prevent future trouble.''

''Right,'' Susan said eagerly. ''Did anybody suspicious come through the lobby today?''

She looked at the clerk. He shied violently.

''How could I tell? People come and go. . . .''

''What about the old man—Tammas. Has he been here?''

The young man hesitated. His eyes sought those of his employer. She snorted.

''So he was here. There's no harm in auld Tammas. He'd never take a penny that wasna his.''

''Who gives a damn about him?'' Jackson demanded impatiently. ''A smart crook would make sure he wasn't seen. Is there a back way into the hotel?''

Relieved to find the investigation seeking more normal channels, the constable took up the inquiry. It was established that there were several ways of getting into the hotel. There was no way of determining when the damage had been done; the chambermaid had finished her work by nine thirty, and no one had seen anything unusual. The constable recorded this unsatisfactory information, and then shut his notebook with a decisive snap.

"You'll be informed, miss," he told Susan. "But since nothing of value appears to be missing . . ."

"I understand," said Susan. "Thanks anyhow."

The constable departed, sweeping away the spectators as he went. The manager lingered. She fixed Susan with a stony stare.

"You'll be leaving on Saturday?"

"Yes," Susan said.

"I trust there will be no further disturbance," said the manager coldly.

When they had all gone, Jackson closed the door.

"Want me to help you clean up? Or do you want to go out? I'll bet you could use a drink."

"No. I'm bushed. I just want to go to bed. You had a nerve, following me," Susan added, with a faint smile, "but I'm glad you did. Thanks for backing me up."

"That's okay." Jackson took her hand. "I'm sorry this happened, Sue. Look, it's none of my business, but if they ask you again, I wouldn't say anything about that poem, or whatever it was."

"It sounds weird, I know," Susan said. "But it's the truth. That crazy old man—"

"Forget about him. Forget about your stolen poem. Forget the whole thing."

"Including you?"

"Including me," Jackson said quietly. "Good-bye, Susan."

He left. Susan sat down on the bed and contemplated the mess. She was trying to decide whether to swear or cry. One or two hard-fought tears did trickle down her cheeks; they were due in part to frustrated anger and in part to the destruction of a dream. Her shining romantic city had turned out to be no different from any other town. Thieves, and cold, suspicious faces, and frightening dark strangers. . . .

"So long, Bonnie Prince Charlie," said Susan sadly.

Chapter 2

Susan had planned to leave Edinburgh on Saturday. It would take at least a day, by erratic local buses, to reach the site of the dig, which was in an inaccessible part of the Central Highlands. When she went to bed on Thursday night, she had almost decided to anticipate her departure by twenty-four hours. It had been a thoroughly disillusioning day, and she couldn't decide whom she hated most—Ed Jackson, auld daft Tammas, the Edinburgh police, the manager, or the pimply desk clerk.

Morning brought sunshine and a rebirth of her normal optimism. After a hearty breakfast (included in the bill) she decided she wasn't going to be defeated by one—or two—unfortunate events. Besides, she had signed up for another bus trip that day.

At the bus station she promptly attached herself to a nice respectable Scottish couple who were on holiday, and she stuck close to them all day. Their cordial goodwill restored her spirits. The wife told Susan all about her children; the husband told Scottish jokes in an accent reverberant with rolling r's. By the time they

stopped at Dunfermline for tea, they were all on the
best of terms and Susan was moved to recite the interminable verses of "Sir Patrick Spens."

> The king sits in Dunfermline town,
> Drinking the bluid-red wine. . . .

The amused Scots cheered when she finished, and
plied her with food. A young pairson needed her nour-
ishment, especially a puir young lassie with her way to
make in the wor-r-rld.

Susan said good-bye to her new friends in Edinburgh
with genuine regret. Mr. and Mrs. Ferguson had given
her their address in Skye and urged her to drop in when
she was in the neighborhood. It was only seven o'clock
when they parted. Susan had no intention of going back
to the hotel so early, not on her last night in Edinburgh.
She had a peculiar-tasting hamburger in a cheap restaurant and then strolled along Princes Street, admiring
the illumination of the Castle, the Scott monument, and
other sights. It was a mild evening, and the streets were
still crowded. She decided to go up to the High Street.
She had never seen it at night.

It was a steep climb, over the bridge by the railroad
station and up the hill, but it was worth it. A new light-
ing system had been ingeniously designed to relieve the
darkness without destroying the atmosphere; it was not
at all difficult for Susan's imagination to carry her back
to 1745, and a handsome Stuart prince holding court at
Holyroodhouse. Or farther back in time, to 1567, the
year that was to prove so fatal to the romantic Queen
of Scots. . . .

There was no barrier now to mark the place where
the High Street became the Canongate, which led on
down the slope to the Stuart palace; but in 1567 it had
been marked by an actual gate, part of the walls that
defended Edinburgh against invading armies. The Neth-

erbow Port was shut at night, and thirty-two men of the
town watch patrolled the streets. It had been after midnight, and bitter cold, on the night of the ninth of February, when a party of men woke the gatekeeper
demanding entry to the city:

"Open to friends of Lord Bothwell's!"

Later, they made the same incredibly damaging request when they asked the gatekeeper to let them out—
damaging because, in the interval, the silent night had
been shattered by a violent explosion. When the
alarmed citizens ran to the house called Kirk o' Field,
to see what had happened, they found two bodies in the
neighboring garden. One was a servant's body. The
other was that of the Queen's despicable young husband, Darnley, who had been convalescing from illness
in that isolated house, for fear that he might infect his
infant son. He had been strangled. And a few months
later, his widow married "my Lord Bothwell."

Susan had pictured the tragedy often in her imagination. She could almost see the Queen's procession
moving along the Canongate toward the palace—the
flaring of torches, the glitter of jewels and gold-trimmed
gowns—for the Queen had visited her ailing husband
earlier that same night. Later, along the same route,
came another, stealthier procession. My Lord Bothwell,
his hard, sneering face half hidden in the folds of his
cloak of "new color"; his confederates staggering under the weight of the heavy barrels of gunpowder.

Bothwell was tried, later, and acquitted. Mary had
never been tried—nor acquitted. History still blamed
her for complicity in her husband's murder. She had
cause enough to hate him. His handsome face concealed a mind both weak and treacherous. He had ac-
companied the band of killers who broke into the
Queen's chamber and slaughtered her Italian favorite.
He had threatened her and supported her enemies. Mary
must have hated him. But had she planned his death?

Susan didn't know. No one knew for certain. But Mary's doom had been sealed that February night in 1567, although it was twenty years later before her graying head was struck from her shoulders by order of her cousin, Elizabeth of England. Mary's countrymen had judged her, as later historians would do, and they had driven her away to imprisonment and eventual execution in England.

Susan paused under the yellow glow of a streetlight and gazed up at the facade of the dignified mansion on her right. It was too bad. She would have had only happy memories of her days in Edinburgh if it hadn't been for daft auld, damned auld Tammas. Now when she remembered Edinburgh, the romance and the charm would be tainted by encounters with hostile constables and leering desk clerks. Being in a dramatic mood, Susan groaned aloud. A strolling couple gave her startled looks. Susan groaned again. Even now, when she was trying to immerse herself in romantic reveries, auld Tammas intruded on her thoughts. If it weren't for Tammas, she could lose herself in legends—see the ghosts of Mary and Charles Edward glimmer eerily in the shadows. The ghost of a girl in a gold-trimmed gown; the ghost of a young man in a ruffled shirt and a coat of bottle-green velvet and a kilt of the royal Stuart tartan. . . .

Of course, Susan reminded herself, they had not worn the kilt in those days. One of Charles Edward's costumes, still to be seen in a Scottish museum, consisted of a short jacket and a pair of the tight trousers called trews. And in Mary's day the Highland chiefs would have worn their belted plaids—inconvenient garments that had to be pleated by hand each time they were put on. The wearer would lie down on the pleated section and, somehow or other, get a belt around his hips to hold the pleats in place. The unpleated upper part of the long rectangle of cloth was stuffed up under his coat, and the ends were wrapped around his shoulders. It must have been worse than putting on a girdle, Susan thought, walking on. A Highland chief caught without his plaid by an enemy would simply have to fight in his shirt, or in his bare hide. A philabeg, or small kilt, as the short, permanently pleated garment was called, would have been much handier. . . .

The movement that caught her eye was definitely the flaring out of a kilt. They were not so convenient after all, especially for a man who was trying to move quickly and unobserved. The flicker of movement crystallized the vague uneasiness that had been bothering Susan for several minutes—an unease that had noting to do with her enjoyably gruesome evocation of Scottish history. She whirled around.

He would have escaped her sight if he had stayed where he was, in the shadow of a doorway. Instead, seeing her turn, he started to run. The tall stooped figure in its threadbare kilt was unmistakable. Susan hesitated for only a moment. The fact that Tammas had the nerve to follow her, after all the other annoyances he had caused her, brought her anger to the boiling point. She ran after him.

Raised eyebrows and stares followed them as they pelted down the street, but no one interfered. Tammas's pace was astounding. He looked like one of the wooden toys that flop their arms and legs when a string is pulled, but he covered ground like a stag. Susan was still some distance behind when he ducked into a side street.

If she had not been so angry she might have been daunted by the darkness of the deserted thoroughfare. It sloped steeply downhill, and the buildings that loomed up like unlighted cliffs on either side appeared to be uninhabited. But the sight of Tammas flapping frantically ahead spurred Susan on.

Ten minutes later her ardor had cooled. She had no idea where she was. It didn't seem possible that she could have gotten lost in such a short time; the High Street couldn't be far, but they had twisted and turned and back-tracked. . . . Once, in the wild pursuit, she had caught sight of a street sign, "Blackfriars Street," which had oriented her and given her a slight chill. Darnley's murderers had come through Blackfriars churchyard on their way to Kirk o' Field. She must have passed right over the site of that ill-omened house.

But that had been several turnings back, and now she was lost herself and had lost Tammas. This street was hardly more than an alley—dark, evil smelling, and utterly deserted. There was a single feeble bulb up ahead, suspended from one of the facades. As she peered in that direction, Susan saw a tall stooped form slip through the pale circle of light and vanish into an opening beyond.

The houses stood tall and silent, close-packed like spectators at a big game. At first Susan thought her quarry had gone into one of them. If he had, she was out of luck. She wasn't angry enough to pound on a locked door, rousing all the neighbors, who would then assure her, in irate chorus, of the harmlessness of auld daft Tammas. But she kept on walking. She was almost opposite the opening before she saw it. Narrow, dark, and quite steeply pitched, from the angle of the small portion of steps visible under the streetlamp, it was the entrance to one of Edinburgh's closes. The name was appropriate in several senses; for the narrow paths, as old as the city itself, were usually dead ends, leading to a court or apartment house.

Susan plunged into the opening. The stairs were steep and rough. The houses edged in on either side, their tall facades as dark as midnight. But she had Tammas cornered now, if the close lived up to its name. It never occurred to her to be afraid of the old man. From the way he had been running, he seemed to be afraid of *her*.

The stairs turned sharply; far above, a glow of faint light became visible. Susan stopped. She had been wrong in her surmise; the close was not closed. At the top there must be an exit into another street—perhaps through a pend, an archway cut through the street floor of a house. There was no sign of Tammas. She had lost him. Either he had emerged into the street above or—uncomfortable thought—she had passed him. The darkness below was thick enough to hide a man if he stood still and pressed himself into some concavity in a wall.

Susan consigned Tammas to perdition and decided to go home. The whole business had become ridiculous.

As she stood there, catching her breath and trying to decide which way to go, something came hurtling out of the darkness below, so close that it grazed her ear. It struck the steps above her and began to roll back down. Susan threw herself to one side. She fell heavily and let out a cry of pain as the stone scored her bare knees. A sound from the black emptiness below completed her demoralization. It sounded like an animal's low growl.

Susan scrambled to her feet and began to climb, although that verb gives little idea of the speed with which she progressed. Clinging to the wall, scrambling four-footed like a cat, gasping and dripping blood from her lacerated knees, Susan went up. The light above seemed to be no closer, but it was the only goal she had. She had almost reached it when a figure stepped out and stood silhouetted before the light.

Luckily Susan was holding on to the wall just then, or shock might have sent her rolling down the stairs. For a second she thought her brain had given way; for the silhouette, featureless as a shape cut out of black paper, was that of a Highland cavalier of the eighteenth century.

Dim light gleamed on the silver buckles on the man's shoes and struck a spark from the hilt of the rapier

slung at his side. The wide cuffs of his coat ended in a
tumble of lace that fell over his hands. Although Susan
could not see it, she knew there must be more lace at
his throat. The man had long hair, tied with a ribbon
at the nape of his neck. His kilt was knee-length; from
the top of one sock protruded an odd shape that Susan
recognized as the hilt of a sgian-dhu, or dagger.

There was nothing unusual about the man's kilt. A
lot of men in Edinburgh wore them, including the sol-
diers at the Castle. But the rest of the costume elimi-
nated the possibility that she had encountered an
ordinary citizen of the town out for an evening stroll.
The obvious explanation never entered Susan's head.
She was in a state of panic, complicated by an overly
active imagination, and she saw a ghost—the shade of
a dead prince, lace at his wrists, reddish-blond hair tied
back in a queue. With a gasp, Susan flung herself into
Prince Charlie's arms.

He was no ghost. The soft suavity of velvet met her
clutching fingers; under it was the solidity of a human
body. He staggered back under the impact and remarked breathlessly, "What the hell—?"

An incoherent interval ensued. The wisps of fantasy
had been driven from Susan's mind by the prosaic comment, delivered in a twentieth-century male voice. The
accent was cultured, with only the faintest trace of a
burr. However, her attempts at explanation were not
successful. She had too many things to explain, and
"auld Tammas," "rocks," "poems," and "Prince
Charlie" were blended in an unintelligible hodge-
podge. Susan was further confused by the identity of
the unknown, who held her, not in a tender embrace,
but off at arms' length, as if he expected her to bite
him. If he wasn't the ghost of Bonnie Price Charlie,
who was he? His retreat had taken him out of the faint
glow of the light, and she still couldn't see his face.

"Just a moment," he said, after a time. "I hope you

won't mind my saying that your narrative is not only difficult to follow, but inherently implausible. I know auld Tammas. Everyone in Edinburgh knows auld Tammas. In his heyday, which was admittedly some years ago, he was a member of one of our leading families, as well as a historian and a writer to the signet. His present mental condition is somewhat eccentric; but under no circumstances could he have behaved in the manner you have described. Tammas may be auld and he may be daft, but he does not hurl rocks at young women.''

There was only one possible reply to this pompous speech. ''Oh, yeah?'' said Susan.

Snatching at one of the hands that grasped her shoulders, she brought it to her cheek.

''Blood,'' said the man, in a changed voice. His fingers traced the sticky trail along Susan's cheek to her ear.

''My knees hurt too,'' she said pathetically. ''I fell down.''

Light flared. Susan blinked, too dazzled to see anything except an expanse of bottle-green velvet and a fall of white lace.

''Hmmm,'' said the man, examining her ear and then her knees with the aid of his cigarette lighter. ''Yes. It does appear that some hard object has scraped the side of your head. How very odd. What the devil are you doing here, anyway? This is no place for a stupid female tourist.''

''I was following auld Tammas,'' Susan muttered.

The stimulus of fear had abandoned her; she felt dizzy and a little sick. She swayed. The lighter went out. As she continued to buckle slowly at the knees, her new acquaintance took her in a reluctant but competent embrace.

''I thought American girls were tough,'' he remarked disagreeably. ''You're bleeding on my lace.''

"It's the other ear," said Susan, without moving. "May I ask why the lace? And the dagger, and the green velvet coat, and the—"

"A costume party, naturally. Do you think I'd appear in this ludicrous rig unless I had to? My aunt is giving the party. Aunt Margaret. I'm late. And it appears I shall be even later. What am I to do with you? I can't leave you here, sprawled on the stairs; someone might trip over you and there would be a nasty accident. I think perhaps you'd better come along with me."

"I'd follow anybody anywhere," said Susan, removing herself from the velvet bosom of the coat. "Even the ghost of Bonnie Prince Charlie."

"Oh, hell," said her reluctant rescuer. "So you're one of *those* Americans."

"What do you mean?"

"One of the Bonnie Prince Charlie romantics. Your great-grannie's name was Bruce, so you deck yourselves out in tartans you've no right to wear and pretend to thrill the skirl of the pipes—whose sound would make any genuine musician howl like a hound. Your Bonnie Prince never really existed, you know. Charles Edward was an arrogant, lackwit Stuart, with a brain the size of a pea and the manners of a swine. You're damned lucky I'm not him—he, I mean. He'd have had you on your back before you could say—"

"Oooh," Susan gasped. "He couldn't have worse manners than you. You conceited Scot, I'll bet I know more about your history than you do."

The shadowy figure laughed rudely.

"Let's not discuss it now, shall we? The moments are fleeting by, never to be regained. I think you'll be a definite asset to the party. Can you walk?"

"My knees hurt. What do you mean, definite—"

"Aunt Margaret will deal with your knees. That's a provocative remark, isn't it? Taken out of context—"

"I'm not going to your damned party," Susan exclaimed, trying to pull away from the hand that had grasped hers and was guiding her up the stairs. "I can't go anyplace looking like this!"

"You'll have to go someplace," the man pointed out, with maddening logic. "And I am going, reluctantly but steadfastly, to my previous engagement. You can come along, or stay. It's all the same to me."

Susan had no intention of staying. The dark incline behind her reminded her of the gullet of a carnivorous animal, waiting to swallow her up. Seething, she stumbled after her guide. Before long they emerged into a narrow, poorly lighted street—not the High Street, but one of the thoroughfares that led into it. Susan's guide dropped her hand.

"Well? Have you made up your mind?"

Susan screamed. It was the first time she had seen his face.

Inhumanly handsome, cold and fixed, it had the same ghastly detachment as that of an effigy on a medieval tomb. No scar or birthmark or physical disfigurement could have been more terrifying than the cold mask of—

"A mask," Susan exclaimed, her terror replaced by furious indignation. "Of all the nerve!"

Her companion's hand went to his chin, where the lace jabot met the bottom of the mask.

"I told you it was a costume party. You are the second most unreasonable female I've ever met. First you're angry because I'm not a ghost; now you object to my wearing a mask. I'd leave you here, except that I'm looking forward to your meeting with Aunt Margaret. She is the most unreasonable female I've ever met. You two should hit it off beautifully. Come along now, I'm really frightfully late."

He turned his back on her and started to walk away.

Susan was not keen on being left alone, but it was not fear that prompted her to follow him. It was the way the pleats of the kilt swung out as he walked and

the arrogant angle of the dress sword slung at his side.
The tartan of his kilt was the vivid red-and-green Erskine sett. When he turned his back and shut his mouth,
he was the quintessence of every romantic image she
had ever dreamed about Scotland. It was impossible to
let him walk out of her life.

The image wavered, however, when Susan beheld
their means of transportation. Gleaming with chrome,
bristling with gadgets, it was an offense to the eye in
itself; and when the gallant kilted figure slammed its
buckled brogue down, the engine bellowed revoltingly
and let off a blast of foul exhaust.

"A motorcycle!" Susan's lip curled.

"A Norton 750," her cavalier corrected. He leaned
back and contemplated the curved handlebars. The frozen mask concealed his expression, but adoration softened his crisp voice. "Isn't she a beauty? I just got her.
Haven't paid for her yet, of course. . . . Hop on."

He had to shout to be heard above the engine's roar.

Susan did not hop on. Her knees were beginning to
stiffen, and they hurt like fury. With as much dignity
as she could muster she mounted the pillion and
wrapped her arms around her companion's narrow
waist. They were off, profaning the antique mysteries
of Edinburgh with sound and stench.

Yet as they went on, crossing the High Street and
plunging into the darkness beyond, Susan was conscious of an inappropriate exhilaration. Her hair
streamed out in the wind; the high, dark houses flashed
by and were succeeded by the walls and trees of a suburban area. Except for the mechanical scream of the
engine, she could almost imagine she was riding horse-
back on a tall stallion that thundered through the night,
carrying two fugitives on a breathless escape. Young
Lochinvar, with his stolen bride on his saddlebow; Mary,
Queen of Scots on the daring midnight flight from Holyroodhouse, after Rizzio's murder. . . . An insane de-

sire to sing came over her. "All the blue-bonnets are over the border!"

She repressed the desire. Such an outburst would only confirm her companion's judgment of her as "one of *those* Americans." He was the rudest, most arrogant. . . . It occurred to her, with a slight shock, that she didn't know who he was. An Erskine, presumably, but that didn't help much.

Without slackening speed, the vehicle suddenly made a right turn. It appeared to be heading straight for a high iron fence. Susan ducked; but the gates were open. There were lights up ahead. They blazed from the front of an elegant country house. The motorcycle stopped with a final defiant roar. Susan's escort gave her a hand down.

He stood for a moment gazing at the house. In the bright light his mask lost its desquieting air; it was merely absurd. It hid his expression, but Susan sensed that he was nervous. His hand fumbled at the lace at his chin and then adjusted the fur-trimmed sporran that hung from his belt.

"I can't go in there," Susan said nervously. "I look awful."

"It's too late now," the masked man said, in equally gloomy tones.

Side by side they mounted the broad stairs. The door was flung open as they approached it. The butler had a face almost as impassive as the mask; it did not change as his eyes swept over Susan's disheveled form and then went to her companion.

"Good evening, Mr. James."

At least I know his name, Susan thought. It was small consolation.

The vast marble-floored hall was lighted by crystal chandeliers. Through an open archway Susan saw a room that seemed to stretch on forever. Large as it was, it was crowded with people. A Viking in a horned hel-

met and long blond braids chatted with a lady in pow-
dered wig and panniered satin skirts; an Indian chief,
complete with feathered warbonnet, walked arm in arm
with an Egyptian belly dancer. However, the majority
of the costumes were Scottish. Susan's first impression
was that she had never seen so many male knees.

The costumes covered all the eras of Scotland's history, from belted plaids and saffron shirts to the philabeg and the short-tailed coats of twentieth-century
evening dress. None of the women wore the kilt, which
was a strictly masculine garment, but they wore the
proper feminine equivalent—long pleated skirts of silk
or fine wool tartan, with matching sashes draped across
the bosom and fastened on the shoulder with a silver
brooch. Susan's dazzled eyes identified the famous tartans: the distinctive Colquhoun green and black, with
narrow red and white stripes; the blue-and-red Chis-
holm; the complex Anderson sett with its varicolored
stripes on a pale-blue ground. Susan sighed wistfully.
James's taunts about tartans had been undeserved; she
was a purist in such matters, and she had never owned
a plaid skirt, since she knew that only those bearing a
clan or sept surname were entitled to flaunt the clan
tartan.

At this moment in her life, however, she would have
pawned her soul to Satan in exchange for one of the
long, graceful skirts—or, indeed, for any costume other
than the one she had on. It was certainly unique. No
one else was wearing a short blue denim skirt and a
soot-streaked sleeveless T-shirt. None of the other bare
knees were bloody.

A woman marched toward them, her full skirts bil-
lowing out with her long mannish strides. She was almost as tall as James; if she had been a few inches
shorter she would have been fat. She wore an old Highland costume, the tartan tonnag over her shoulders
matching the pattern of her long pleated gown. The hair

twisted into a heavy knot at the nape of her neck was gray, but her thick brows were solid black, and they were drawn together in a scowl. Susan had no difficulty in recognizing "Aunt Margaret." She slid behind James. He was big enough and broad enough to conceal her slight form, but she sensed she was too late. Her hostess had already seen her.

"Chicken?" James inquired softly, from under the frozen simper of the mask. "Come out and face the music. Tell her she looks like Flora MacDonald, that should do it. She's another Bonnie Prince Charlie type. You two should get along fine."

He struck an attitude, one hand on the hilt of his sword. The other hand dragged Susan ruthlessly out into the open.

Aunt Margaret stopped in front of the couple and looked her nephew over, from his silver-buckled brogues to the crown of his dark head.

"At least you had the decency to wear a mask," she remarked.

Only her feeling that she must uphold the reputation of the entire United States, from sea to shining sea, kept Susan from turning tail. But she had underestimated Scottish hospitality and class breeding. Margaret turned to her and the grim visage shaped itself into a smile which, if strained, was nonetheless gracious.

"I'm so glad you could join us, my dear. What an original costume! I'm afraid its significance isn't immediately clear to me, but its effectiveness—"

"Aunt M.," said James loudly. "Don't be sarcastic. The lady is not trying to emulate a victim. She *is* a victim. That's real blood."

"My poor child!" Margaret's artificial smile was replaced by a look of burning sympathy. "It's that ghastly motorcycle. I knew you'd kill yourself one day, Jamie; what a pity you couldn't injure yourself, instead of an innocent passenger. Did you fall off—er—I don't believe I caught your name.''

"Please call me Susan. It wasn't—uh—Jamie's fault. In fact, he rescued me.''

"A likely story," said Jamie's aunt. "But we mustn't stand here discussing the cause of your injuries; come straight up, child, and let me put something on those scrapes. Good heavens, your face is cut too.''

Susan was swept away, up the curving staircase and into a handsomely appointed bedroom. Her hostess shrieked loudly for her maid, but she did the dirty work herself, wiping off dust and blood and applying iodine lavishly. Her big, clumsy-looking hands were surprisingly gentle. It was a pity, Susan thought, that Lady Margaret—for so the maid had addressed her mistress—had been prevented by her exalted social position from seeking gainful employment. She would have made an excellent nurse. In an earlier and more violent era she would have been quite at home striding through the heather with a fugitive prince or defending a besieged castle for her absent lord, as some termagant ladies of history had done.

With such thoughts occupying her mind, Susan found it easy to introduce the subject of Flora MacDonald. As James had predicted, this proved a sure way to Lady Margaret's heart. She was delighted to find Susan so well informed, and took her into the sitting room to show off her greatest treasure—a withered, wrinkled glove that had once enveloped the fingers of the Stuart prince. Susan's private opinion was that if Prince Charlie had worn all the gloves cherished by his devotees, he must have changed them six times a day; but naturally she did not express this radical idea aloud. She and Lady Margaret were fast friends by the time they descended the staircase, arm in arm.

James was waiting for them at the foot of the stairs. It was a pity, Susan thought, that he insisted on wearing

the silly mask; without it, he would have been a handsome figure of a man. The thick dark hair was his own,
not a wig; his narrow hips and broad shoulders suited
the romantic costume admirably. The lace at his wrists
framed hands that were beautifully shaped, in spite of
the bruised knuckles and the recalcitrant traces of oil
smears. His legs weren't bad, either. Susan reminded
herself to tell James so. He wouldn't appreciate the
compliment.

"So fortunate that Jamie had found a sensible girl
like you," said Lady Margaret. "Perhaps you can bring
the boy to his senses. His father is in the right, I agree
with his view absolutely; but although Seumas is my
own brother, I must admit that he doesn't know how to
handle a boy like Jamie. They are both horribly stubborn. All the Erskines are stubborn. Except for myself,
of course."

Lady Margaret didn't bother to lower her voice; and
although Susan didn't think her comments could have
been overheard amid the noise below, she felt some
delicacy about being made the recipient of such personal confidences. But she could hardly admit now that
she was there under false pretenses; that she had never
met James before that night, and that she had not the
faintest idea what Lady Margaret was talking about.
She couldn't help being curious, though. Why were
James and his father at odds? And most intriguing of
all, what was the meaning of Lady Margaret's strange
comment about James's mask? Why was it preferable
for him to hide his face?

The mask gave nothing away, but James's comment,
as they joined him, made it clear that he had heard his
aunt's remarks.

"Do shut up, Aunt M. Must you discuss family matters with every passing stranger?"

"How can you call dear Susan a stranger? She is

remarkably well informed about Flora MacDonald and the Forty-five. Do you have Scottish blood, my dear?''

"I don't think—"

"Somewhere in the background, no doubt," said Margaret comfortably. "Oh, dear, there's the Innes boy trying to do some strange kind of sword dance. I must stop him before he chops off someone's sporran."

She plunged into the melee in the drawing room.

Susan and James contemplated one another. Or, to be more accurate, Susan contemplated the mask, which faced her with a conspicuous lack of interest. There were holes under the perfectly arched brows, but she couldn't see the eyes behind the holes.

"Can I go home?" Susan asked.

"I can't leave yet."

"Taxi," Susan suggested, with an inner qualm as she remembered the emptiness of her purse.

"If you can stick it for an hour or so, I'll run you home. There's food in the green parlor and dancing in the ballroom. Which will it be?"

"Food," Susan said. It had been a long time since that hamburger.

The groaning buffet made her forget her qualms about remaining. She stuffed herself shamelessly, and drank champagne. James watched. He couldn't eat without removing the mask, and apparently, he would rather starve than do that. The champagne made Susan feel very happy.

"What are you and your dad fighting about?" she inquired sociably, through a mouthful of smoked eel.

"None of your business."

"The usual, I suppose," said Susan wisely. "He can't understand your ideals, and your— What are your ideals? Do you have any? Hic."

The hiccup surprised her. She covered her mouth with a guilty hand. James began to laugh. The sound echoed hollowly from behind the mask.

"You've had enough. Let's dance, that should work off some of the alcohol."

The dancing turned out to be solidly ethnic—reels, jigs, and strathspeys. If James had hoped to catch Susan off guard, he was disappointed. She belonged to a Scottish dancing group back home, and after watching the complex figures for a few minutes, she dragged James straight into the intricacies of the reel. She danced much better than he did; he kept tripping over his feet, and she had to keep shoving him back into place. He was the first to admit defeat and suggest that they go into the garden for some fresh air.

It was a lovely night. The glow of the city lights warmed the sky to the south. The night breeze stirred the trees and cooled Susan's hot cheeks. She sighed happily.

"I'm having a wonderful time!"

"Yes, I know." Elbows on his bare knees, James stared moodily at the ground. "I take it you have forgotten about the attempt on your life."

"I wish you hadn't said that. I really had forgotten. But I don't think he meant. . . . What am I going to do about the old fool?"

"Tammas? That was a preposterous story, you know. What happened really? You can tell me the truth."

Susan told him the truth. It did sound preposterous, even to her. But as the narrative proceeded, she realized that it was having an extraordinary effect on James. By the time she reached the moment of their meeting, he was sitting bolt upright. The expressionless face turned toward her did not hide the absorption that fairly radiated from him.

As for Susan, the retelling had the cathartic effect of a good long session with a psychiatrist.

"After all," she concluded sheepishly, "I don't know why I got so uptight about it. Feeling like a stranger in a strange land, I suppose. I'm leaving town tomorrow, so. . . . Maybe the deal with the rock tonight was an accident. Or maybe the poor old guy gets frantic when he's cornered. I should just forget it, right?''

James replied with an ambiguous sound, half grunt, half growl. The mask continued to face her with its frozen smile, and Susan said irritably,

"Actually, the craziest thing about this whole business is our relationship. Do you realize I've never seen your face? I wouldn't recognize you if I met you on the street. No one else is wearing a mask; why you? And why did your aunt make that crack about it? Is there something about your face—''

She stopped, fearing she had committed the cruelest of social blunders. Maybe there *was* something about the face this man kept concealed even from his friends. If he was deformed, or hideously ugly . . .

"Oh, that,'' said James uncomfortably. "Well, my face is . . . that is to say . . .''

"I'm sorry,'' Susan mumbled. "I mean, I'm really awfully sorry if I—''

James laughed. "No, no, you poor innocent child. It isn't what you're thinking. Your tastes in literature must be perfectly frightful. Are you ready? Behold!''

His right hand swept the mask away.

The light from a lantern dangling from the tree overhead allowed Susan to see his face clearly. It appeared to have the regulation number of features. One nose, generously shaped; two brown eyes, under even dark brows; a mouth. . . . Susan assumed there must be a mouth. She had heard it speak. Its shape, and that of the lower half of James's face, was obliterated by a short bushy beard and untrimmed moustache of a type that looked vaguely familiar. It reminded her of someone— some historical character, naturally. Susan stared in fascinated silence, trying to isolate the resemblance. Then she had it. Of course. Civil War generals. The Confederates particularly had favored such hirsute adornments.

James's beard was shorter than some she had seen in old photographs. It had been hidden by the lace at his throat and the elongated chin of the mask. But it blurred James's features as effectively as Longstreet's and Jeb Stuart's beards had done.

James began to squirm uncomfortably under her concentrated regard. He rose to his full height, the pleats of his kilt rippling, and untied the ribbon that held his hair back. The long dark locks swung down over forehead and cheeks. There was almost nothing to be seen of his features now except the Roman contours of his nose, protruding from the brush like a barren rock out of a fuzz of gorse.

"Well?" he said.

"You look," said Susan, "like General Jeb Stuart in drag. . . . Oh, Jamie, I'm sorry, I didn't mean to say that, it just—"

James sat down.

"If you'd just cut off the beard," Susan began apologetically.

"There is," said James flatly, "an excellent reason for the beard. Never mind what it is. It is none of your affair. But your rude, uncouth comment expresses my aunt's sentiments rather well. In deference to her feelings I hid the beard tonight. I am trying to ingratiate myself with Aunt Margaret. I need to ingratiate myself with Aunt Margaret. She has considerable influence with my father, and at the moment he and I are not on the best of terms."

"He doesn't know about the Norton 750?"

"Oh, that. No, he doesn't. But that's the least of my problems with the old. . . . Damn it, how did we get onto that subject? We were talking about you and Tammas."

"Me and Tammas be damned," Susan said ungrammatically. "I don't want our names joined, if you please. Forget about him. I intend to."

"Aren't you even curious?" James asked. "I am. It's the damnedest story I ever heard. You're absolutely certain about the poem?"

"Of course I'm certain. 'And I a man, and lacketh libertee.' James the First, born 1394, reigned from 1406 to 1437. . . ."

"When, one presumes, he died. Ninety-four from thirty-seven. . . . He was only forty-three."

"Your kings died young. And violently. I mean, I enjoy the romantic legend, but I wouldn't want to be transported back to any period in Scottish history. The Scots were a bloodthirsty crew of illiterate barbarians. It took the English to civilize you."

She meant to be offensive. She did not succeed. The hairy head nodded emphatically and James said,

"Quite right. The Union was the greatest thing that ever happened to Scotland. If I could only convince my infantile parent of that. . . ."

"Aha," said Susan. "So your dad is a Nationalist. Like Tammas. Which brings us back to Tammas, doesn't it? I've got a theory. Maybe the poem is, like, a password. A call to arms for the Nationalists—"

"Now just a moment. You talk about them as though they were an underground movement. The S.N.P. is a recognized political party, you ignorant foreigner. Like your Democrats and—what's the other one? Oh, yes, the Republicans. The Nationalists won seven Parliamentary seats in the last election, quite legally; they don't run about shooting people, like the bloody idiots in the I.R.A."

"I've never heard of any violence in connection with your Nationalist movement," Susan admitted. "Which is surprising, in a way. The Scots came from Ireland originally, and Lord knows, Scottish history up to the nineteenth century was violent enough."

James snorted. "Violence is stupid. No Scot would toss a bomb into a crowded café."

"Too thrifty," Susan suggested.

"If you like," James said stiffly. "Blowing babies to bits is rather wasteful, isn't it? Somehow the point of the exercise has always eluded me."

"I'm sorry," Susan said, after a moment. "It's not a laughing matter, is it? All the same, there must be a few fanatics in your Nationalist movement. Every organization attracts some nuts; there are radical wings even in our political parties."

"Oh, certainly. The S.N.P. includes a wide spectrum of opinion. The basic demands are reasonable enough; even I agree with some of them. I mean, we have no governing body of our own. It's unfair to have purely internal Scottish affairs dealt with by a body in which Scots are a minority. Your states have greater autonomy than our entire nation. All we want is the right to handle our own—"

"We? You know, Jamie, I think you're a fraud. I'll bet you'd be a Nationalist yourself is your dad weren't on that side of the fence. It's a typical adolescent reaction to reject your parents' opinion because you—"

"Do you mind not commenting on my private affairs?" James interrupted angrily.

"Okay, I apologize. But you haven't answered my question. If the moderates only want greater autonomy for Scotland, within the Union, what about the extremists? Independence, I suppose."

"Independence is only a political slogan. It's an impractical idea. What the world needs is greater international unity, not a lot of little countries that bicker among themselves and are too poor to give their people a decent standard of living. Why, we're heading right back into the Dark Ages, setting up dozens of petty independent states. Most of the revolutionaries don't want freedom, they just want a chance to be boss. People have to learn to live together, whether they like it or not. It's becoming a matter of sheer survival, with

every damned fool building atom bombs. Most of the
wars in the last ten years have resulted from such ill-
advised political divisions—the Near East, Ireland, Viet
Nam, Pakistan and India. . . .''

One lean brown hand swept the hair away from his
forehead. His eyes glowed. His enthusiasm amused Susan; she was inclined to agree with much of what he
said, but she had no intention of admitting it.

"Now you're getting off the subject," she pointed
out. "I suppose your father, and Tammas, are all for
independence."

"Worse," James said darkly.

"According to you, nothing could be worse."

"More insane, then. Nobody knows what Tammas
wants. I doubt that he knows himself. He's a Royalist,
but he wants independence for Scotland; presumably he
yearns to restore the Stuarts, if there are any of them
left. He's a lunatic, admittedly, but he is perfectly
harmless—"

"So everybody keeps telling me."

Silence descended like a damp fog. In the tree above
them a sleepy bird chirped questioningly. Finally James
stirred.

"All right," he said. "Let's go around and have a
talk with him."

"Tammas?"

"Tammas."

"But I—"

"You're not afraid of him, are you?"

"Yes. He looks like John Knox."

"Ridiculous."

"Well, he sounds like John Knox."

"Nonsense. He's the exact antithesis of Knox. I
imagine he's the only man alive who still believes in
the divine right of kings. He belongs to some daft
secret society called the Knights of the White Rose;
they drink toasts to the King over the Water and the

memory of Charles Edward Stuart. Good God, he's another romantic; you two ought to hit it off beautifully.''

"Why did he throw a rock at me?"

"We'll ask him."

"You ask him, next time you see him. I want to go home."

"I'll take you home. By way of Tammas's—pad is the word, I believe."

The voice was calm, but Susan recognized the Erskine stubbornness. She sighed.

"Oh, all right. Do you know where he lives?"

"Certainly. He's a friend of—"

James stopped.

Susan didn't ask him to finish the sentence. She thought she knew how it would have ended.

The streets were dark and quiet; the city might have been abandoned in fear of plague or invasion, for all the signs of life it displayed. In the older section of Edinburgh, behind the careful restoration of the High Street, age had deteriorated into squalor. The houses would be almost as black in the sunlight as they were at night; like the gravestones of Edinburgh, their stone facades had been darkened by centuries of soot. They were tall houses, some of them seven stories high: the "lands" of a growing city forced to build upward because of the natural barriers that restricted its outward expansion.

Tammas lived in one of the most run-down areas. Even in the darkness Susan could see the piles of garbage, the broken paving stones and crumbling doorways. James left the cycle chained to a lamp standard. Its glass panes were all broken, and shards littered the pavement beneath. He plunged into a close that lived up to its name, being also dark and foul smelling. Clinging to his arm and stumbling blindly, Susan decided he must have eyes like a cat's. She couldn't see a thing. When he stopped and knocked on a door she took the door on faith; her eyes beheld only a solider darkness. She was standing in a puddle of some liquid she preferred not to identify.

James knocked again.

"Maybe he's not here," Susan said. "Maybe everyone's asleep. He's not the only person living in the house, is he? If his room is at the back, or up above, you'll have to wake up the landlord—"

"This is his private entrance," James explained, in a low voice. "The main doorway is farther on. The house is condemned, so there aren't many occupants, and most of them will be sleeping off their nightly binge. He must be here. Look, there's a streak of light at the window."

Susan's eyes, now more accustomed to the dark, were able to distinguish the outlines of a narrow window on her right. It was boarded up, or else heavily shuttered, but narrow parallel lines of light could be seen. The light was very dim; she thought it must emanate from a candle or lamp, or maybe a twenty-watt bulb. To judge by the lights in her hotel, the use of anything over twenty watts would be regarded as wanton extravagance in Scotland.

James continued to knock. Not daring to shift her feet for fear of stepping in something even worse, Susan sighed.

"He's not going to answer. Give up, Jamie; I don't want to see him anyway."

James muttered something and gave the door an impatient shove.

It swung slowly inward, with a creak of rusty hinges.

There was no hall or vestibule. The door opened directly into a vast chamber whose far corners were untouched by the light—the twenty-watt bulb Susan had postulated was hanging from a beam so far overhead that the light resembled that of a distant star. Large as it was, the room was crammed with objects. All the furniture was old, and most of it was falling apart. Three-legged chairs leaned drunkenly against the wall. Tables sagged under the weight of books and papers. The spaces not filled with furniture were piled with an incredible collection of newspapers, magazines, rotting books. Susan had heard of such places, but had never seen one—the aerie of a miser, an eccentric, a hoarder of trivia. The man had never thrown anything away, not even the stones that had fallen from his crumbling walls. Piles of them were stacked along the sides of the room.

Yet for all its clutter, the place was surprisingly clean. There was no smell of decay, no scraps of rotten food. The room had once been beautiful. Fragments of carved paneling still clung to the walls, and the ceiling, more amply illuminated than any other part of the room, had beams with traces of gilt and faded paint. A glance at the wall to the left showed Susan the shape of what had once been a staircase. The room had been the entrance hall of a house formerly inhabited by wealth and nobility.

The place appeared to be uninhabited, but it was impossible to be sure, since walls of tottering, yellowed newspapers concealed all but the immediate area. James closed the door and started forward along an aisle between the stacks of papers. He did not call out. Susan sympathized; she too was reluctant to shatter the dusty, shadowy silence with sound. Yet Tammas must be here; he wouldn't have gone out and left the light on, using up costly electricity. Probably he had dozed off.

James came to a sudden halt. Susan was behind him; the aisle was too narrow to permit them to walk

side by side. But she could see what had stopped
him and had stiffened his shoulders into a rigid line.
He was staring at the floor. Its worn boards were stained
and scraped. But this stain was different. It was still
wet. The light made it glisten darkly, thickly. Like oil,
or some other viscid substance. Like . . . blood.

Chapter 3

Susan started backing toward the door.

"Let's go," she said, articulating with difficulty. "Let's go *now*. I don't want—"

"To get involved? An American disease, I believe— fear of getting involved."

Susan shut her mouth and stiffened her spine. James was right, of course. If the horrible stain was what she feared, it had to be investigated.

The stain was not a single spot, it was a trail, smeared and sticky. They followed it along corridors walled shoulder-high with roped bundles of newspapers. It was like a ghastly symbolic maze in a surrealist film— humanity trapped within the sterile walls of modern futility, or something equally depressing.

Then they saw the shoe. Only the sole was visible. It had been patched and repatched; a hole had been worn through the latest patch. James jumped forward. Susan followed more slowly. She did not doubt that there was a foot inside the shoe that lay at such an awkward angle; and she was right.

The lean old body lay face down on the floor, arms stretched out above its head. Tammas had been crawling toward the far wall.

James knelt down. He had limited space in which to operate; his movements were controlled and economical. After a few moments he looked up.

"He's dead. The body is still warm."

He got to his feet. He had turned the old man onto his back, and the glazing eyes seemed to be staring straight at Susan. Faded and clouding as they were, they were blue. Once they had been bright and alive, like bluebells and cornflowers. Once Tammas had been as tall and young as the man beside her. She was surprised to feel tears sliding down her cheeks, but she knew she was not grieving over the death of a man she scarcely knew so much as mourning the inescapable tragedy of old age.

"How . . ." she began. Her voice was unsteady. James understood what she wanted to say.

"Stabbed," he said. "Through the back. It took him some time to die."

"It was . . . murder, then."

"Yes. He crawled this way—not toward the door, and help. Why?"

"I don't suppose he was thinking very clearly."

"No. All the same . . ." James searched the room with his eyes. "There's no exit at this end, no telephone. Only a blank wall. If you can call it blank, with all this debris piled up. Tools, building materials, scraps of wood. . . . What do you make of these?"

He indicated the objects with the toe of his shoe.

"A hammer and a rock. What's to make of them? Part of the debris?"

"They slipped from his hands when his fingers relaxed," James said in an even voice. "He got them from the junk by the wall. Selected them. Why?"

Without waiting for an answer, he stepped over the

fallen man and squatted down by the two objects. He didn't touch either one of them. After a moment he straightened up and stood staring at Susan.

"I don't know why," she said. "We're wasting time, Jamie. We must call the police. A doctor, too, I suppose, although . . ."

"The police," James repeated.

"The cops, the fuzz, the forces of law and order. Whatever you call them. Please, Jamie, I can't—I can't stand it much longer. Let's get out of here."

"What? Oh. Yes. Certainly."

He stepped back over the body. His shadow, falling across the upturned face, gave the stiffening muscles the illusion of movement; for a moment it appeared as if the dead man were about to speak. Susan turned and fled. When she reached the comparatively clear space in the middle of the room, under the hanging bulb, she waited for James, only to see him turn to the heaped kitchen table.

"Poor old man," she said softly. "What a way to go. . . . I suppose one of the local hoods thought he was hoarding money along with all this trash."

"Nothing here." James abandoned the litter on the table. "No, Susan, that won't wash. No local crook could have been under that illusion. Tammas never had a penny. He lived on handouts. Contributions to the cause, as he called them. Look here, Susan, don't you see that there is something extremely odd about all this?"

"What?"

"The theory of a thief won't work. Such an individual would have torn the place apart looking for money. It may look untidy to you, but nothing is out of place. There's not even any sign of a struggle. Tammas was no weakling, for all his age; he wouldn't have stood like a Christian martyr while some stranger stabbed him."

Susan stared at him, her lips parted. "What are you saying?" she asked.

"This door was always bolted at night. Tammas was no fool; he knew the neighborhood. He must have let the murderer in. They walked from the door together, as far as . . ." James returned to the spot where they had seen the first bloodstain. "Here. Tammas was leading the way. Would he have turned his back on a nasty-looking stranger?"

"If the man threatened him with the knife—"

James snorted. "Marched him along with a knife at his back? Obviously you've never tried to intimidate anyone that way."

"My experience has been terribly limited," Susan admitted.

"It isn't very effective," James said. "No. What you do is, you hold the knife at the victim's throat, while you're standing behind him. The throat is the only area where you can be sure of hitting a vital spot. The carotid artery—"

"I wish you would change the subject," Susan said weakly.

"I'm trying to make a point. If Tammas had been running away from his killer when he was stabbed, I would expect to see some signs of a struggle here. The space between these papers is narrow, and the piles are unstable. They would topple if you leaned against them. A man running for his life, falling heavily, ought to have dislodged some of them. He must have been standing still or walking slowly; the killer had time to catch him and lower him to the floor. And then . . ." James walked on a few steps. "Then the killer left. But Tammas wasn't dead. He started crawling, dragging himself along. There's a big pool of blood just here. I wonder. . . . Yes. Here it is. The murder weapon."

With the toe of his shoe he nudged it out of the crack

between two stacks of papers. The blade was darkly smeared. Susan looked away.

"Tammas pulled the knife out," James went on. "Not a bright thing to do, but, as you say, he wasn't thinking clearly. There wouldn't be much bleeding from the wound until the blade was withdrawn. Then he crawled farther. What was he looking for?" James stared toward the far end of the room, where the old man's body lay behind the barricades of paper. "A hammer and a rock. Blunt instruments, both of them. But we know he wasn't killed with a blunt instrument. What message was he trying to convey?"

"You've been reading too many thrillers," Susan said. "James, this is indecent—standing around playing the Great Detective while the poor old man is lying over there dead. We've got to go for help."

"Mmm," James said vaguely. But he didn't move, except to push the hair away from his face. His eyes were narrowed and very bright. They scanned the room in a searching survey.

Susan pushed past him. In the narrow space she trod on the bloodstain and was sickened to feel her foot slip. Recovering herself, she made for the door. James caught her arm as she was about to open it.

"Don't rush off in all directions. There's no point in raising the alarm here; the local populace doesn't respond to cries of distress. We'll have to go back to the cycle."

It took James rather a long time to unlock the chain. He helped Susan onto the motorcycle and they took off. Susan could hear him mumbling to himself, but she could not make out the words. Conversation was out of the question until they stopped. James chained the bike to a railing, and Susan followed him into a narrow passageway. She was under the impression that he was looking for a police station, and it was not until he turned into a doorway, capped by a half-obliterated carved crest, that she protested.

"This isn't a police station. Where are you—"

"Sssh." James fumbled with his keys. "This is where I live. We've got to—that is to say, the police station isn't—isn't open at this hour."

Susan was still gaping at this absurdity as he pulled her into a darkened hallway and through a door on the right.

The room was also dark. Susan heard James fumbling around, swearing in an abstracted monotone. Finally he switched on a light.

It was a typical bachelor's room—unmade bed, unswept floor, a litter of empty beer bottles, open books, and record tapes. A guitar lay on the floor near the door. It, and almost everything else, was covered with a thick coating of dust.

"What a pigsty," Susan said critically. "Jamie, what are you trying to pull? Even in this backward country, police stations are open twenty-four hours a day. You must think I'm a moron."

James stood by the desk, his hand still on the lamp.

"You aren't afraid of me, are you?"

Susan considered the question. It was the first time it had occurred to her that she might have reason to be afraid; but the accumulated facts suddenly washed over her and took her breath away. The coincidental meeting, the discovery of Tammas's body, the interest of this stranger in her affairs. . . . And now her presence, alone and unprotected, in the stranger's room.

"No," she said, with perfect truth. "Should I be? What did you have in mind?"

James let out a long breath, and his shoulders relaxed. Susan realized, however, that there was some chagrin mingled with his relief. Perhaps it would have been more tactful of her to scream a little. Men did love to think they were dangerous.

"I don't want to go to the police," James said.

"Why, for God's sake?"

Whatever the excessive growth of hair and beard were meant to conceal, they certainly made it difficult for anyone to read James's expression. Susan could see only his nose and the gleam of his eyes amid the brush. He pushed the hair back with both hands, and she realized that he was trying to look ingenuous, open, trustworthy and honest. The moustache waggled as the corners of his mouth stretched in an exaggerated smile. There was a faint sheen of perspiration on his exposed forehead.

"What makes you so anxious to be law-abiding? I thought your generation in the States was suspicious of the fuzz."

"My generation!" Susan said indignantly. "It's the same generation as yours, unless I'm much mistaken. What makes you so anxious *not* to be law-abiding?"

"It's so pointless! We can't tell the police anything they won't be able to figure out for themselves. But they'll make a big thing of it, possibly demand that we stay in town. Didn't you say you had to report for this dig of yours on Sunday?"

The point was well made, and Susan's face showed that she was struck by it. Encouraged, James went on.

"I mean, it's just a waste of our time. I—uh—I have to go north myself tomorrow. Today, that is. I could run you up on the Norton. Save you the bus fare. But if we report to the police, we may be stuck here for days. It isn't as if we could do anything for Tammas."

"No. We have to go to the police, Jamie. I couldn't stand thinking of him lying there, maybe for days. . . ."

"Of all the sentimental rubbish! Damn it, your chin looks just like Aunt Margaret's. You don't seem to realize the position you'll be in if the police learn that you went to see Tammas tonight."

"What do you mean?"

"I don't want to alarm you," James said. "But look

at it from an impartial point of view. You accused Tammas of accosting you on the street; then of searching your room. It's a matter of record. Well, don't you see, the behavior you describe is totally out of character for Tammas. He is—was a misogynist—scared to death of women—and the gentlest character alive. And now he's dead—murdered—''

"Are you—trying—to say—"

"No, no, I'm not accusing you of killing him! After all, I'm your alibi. But what if the police don't believe me? What if they decide you had an accomplice, who bumped the old chap off after you had taken considerable pains to establish that he had finally gone round the bend?''

"But why? Why should I do such a thing?''

"God knows. Oh, I'm not saying you're in danger of being condemned for a crime you didn't commit. You'd be cleared eventually. But if the police ask you to—you are familiar with our phrase, 'to assist the police in their investigations'? It wouldn't do your reputation a lot of good, here or in the States, if that should happen. And it might be . . . unpleasant. They'd fetch in a battery of alienists to examine your subconscious, and by the time the lads got through you might begin to think you had stabbed Tammas because he was a symbol of some damned Freudian nightmare. Honestly, Susan, if there were any useful purpose to be accomplished by reporting his death, I'd say go ahead. But under the circumstances . . .''

Susan rubbed her bare arms. She felt cold. There were plenty of flaws in James's argument, but she was not affected by logic or the lack of it; she felt like an alien in a strange country—small, helpless, and lonely.

"All right,'' she said weakly, "But . . .''

"No buts.'' James crossed the room. He patted her on the shoulder, rather as he might have patted an obedient dog. "Good girl, Susan. I'll just get a few things

together and then we'll run around to your hotel and
get your—''

"In the middle of the night? They'll think—''

"They think! What think they? Let them think!''

"The verb is 'say,' '' Susan remarked. '' 'They have
said. What say they? Let them say!' And it would be a
Scottish motto, of course. The sheer arrogance of
it . . .''

She watched, with an unflattering lack of interest, as
James began to divest himself of his evening attire and
the conspicuous tartan of his clan.

II

They were halfway to Stirling, and the sun was well
up over the purple peaks ahead, before Susan began to
get her wits back. James had taken advantage of her
shocked state to lead her around town like a puppy he
wanted to train. Checking out of the hotel had not been
pleasant; the knowing grin of her erstwhile friend at the
desk, when she came in with the dawn, made her want
to slap his face. Her suitcase was too big for the cycle,
so she had to bundle a few necessities into her knapsack
and arrange to have the big bag sent on. James had
behaved oddly about that. He had hesitated and mumbled, and suggested the Left Luggage desk at the station, over Susan's outraged objections; then an idea had
apparently occurred to him, and with a mutter that
sounded like ". . . be able to trace you in any case,''
he had agreed.

Now, wearing James's extra helmet and sheltered
from the wind of their passage by his body, Susan found
that the fresh air was blowing some of the fog from her
brain. Trace her? Presumably the police were the missing subject of that sentence James had mumbled. There
was no tangible clue to link her with the crumbling
mansion where Tammas's body lay, with its sightless

blue eyes staring up at the faded pink goddesses of a more ribald era; but it was possible that when the body was found the police might remember her accusations and want to ask her more questions. Well. . . . If they did, they could just come after her. She was no fugitive; she had checked out in the orthodox manner, if at a somewhat unorthodox hour. But that could be explained by James's offering to give her a ride. A poor young student wouldn't pass up a free lift. She was not running away. She had nothing to hide. . . . Well, not much. And if the police got sticky about her accusations she could . . . not retract them exactly, but imply that she had been mistaken.

Susan was not at ease about her situation generally; but the most serious cause of concern was the man to whom she clung with such necessary ardor. James was up to something, she had no doubt of that. He knew something she didn't know. But when she tried to think of him as a conspirator, using her for some evil purpose of his own, she almost laughed aloud.

She had to admit this was an interesting way of seeing Scotland. The scenery had been mixed: the spreading, grimy suburbs of Edinburgh had been succeeded by oil-storage tanks and refineries, then by farmland. And up ahead the hills began, purple in the morning light—Stirling Rock and the Ochils and, shadowy outlines lost in distance, the towering giants of the Highlands. There was the true home of the clans—MacGregor, MacNab, Buchanan; the battlefields of Killiecrankie and Culloden; Glencoe, where the MacDonalds had been massacred in cold blood by men they had entertained as honored guests; Scone, the ancient capital, whose sacred Stone had been raped away by an English conqueror. Some of the most romantic figures in history and literature had roamed the rocky glens: Rob Roy MacGregor, Graham of Claverhouse, Robert the Bruce

and William Wallace—not to mention Bonnie Prince
Charlie.

The glens had also been the scenes of massacre, murder, and wretchedness. The clans had preyed on one
another like Sicilian bandits, murdering men, women
and children with an unchivalrous lack of discrimina-
tion. The infamous Highland Clearances had evicted
thousands of people from the lands their families had
farmed for generations and sent them out to starve without help or mercy. MacBeth had probably been slan-
dered by William Shakespeare, who had maligned
equally well-known historic personages; but Duncan
had died violently on the field of battle, and his was a
typical end for a Scottish king. It was a wild, bloodthirsty history.

By late afternoon, Susan had forgotten romance, history, and everything else except the vast discomfort that
covered her body like an expanded toothache. Once
upon a time she had rather enjoyed motorcycle riding.
She could even drive one herself. But she had never
ridden one for such a long period of time. He had
stopped only once, for a hasty lunch, which Susan regretted as soon as the cycle started up. Her insides had
subsided eventually; they had to, since James refused
to stop. Now she was hungry again.

Late as it was, the sun was still well above the horizon, but that horizon had risen considerably in height.
They rode through mountains that closed in around the
narrow glens like contracting fingers. The Highlands
still retained an aura of remote majesty, in spite of the
invasion—or contamination—of the tourist trade. Susan
began to have dismal forebodings about the inn where
she meant to spend the night—if they ever reached that
hypothetical spot.

She was saved by the tea break, an indulgence no
Briton, Scot or Englishman, would give up for anything
less than an erupting volcano. James had bought extra

food when they stopped for lunch. They ate it by the side of the road. Its narrow paved surface was the only break in an overwhelming display of nature in the raw. The hills were rounded and covered with sparse vegetation; beyond, Susan caught glimpses of higher mountains, stark and bare, with only the white frill of an occasional waterfall to break the severity of the brown flanks. A burn ran along the road, chuckling and bubbling over clean-washed stones. The air was cold and clear, and so rarefied it seemed to sting her throat. There was not an animal to be seen, except for the black, gliding form of a bird of prey high overhead.

"Where am I?" Susan asked plaintively.

James swallowed the last of his sandwich.

"Somewhere in the Grampians," he answered. "We're heading for the Perthshire–Inverness-shire border, where the Sow of Atholl and the Boar of Badenoch lift snow-clad heights out of the mist. The bleak Pass of Drumochter, fifteen hundred feet high, marks a land of trackless wastes, uninhabited save by the deer and the grouse, the wildcat and the eagle! That guidebook is twenty years out of date, though," he added, abandoning the tour-guide voice. "Did you say your chum Campbell is looking for the Picts? What makes him think he'll find them out here? I thought they were little chaps who painted themselves blue and rushed the Romans, down by Hadrian's Wall."

"They weren't little; they were tall and redheaded. And they may or may not have painted themselves blue. Tattooing is a fairly common practice among primitive people. They did fight the Romans, but they lived in the north as well. At one time the Pictish tribes covered most of modern Scotland. For heaven's sake, you ought to know about them. Don't you study them in school?"

"I have struggled, with moderate success, to forget what I learned about Scottish history," James replied.

He stretched out at full length, his hands clasped beneath his head.

"Well, they're your ancestors. It wasn't until the fifth century that the Scotti came over from Ireland and established the kingdom of Dalriada in southwest Scotland. They fought the Picts and intermarried with them for centuries, until Kenneth MacAlpine defeated the last Pictish king and became king of the Scots and the Picts in 824."

"Show-off," said James. He closed his eyes.

"It's true that very little is known about the Picts," Susan went on. "They left no written records—none that we can read, at any rate. Even their spoken language is hypothetical. But they weren't bare-bottomed barbarians; they had kings and cities—and churches, after they were converted to Christianity. Their monumental art, which consists mostly of carved stones, is very sophisticated. Yet there are no true Pictish sites known, and no burials."

"I do have faint recollections of some lecturer babbling about burials," James admitted. "You archaeologists are a ghoulish lot, aren't you?"

"The richest finds come from graves. Like the Sutton Hoo treasure—even you must have heard about that. It was an Anglo-Saxon ship burial—or maybe a cenotaph, since they didn't find any traces of the body. It's been dated to the seventh century. The Picts were still going strong at that time, and I don't see any reason why their kings shouldn't have owned equally beautiful things—silver bowls, jewelry made of gold and garnets and enamel. Of course a lot of the rich burials were looted in antiquity, but Professor Campbell thinks some graves, and some town sites, must have survived. He's one of the world's foremost authorities on the Picts. Here." Susan took her copy of Campbell's book from her purse and thumped it down on James's chest. "This is his magnum opus."

James opened one eye and rolled it down toward his extremities. He picked up the book, but after a single cursory glance he returned it to Susan.

"It looks horribly dull. Also dog-eared. Do you carry this everywhere with you?"

"It is dull," Susan admitted. "Campbell will never become a best seller. But I think he's right. The Picts must have left some physical remains. We just haven't found them yet."

"But why look up here?"

"Campbell has a lead—one of the carved symbol stones, which was recently found in a crofter's yard. He's been pretty closemouthed about the discovery; archaeologists always are when they think they're on to something. But he's no fool, even if he is hung up on his darling Picts, so I assume he must have good reasons for choosing this site."

"But this place—this village, you keep talking about—isn't on the main road. How were you planning to get there?"

"Bus to Blair Atholl," Susan said. "Then another bus—or two. Maybe I could have hitched a ride. I am also capable of walking if I have to."

"I don't believe in your village," James muttered. "There is no such isolated place left in the Highlands."

"It isn't really a village, just a few houses. There used to be a castle or manor house or something near the site. It has been abandoned for centuries, but apparently a few people still scratch a living up here."

"Poaching, probably."

"Well, I don't blame them if they do. I mean, the Nationalists have got a lot of legitimate gripes. Like the taxi driver told me all the salmon streams are rented out to rich English sportsmen. A man can't even fish in his own burn without getting arrested! I think that's terrible."

"It's a pity you and Tammas got off to such a bad

start,'' James said. He sat up and began to gather up
the remains of their snack. ''Your opinions resemble
his to an alarming degree. Let's get on the road. I'm
not sure how long it will take me to find this damned
place, and if we don't find it by dark we may as well
forget it.''

''I don't know why you're doing this,'' Susan said.
''I told you to drop me in Blair Atholl. Wherever you
are going, you must be out of your way.''

''Oh, that's all right. I've become interested in your
Picts. What are your colleagues like?''

''I wouldn't know. I've never met any of them. I suppose most of them are graduate students of Campbell's.''

''Will they be there when we arrive?''

''Some of them ought to be. We're supposed to start
work Monday morning. The eager beavers will probably arrive early.''

''Let's hope we'll be among them.''

Somewhat to Susan's surprise, they were. A few miles
farther along the road she recognized a cairn of stones
that had been mentioned in her directions. A stout
branch had been thrust into a gap between the stones;
pinned to its tip was a fragment of bark with a crudely
drawn hand. The finger pointed toward an unpaved track
that was barely wide enough for a small car.

''Somebody must be here,'' Susan said, cheered by
the jaunty makeshift sign. ''Wasn't it nice of them to
leave a signal?''

''Nice,'' James agreed sourly. He turned into the
track.

It wound through a stand of stunted pines for almost
a mile before turning abruptly into a mountain path
along the flank of a hill so steep it seemed about to
topple over onto them. James swore as a flung stone
scratched the gleaming chrome.

The track turned around a shoulder of rock and widened. A level, meadowlike expanse, some fifteen acres in extent, was crossed by a small stream. Two or three houses huddled close to the side of the hill, and beyond the meadow the great peaks of snow-topped mountains reared their heads into the gaudy sunset. At the far end of the parkland, tumbled heaps of gray stones could be seen.

Susan gasped with pleasure. "Isn't it beautiful?"

"A pint of beer would look a lot more beautiful."

Susan surveyed the low stone houses squatting mistrustfully against the hill.

"They said there was an inn."

"There must be one," James agreed. "That looks hopeful."

The house he indicated was larger than the others, with dormer windows in the steep-pitched roof. An extrusion under the eaves might have once been a sign, before wind and rain had scoured its surface clean.

They chugged slowly along the "main street."

"No television aerials," Susan said. "It's the first place I've ever seen without them."

"I don't suppose reception is very good up here," James said. "Radio as well."

He sounded quite cheerful. Susan attributed his rising spirits to the proximity of beer.

The door of the inn was uncompromisingly closed, but it was unlocked and yielded to James's thrust. The room within was almost dark, so narrow were the windows. Susan knew the winter climate must be bitter, but she found it hard to understand how anyone could close a door on a bright summer evening and that glorious view.

As she stood blinking on the threshold, the first thing that caught her eye was the welcome glint of bottles on shelves behind a rough counter. Before she had time to see more, a voice hailed them from out of the gloom.

"Colleagues? You must be; no one else would come
to this ghastly hole. Enter, friends. What'll you have?"

Susan stumbled across the threshold and felt a hand
catch hers. A face peered out of the shadows—a tanned
young face topped by bright-red hair.

"Ewen MacGregor," said the face. "And this"—indicating a man who stood behind the counter—"this is
Andrew, our genial host. Observe his beaming countenance and air of bonhomie."

Susan laughed. Andrew's glum face became even
glummer. Without comment he turned and began to
make splashing sounds with liquids and glasses. Ewen
steered Susan to a table, one of three that stood against
the wall.

"The amenities include chairs," he remarked, pulling one out for Susan. "And a loft with a fine heap of
musty straw. I hope you have a sleeping bag. The alternative is a blanket that has comforted many an ailing
ewe in her time. I've been in residence since last night.
I regret it. But there is one saving grace. . . ."

He picked up one of the glasses the innkeeper
thumped down on the table and buried his face in it,
coming up with a foam moustache. The others followed
suit. It was excellent beer.

"Once again, please," said James, putting down an
empty glass.

"And what about a little light, Andrew?" Ewen
added. He smiled at Susan. "I'd like a better look at
what appears to be a second saving grace."

Andrew spoke for the first time. "There's three mair
hours o' daylight. I'll not waste the current."

"But the sun is outside," Ewen protested, winking
at Susan. "It hasn't a hope of getting in."

"Then gae oot," said Andrew.

"Not a bad idea." Ewen rose. "What about it, com-
rades? We might walk up and have a look at the site."

Sunlight showed Ewen to be a tall, heavily built man

with the high cheekbones and prominent nose of the
Celt. Freckles and a wide grin gave an ingenuous look
to features that were otherwise roughhewn and rather
forbidding. He gazed at Susan with obvious approval as
they walked across the road toward the ruins.

"This is a pleasant surprise. Old Campbell is noto-
riously prejudiced against female students. Ellie is the
only other girl he accepted for this excavation. Ellen
Glascow," he added, as if they ought to know the name.

"I'm glad there's another girl," Susan said.

"You don't know Ellie?" Ewen looked at James, who
shook his head. "She's from Auld Reekie. I'm Dundee
myself; one of the old boy's prize students, if you can
believe it. You're not one of our crowd, so I assumed
you were from Edinburgh too."

"James isn't going to be on the dig," Susan said.
"He was kind enough to give me a lift up here. And I
guess he's stuck for the night."

Ewen said cheerfully. "He can share the ewe's blanket."

He grinned at James, who gave him the sort of look
Queen Victoria might have given an impertinent housemaid. Susan decided it wasn't worth the effort denying
the perfectly reasonable assumption Ewen had made
about their relationship.

"Who else is here?" she asked.

"Peter MacNab is the only other one so far. He's at
the site; spends all his time there. A dedicated soul. A
genuine ass. A damned good archaeologist. I'll be delighted to introduce you—when I learn your name."

Susan told him.

"I'm from Illinois," she added. "One of my teachers
is a buddy of Professor Campbell's. Didn't he tell you
I was going to be here?"

"He doesn't tell anyone anything," said Ewen. "Except a lot of boring facts about the Picts. Don't let it
worry you, love. Campbell is a closemouthed sort of

bloke, but he knows what he's doing. You just show up
and dig where he tells you. That's all. There's nothing
else to do, actually. Talk abut being cut off! This place
makes Skye look like Hyde Park. The people are a peculiar lot—inbred, and all that. They dislike strangers.
I don't know how our chief talked Andrew into taking
us in. Blackmail, perhaps.''

"No radio?" James asked. "No newspapers?"

Ewen laughed.

"Andrew has a radio. He turns it on once a week to
catch the football scores. But we aren't allowed to listen. He seems to think the cost increases in direct ratio
to the number of people who are listening. Every third
day he drives to Kingussie for supplies, and, if pressed,
will fetch a used copy of *The Scotsman*. That's our com-
munication with the outside world. I find it quite rest-
ful. If there's an atomic holocaust we won't know about
it till it's too late."

They had reached the outer rim of the ruins. Ahead
stood a low stretch of wall, with half of a delicate stone
arch still in position. Ewen stopped.

"Peter!" he bellowed. "Hoy! Where are you? We've
got company."

A brownish lump, which Susan had taken for a
medium-sized boulder, now moved and revealed itself
as the upended rump of an exceedingly tall young man.
He blinked at them from under a mop of dark hair as
long as James's. His narrow face was clean shaven except for the inevitable stubble of beard; male excavators
usually welcome the excuse to go unshaven for the
course of a dig, and some raise handsome beards. This
beard, if it ever reached maturity, would not be handsome. It was a mixture of red, brown, and black.

"You're not Ellen," Peter remarked, staring at Susan.

Ewen performed introductions, added, "Susan is
from the States. An encouraging sign, wouldn't you say?

Who knows what other unexpected treats our beloved leader may have in store for us? A Persian houri, perhaps, or a busty Italian lovely?''

Peter, accustomed to his colleague's flippancy, didn't even glance at him. He continued to stare at Susan.

"The States? With whom did you study?"

"Dr. Bliss. Arnold Bliss."

Peter nodded. "A reasonably decent scholar. But his interpretation of the Regus A material—"

"Shut up," said Ewen. He added, to the others, "Peter is probably the dullest human being you'll ever meet. Talks of nothing but archaeology. Don't let him start."

Unperturbed, Peter returned to his interrupted activities, and Ewen led the other two toward a sizable heap of stone at the southwest angle of the open space.

Susan was getting excited. This was her first real dig, except for a summer in Virginia excavating a much-worked-over Indian mound, which had yielded nothing more exciting than arrowheads. This site appealed to the romantic in her as well as the professional, for the fragmentary walls were clearly much later in date than the hypothetical Picts—in whom Susan had to admit she had very little interest. The structure that had once stood here was medieval in date, that much was obvious from the remaining stonework, but its exact nature puzzled her. The broken arch suggested a church, yet other clues implied a more secular structure. Surely that gaping hole between two stretches of wall had once been the gateway of a fortified castle.

She stumbled. Ewen caught her and set her on her feet with a smooth, effortless motion. He grinned sympathetically.

"The first time for you? It is exciting. And this looks a rather hopeful site."

"For the Picts?" Susan asked. "If this wall isn't tenth or eleventh century, I'll eat it."

"Quite right," Ewen said. "There was a small castle

here once. And a sizable chapel, rather large for a provincial nobleman, unless—"

"Unless it was erected on the site of an earlier church," Susan interrupted eagerly. "A spot hallowed by earlier worship, dedicated to a saint. . . ."

"Very good." Ewen squeezed her arm. "That's what dear old Campbell thinks. The problem is a bit complicated," he added, nodding amiably at James, who was listening with a bored expression, "but it involves Saint Ninian, who is supposed to have converted the Picts at some time in the mists of antiquity. The sources mention a Casa Candida, or White House, founded by Ninian, and sure enough, remains of an early sanctuary were located which had whitewashed walls. In his early probing at this site Campbell claims he found similar walls. Add that to the symbol stone, which our jolly innkeeper was using for a cattle trough till Campbell stumbled over it—literally, if apocryphal accounts are to be believed—and you get . . ."

"Picts," Susan agreed. "Wow, what a coup that would be."

"Coup isn't the word. It would be a bloody revolution, if we could turn up a genuine Pictish site. It would make Campbell the grand old man of British archaeology, and it wouldn't do us any harm, either. The thing that makes this site particularly promising is its isolation. The castle was abandoned sometime in the fourteenth century, and nobody has been here since except for the crofters. They vandalized the castle for their houses—you probably noticed that the stones of which the inn is built come from here. But that's all they did. They're a dull lot; it wouldn't occur to them to dig for treasure—"

James started and slapped at his arm as if an insect had stung him.

"Treasure?" he repeated. "What sort of treasure would be hidden here?"

"Oh, Lord, all sorts," Ewen said sweepingly. "If the castle was destroyed by an enemy, the owners might have buried the family plate in the dungeon before dying on the walls. Of course Campbell is praying for a hoard of Pictish treasure, like the one that was found in Shetland, only bigger."

"That one wasn't bad," Susan said. "You mean the Saint Ninian's Isle treasure? There were half a dozen silver vessels, among other things, and some beautiful silver brooches."

"Silver," James said stupidly. "There was gold in the Sutton Hoo burial."

"That was in Suffolk," Ewen answered. "Same date, different culture. Actually, the Picts go back to God knows when. Fifth century at least. The Sutton Hoo material is unique, of course, but a Pictish equivalent— an undisturbed royal burial—would be worth even more. I'm thinking of its historical value, but it would be worth a fortune on the illegal antiquities market—which is why we can thank the Lord that our local peasants aren't as up to date as their peers in Italy and Greece. One can't blame the poor devils, in a way; they've been exploited by the gentry for generations, and they feel they have a right to anything that is found in their fields. All the same, illegal amateur digging is disastrous for archaeology."

He broke off with a self-conscious laugh. "Here, I'm beginning to sound like Peter. Don't want to bore you with our professional chatter, chum."

James's expression could hardly be called bored. Distracted might be a more accurate word. His eyes were wide and wild, his eyebrows elevated. His lips moved in silent commentary.

"What's the matter with you?" Susan asked sharply.

"Looks as if he's just remembered an important job he forgot to do," Ewen remarked. He glanced at Susan. "Actually, I think he might easily make it back to civilization tonight, if he left at once. Quite an easy run, really.''

''Hmm,'' said James, coming back to life and giving Ewen an unfriendly look. ''Not that I want to accuse you of ulterior motives, chum, but perhaps I had better stay the night. Only I wouldn't want to deprive a legitimate archaeologist of his or her share of the sheep blanket.''

''There are plenty of blankets,'' Ewen admitted. He looked downcast, but only for a moment; his normally ebullient personality reasserted itself, and he gave James a sheepish smile. ''It was worth a try. . . . No, actually, I don't expect any other members of the group will arrive now before tomorrow. So feel free. I expect you'd like something to eat. Let's go back and see what atrocity Mrs. Andrew is preparing for supper. It will be something with mutton in it, you can be sure.''

As they headed back toward the inn, Ewen tactfully fell behind. James's response to his not-so-subtle hint had confirmed his assumption about the relationship between the pair, and he was giving them a chance to sort out their plans for the night. As soon as he was out of earshot James hissed out of the corner of his mouth,

''We've got to talk.''

''What about?''

''Good God, woman! Have you forgotten what happened to Tammas?''

''I wish I could. What's bugging you? You haven't said a word about it all day, and now all of a sudden. . . . I can't figure you out. What are you doing here, anyway? I thought you were going to drop me and go on your merry way. Where are you going, if I may ask?''

''Home,'' said James.

''I thought you lived in Edinburgh.''

''You don't suppose that hole in the wall is where I

was born and raised, do you? I've a home like anyone else. It isn't far from here. A bit south of Loch Ness.''

''It figures,'' said Susan. ''The monster and all. . . . Well, we'll talk, but not until we've eaten. You'll be in a better mood with something in your stomach.''

She had the final word. They had reached the inn and Ewen was closing in on them.

The interior of the room was darker than before. Ewen switched on the light. There was no objection from the host, for the simple reason that he was not present. Doubtful odors, issuing from another room, indicated that supper was being prepared. It definitely included mutton.

Conversation with Ewen was not difficult. He could probably carry on a solo discussion with himself. Susan talked with him about the problems of the site and found him well informed under his flippant exterior. James was only present in body. He said not a word, but seemed to be engaged in some painful inner debate. That it was painful Susan could not doubt. His brow was furrowed; even his moustache seemed to droop.

The walls were so thick and the door so heavy that they had no warning at all. The door opened and the newcomers were there, peering across the threshold.

The first was a girl, and Susan knew she must be the aforementioned Ellie. She was about Susan's age, but there the resemblance ended. Susan was reminded of a moth—one of the insignificant little night flutterers called dusty millers. The girl's hair, of an indeterminate tannish shade, brushed out on both sides of her face and was flattened on top by a band of woven fabric. Her features were small and pinched; her face tapered abruptly to a narrow, pointed chin. The face seemed three quarters eyes, thanks to the big horn-rimmed glasses; it was insectlike and oddly endearing, as are the faces of some of the smaller moths. Ellie was wearing shorts and a coarse blue shirt, which was wrinkled

and sweat-stained. Her meager shoulders were bowed
under the weight of a bulging knapsack. But the most
striking thing about her was the expression of abject
terror that whitened her face as soon as her eyes lit on
Susan.

The young man behind Ellie was taller, but not much
broader. He was bearded, though not so affluently as
James; his hair and beard were fair, and his nose had
the magnificent curves usually attributed to the peoples
of the eastern Mediterranean, but which are often found
in the Highlands.

He shoved at Ellie, who seemed to be rooted to the
spot. She moved to one side, never taking her eyes off
Susan. Her companion stepped into the room. He was
smiling and had started to slip his shoulders free of his
pack when he too was struck with speechless consternation.

Ewen greeted the newcomers with a roar of delight.

"Ellie and Dugald! I'd given you up. What did you do,
walk from the main road? You're just in time for some of
Andrews' ghastly stew. But first, what about—"

It was finally borne in upon him that something was
wrong. Dugald raised his arm and pointed at James.

"Ewen, you fool, don't you know who he is? That's
Erskine. The Edinburgh murderer!"

Chapter 4

Susan felt as if the curtain ought to come down on the frozen tableau; no author could have invented a more effective ending to a scene. Unfortunately, this was not a theater. Sooner or later, someone would have to do something. Susan looked at James. He was staring at Dugald, but his look of outrage indignation was slightly overdone.

Ewen was the first to regain his voice. Emotion made him revert to pure Scots.

"Ye're daft, mon," he bellowed. "Daft! What are ye havering aboot?"

"It—it was on the telly," Dugald stuttered. "In a hotel in Blair Atholl, a few hours ago. He stabbed an old man—killed him. The sgian-dhu had the Erskine crest—"

"What?" James shouted.

"That's not proof," Ewen said slowly.

"He was seen," Dugald insisted. "Seen leaving the house in the middle of the night. Along with a lassie—" His rigid arm swiveled toward Susan.

"Man, you are out of you mind," Ewen exclaimed. "Susan isn't . . . Susan doesn't . . ."

"Oh, but she is, and she does," said Ellie. Her soft, precise voice sounded strange after the shouts of the men; but it held a quiet malevolence that was even more threatening. "I don't know Mr. Erskine, but I know about *her*. She's wicked. Evil and treacherous. Don't let her get away."

"You know her?" Ewen asked dazedly. "How could you? Where did you meet her?"

The thick lenses of Ellie's glasses flashed as she turned her head away.

"I—I know about her. I didn't say. . . . Can't you take my word? She's a murderer!"

"Jamie," Susan said urgently. "I think I know who—"

"All right, Susan." James stood up, pushing his chair back. He nodded at Dugald, who had finally freed himself of his knapsack and was dancing up and down waving his arms and uttering incoherent challenges. "I'm Erskine, all right. I suppose Dugald has seen me around the University. His face is vaguely familiar to me. But the rest of it is all wrong. We've been framed. I don't know who framed us, or why, but I'm going to find out. And I suspect some of the answers start right here. Damn it, can't we sit down and talk like reasonable people? I'm as anxious to discover the truth as you are."

"Hmph." Ewen rubbed his chin. "I've never been one for turning a man over to the police. Start talking, Erskine. Shut up, Ellie. And for God's sake, Dugald, stop dancing about."

Dugald had closed the door, presumably to keep the miscreants from escaping, but they might have heard the sounds outside if they had not been so preoccupied. The opening of the door took everyone by surprise and sent Dugald staggering back against the bar.

The man who stood in the open doorway seemed to fill it, psychologically if not physically. Susan didn't

recognize him at first. He was out of context. She had
not expected to see him again, certainly not here. After
a moment she finally found the name.

"Ed Jackson!"

The cool dark eyes focused on her.

"Jackson, yes. From Interpol. It took me a while to
track you two down. I didn't think you'd be stupid
enough to come here."

"Inter——" Dugald began.

Jackson waved him to silence.

"These two are wanted for murder. Ah, I see you
know that. What you don't know is that there are international ramifications. This girl. . . . Well, that's not
your worry. But assisting the police is. You, there—"
He gestured at Ewen. "Tie him up. And do a good job
of it, I've no intention of driving back to Edinburgh
with him loose in the back seat. Come on, move!"

"But—" Ewen's voice had risen a full octave.

"The alternative is for me to immobilize him," Jackson said coldly. "He won't like it. Unarmed combat is
one of my many specialties."

"Wait a minute!" Susan moved toward him. "You
can't—"

He struck her across the face, a crisp openhanded
slap that sent her reeling.

James jumped at Jackson. Ewen grabbed him, wrapping long arms around his body and pinning his hands.
They struggled, mouthing breathless interjections. Finally James gave up.

"*Et tu, Brute,*" he said unoriginally. "Susan, are
you hurt?"

"Yes," said Susan, from the bench to which she had
been flung. She rubbed her stinging cheek.

"Brutus be damned," Ewen panted. "I'm no ally to
a murderer, Erskine. Just stand still now, like a good
lad, while I tie you up. Would you rather be skelped by
that fearsome man there? No, surely you would not, it

would be a foolish act. Just be still. . . . Good lad, now. . . .''

He removed his grip and smiled reassuringly at Jackson, who was watching the performance with ill-concealed impatience and no amusement whatever.

''Rope,'' said Ewen, looking around the room. ''Wouldn't you know that there's never a wee rope about when it's needed. What. . . . Ah.''

He unbuckled his belt and pulled it free. James retreated, one slow step after another; Ewen followed him, clutching his trousers with one hand, waving the belt like a leash, and mumbling encouragement.

''Stand, that's a good lad. It willna hurt. . . . Not. . . . Damn these trousers!''

Susan overcame an insane desire to laugh. It was quite obvious to her what Ewen was doing. She didn't know why he was doing it; she only hoped Jackson was not sufficiently acute to anticipate the next move.

Ewen had maneuvered James across the room toward the bar. Dugald was still near the door, staring like a man bereft of his wits. With a sharp, profane word, Jackson started forward. At the same moment Ewen's pants dropped. Susan had a flashing glimpse of gaudy tartan shorts, but she did not have time to study the effect with the appreciation it deserved; Ewen stumbled, clutching with both hands at his recalcitrant garment. He fell against Jackson. The two crashed to the floor.

Whirling around, James hit the staring Dugald smack on the chin, and followed it up by a nasty blow in an illegal area. Dugald joined the pair thrashing around on the floor. James caught Susan's wrist and yanked her out the door.

He slammed it shut, looked wildly about, and picked up a stout piece of kindling from the wood stack by the steps. He wedged the stick into a crack in the stone step so that it was braced against the door.

Jackson's car, a tan Morris, was parked by the steps.
"The car," Susan gasped. "Let's take it."

James didn't even bother to answer. He was already
busy with the car, and as he raised the hood Susan
realized the folly of her suggestion. Only an idiot would
have left the keys in the ignition, and Jackson was no
idiot. Starting the car without keys would take time,
and they had none. It would also leave the pursuers with
a vehicle of equal speed—the motorcycle. One of the
vehicles had to be disabled, and James proceeded to do
this without delay and without finesse. The terrain, like
that of most of Scotland, was littered with stones. James
grabbed the biggest he could conveniently lift and threw
it into the engine of the car. A satisfactory cracking,
splitting sound ensued, followed by a hiss and a spout
of liquid.

"Hurry," James yelled, running for the motorcycle.
The door of the inn vibrated as something heavy struck
it from within.

They were off down the pebbly track amid a storm
of dust. Susan closed her eyes and hung on.

When they swung onto the main road James increased speed. Conversation was impossible and unnecessary. The main thing was to get as far away from
the inn as possible in the shortest possible time. That
time would be very short. Immobilizing Jackson's car
had given them a few extra minutes; but there must be
other means of transportation in the village, and there
definitely was a telephone. Susan had seen the wires.
Jackson wouldn't know whether they had gone east or
west on the main road, but he could call and have road-
blocks set up at both ends.

Susan moaned. Her stomach hurt. The pain was not
caused by fear. She was hungry. Even mutton stew
would have tasted good, and she had a feeling it was
going to be a long time before she got anything to eat.

II

They lay in a moonlit clearing under the shelter of a pine. The sharp, aromatic tang of the fir trees blended with the exquisite clarity of cold mountain air. Wrapped in one another's arms, they watched the moonlight silver the darkness of night.

"I'm hungry," Susan said.

"You had the remains of the ham sandwich."

"A lot of help that was."

"What do you expect me to do, run out to the nearest café and fetch you a snack?"

"I'm cold."

"I," said James, "am doing all I can to remedy that."

"It's not enough. You are the most ill-equipped fugitive I've ever heard of. No food, no sleeping bag, no blanket, no—"

"I am not a seer. How the hell did I know we'd have to run for it?"

He shifted position, pulling her closer to him and wrapping the folds of his jacket more tightly around her. The movement brought Susan's cheek into contact with his beard, and she swore. The beard had been the final disillusionment in a generally annoying day. Beards were supposed to be sleek and silky and sensuous. James's beard felt like a bristly doormat.

"I should think you'd be tired enough to forget food," James said. "God knows how long it's been since we slept."

"You don't seem to be that tired," said Susan pointedly. She reached back and shifted James's hand.

"You *said* you were cold. There's one activity that is particularly—"

"I think men are crazy," said Susan. "How can you think about that at a time like this? Anyhow, your beard turns me off."

She felt James stiffen in outrage, and added, in a more conciliatory voice, "We've got a lot to talk about. How are we going to get out of this mess?"

"You said you were too tired to talk. You said you—"

"Stop quoting me! We might as well talk; I'm too tired to sleep. Where is this place we're heading for? I'll bet you're lost. Since we turned off the road we've been winding all over the forest primeval. You can't possibly—"

James sat up. The insult to his beard still rankled; he let Susan's head drop to the ground with a thud.

"Damn it, I can't sleep either. And," he added meaningfully, "it isn't because I'm hungry. As for our destination, I told you. I'm going home. Not to the castle, because they may be expecting me to go there—"

"The castle!"

"It's a small castle," said James defensively.

"Are you anybody—well—anybody important?"

James laughed. "Good Lord, no. We're the most obscure branch of the Erskines. Never had a bean, or an office worth mentioning. The castle is a crumbling ruin. I'd swap it for a nice modern flat any day. Especially now. It's probably surrounded by police."

Susan turned onto her back and clasped her hands under her head. She had never seen such brilliant stars. They looked as if they were caught in the boughs above, like scattered diamonds.

"Jackson seems to know all about us," she agreed. "He's probably got some of his men staked out on your home ground."

"We had better have a talk, at that," James said. "You didn't believe that rot about Interpol, did you?"

"Well . . ."

"If Jackson is the chap you encountered, oh, so accidentally, on that bus tour you told me about, he's a phony. How could he possibly take you for an international crook?"

"That was after Tammas gave me the message," Susan said. "Obviously he mistook me for someone else. Jackson could have made the same mistake. What baffles me is how Tammas could have made such a booboo. I have a hunch, now, as to whom he took me for; but there's no resemblance between me and that scrawny little wench. I mean, I'm not conceited—"

"Oh, no," said James.

"Tammas was a rotten conspirator," Susan said stubbornly. "I wouldn't have anyone that sloppy in *my* conspiracy."

"Evidently someone else felt the same way," James said.

The shiver that ran through Susan's body was not induced by the cool night air.

"Let's take it from the start," James said. He leaned back against the bole of a tree and clasped his hands around his bent knees. A single shaft of moonlight, which left the rest of his body in shadow, outlined the long, curled fingers and brought out the ridged musculature and bone structure of his wrists, whitening them like the marble hands of a knight's effigy.

"A good deal of this is conjecture." James went on. "But it fits together rather well. The paper Tammas gave you was a message. Only he gave it to the wrong person. Now I don't believe in this double business; and even if you did have a twin somewhere, it would be too wild a coincidence if you were both in Edinburgh at the same time. So why did Tammas select you? The only possible answer is that he was told to give the message to a girl—any further information would be wasted on Tammas—who was doing something, or wearing something, that would identify her. The only thing about you that distinguishes you from all the other young females in Edinburgh is your archaeological background. Were you by any chance carrying that book the night you saw Tammas? The Penguin?"

"I don't remember. I might have been. I probably was."

"You probably were. Anyhow, let's assume, for a starter, that Tammas had been told to pass on his message to a contact who carried something connected with the dig, or the Picts, or Professor Campbell. Presumably that contact was Ellie. Only you showed up first, so you got the message. Ordinarily, the error wouldn't have mattered. The quotation is meaningless on the surface; a normal tourist would have thrown the paper away and forgotten about it. But you aren't normal. You're a frustrated romantic who knows Scottish history cold, and who has memorized thousand of lines of useless poetry. Several days after the event you were able to quote the lines and give the source. Now think, Susan. Who else knew you were able to do that?"

"Oh, God," said Susan. She sat up and wrapped her arms around her shivering body. "Me and my big mouth! Everybody in the hotel could have known. I spouted off in front of the policeman and the clerk and the manager and . . . Jackson. He was there when I got mad and started babbling about James the First and *The King's Quair*. But that wasn't when he first discovered my expertise about Scottish poetry. He followed me on that bus tour. . . . How do you suppose they found out about me?"

"I can think of several possibilities," James said. "Perhaps Tammas followed you back to your hotel that night. Or—here's an idea—when Ellie turned up, the conspirators learned that an error had been made. Campbell hadn't mentioned you to Ewen, but he might have done to Ellie. Once they knew your name it would be easy to locate you. Jackson trailed you to the bus station. . . ."

". . . to find out who I was and how much I knew," Susan finished the sentence. "The bus was half empty; he could have bought a ticket at the last minute. Looking back on our conversation, I can see that he was pumping me. And what did I do? I quoted obscure Scottish poets at him all day long? He made love to me so he could search my purse—looking for the message or any other incriminating evidence. . . ."

"That must have been his only motive," James agreed, in a singularly unpleasant voice. "So he made love to you, did he? Are you certain you can tell the difference between mad passion and homicidal mania?"

"A certain doubt did pass through my mind at the time," Susan admitted in a small voice. "He seems to have a rather hasty temper. I can see why he was mad. He must have thought I was leading him on. But he couldn't risk strangling me then, in a public place, with the bus waiting. So he followed me to the hotel to—to—finish the job?"

"I doubt that," James said calmly. "It wasn't your knowledge of Scottish poetry that worried Jackson. You might still be an innocent bystander. He was afraid you might be more than that—a rival conspirator. He had to get a look into your purse to see if you were carrying a false passport, or a gun, or any of the other useful items conspirators habitually carry. I suppose during the—er—encounter, he managed to ascertain that you were not concealing a weapon on your person?"

"I suppose he did," Susan muttered. Her face was hot. She was glad the darkness concealed it from James.

"He found nothing," James continued. "But he still wasn't certain; you must have confused the hell out of him with your little quotations from the poets. You look, and behave, like a baby-faced innocent, but to a suspicious mind your boasts must have sounded like veiled taunts. Jackson followed you to the hotel because he was still in doubt, and he arrived on the scene to discover that poor auld Tammas had done it again. In attempting to correct his initial error, he had committed an even more serious mistake. By going to such lengths to retrieve an otherwise meaningless scrap of paper, he had emphasized its importance.

"You proceeded to clear yourself, in Jackson's eyes, by telling the police about the quotation. You wouldn't have been so candid if you had known that it was significant. But the incident convinced Jackson that Tammas was no longer dependable. So—exit Tammas."

"It makes sense," Susan agreed gloomily. "So Jackson is not a policeman. He's a bad guy. One of *them*—whoever they are. I think I'd rather be chased by the police than by a nameless gang of professional criminals."

"We are being chased by both," James pointed out. "The professional touch is evident in the quickness with which the conspirators took advantage of our discovering Tammas's body. They may have been in the neighborhood when we arrived—the body was still warm. They let us go, which was clever of them. Two more murders wouldn't have been a bright idea. If you were killed, after having made a public outcry about your encounter with Tammas, the police might be moved to investigate Tammas's recent activities. The gang decided to put us out of action in a more subtle manner. They substituted my sgian-dhu for the knife that had been used—swiped it right out of my room after we left. It wouldn't be difficult to bribe a witness to say he had seen us. Now that we're fugitives, we are fair game. We could be killed resisting arrest; we could have a fatal accident during our wild escape; we could even disappear, permanently, if Jackson catches up with us out here. It's not hard to hide a pair of corpses in the Highlands."

"You are the most cheerful conversationalist." Susan groaned. "Why don't we give ourselves up, then? If your theories are right, we'd be a helluva lot safer in jail."

"Undoubtedly. But we'd also be out of action. I don't believe we could be railroaded into a prison sentence for a murder we didn't commit, but arguing with the police is not my idea of how to spend the summer. You see what all this implies, don't you? Our unknown adversaries don't care whether we're dead, or simply preoccupied. Their plans will come to head within a certain period of time. They want us out of the way until the job is done."

"What job? What is the point of all this?"

"That's a good question. Let's get back to the archaeological clue. And if you think my theories thus far are based on insufficient evidence, wait till you hear the rest. I think there are two groups of what you childishly refer to as bad guys. Tammas was daft, but he was not a criminal in the ordinary sense. It's impossible that he could have had anything to do with a cold-blooded rat like Jackson. I tell you, that chap is a pro. He wasn't bragging when he said he was a specialist in unarmed combat. I'll wager he's pretty good at armed combat too. He was carrying a gun; did you notice the way his jacket bulged? Ewen saw it; that's why he grabbed me, to keep me from getting shot."

"God bless him," Susan said devoutly. "I wondered why he helped us get away."

"I don't think he knew himself. He took rather a fancy to you, and he didn't like Jackson's looks—or the gun. I doubt that Ewen is mixed up in the plot, but somebody on that staff is."

"Ellie."

"Ellie. She gave herself away with her innuendoes about you, but I have a feeling she honestly believes we killed Tammas. She's not a professional crook either. Therefore she must be a member of Tammas's organization."

"How could he have mistaken me for her, if she's one of his group?"

"You don't know these people," James said wisely. "The Innocent Fanatics, one might call them. They simply adore playing silly tricks and behaving like stage spies. The organization is probably divided into cells, like the Communist underground. No member knows more than two other members, and they communicate by means of cryptic idiocies like the message you got."

"You sound as if you knew a lot about the organization," Susan said suspiciously.

There was a slight pause before James replied.

"Merely logical surmise."

"Hmm. All right, then; the Innocent Fanatics are one group. How do you suppose they got mixed up with Jackson? Innocent he is not."

"An excellent question." James sounded very smug. Susan peered at him through the darkness, trying to see his face.

"I know what you're thinking," she said. "When Ewen mentioned treasure, you stiffened like a pointer."

"What else could it be? Professional criminals wouldn't be interested in Tammas's wild plots. One thing attracts those types—money. You know and I know that there's a fortune being made out of illicit archaeological smuggling these days. There is something buried in those ruins that means big money."

"But Tammas wasn't interested in money," Susan argued. "Whatever your treasure may be, it has some appeal beyond mere cash value."

"Possibly. but I don't think we'll get anywhere speculating about its nature. We haven't enough information. The question is, what are we going to do about all this?"

"The police—"

"Would you care to explain our theories to a local bobby in your home town?" James inquired politely. "Our lads are no more imaginative, darling."

"You mean we should—"

"Look here, my girl, I'm not aching to play young detective. We haven't any choice. I don't give a damn about saving one of Scotland's archaeological treasures; I just want to keep my valuable hide unholed. If we don't stop them, they'll stop us. Jackson is efficient enough to scare me, and he can't be the only one of them. There's one clue we haven't discussed, but it must be important, or they wouldn't be so anxious to quiet you. The quotation, Susan. What meaning does it have?"

"I can't think. I'm too hungry."

"All right, then." James pushed himself to a standing position. "We may as well get on. I thought some rest would be a good idea, but I can't seem to sleep either. The trails are bad in the dark, and we'll have to do most of it on foot. Are you game?"

"I'll do anything," Susan said, "that will bring me to something to eat."

III

In the following hours she was to regret this statement. The motorcycle had to be abandoned; its description had undoubtedly been circulated to every policeman in Scotland. They pushed it into a rocky hollow and piled branches over it so that no sparkle of chrome could betray its presence. James lingered over the job, arranging the camouflage with tender care, until Susan remarked sarcastically,

"Why don't you shoot it? It would be the kindest thing to do."

After that, James allowed her to carry her own knapsack. He had an electric lantern, but he wouldn't use it except in the roughest areas. The moonlight helped a little. Under its eerie glow they plodded through the gorse and heather of upland moors. That was the easy part. After the moon went down the terrain changed.

Some of the slopes were so steep they had to be traversed on all fours. One section involved a bit of rock climbing that would have been nasty enough in daylight. In the dark it was utterly foolhardy; Susan could not have managed it if James had not relieved her of her pack and guided her every step with infinite patience. "Three inches down . . . now a bit to the left, that's got it, your toe in that crevice . . . Now let go with your right hand, it's okay, I've got you. . . ." Her hunger was no longer a joke. Exertion and nervous fatigue had burned up her reserves and she began to feel lightheaded as she staggered after James.

Finally the interminable night ended, not in the spectacle of sunrise, but in a gradual lightening of the air. Susan had sunk into a haze of weariness, plodding along one step at a time, without thinking of anything beyond the next impossible step. When James stopped she walked into him. He put his arm around her shoulders and pulled her to his side. His face was an ugly shade of gray from sheer fatigue, but he grinned cheerfully at her.

"Almost there, love. You're a Spartan. Can you keep it up for another ten minutes? Bed and breakfast at the end of it all."

Susan nodded. She sought numbly for a suitable response. "I'm sorry I said that about your beard," she muttered.

Her knees began to sag, in spite of her best efforts. James tightened his grip.

"Look there," he said, and pushed aside a branch.

They stood on the edge of a sheer drop. Down below lay a small glen, long and winding, but so narrow Susan could have thrown a ball and hit the opposite cliff. At the far end, where the glen broadened out, stood the castle, on its own small hill. It might be as ruined as James had claimed, but distance lent it perfection. Lichen and ivy stroked green fingers along the soft gray stone of the walls, which were reflected in the mirror-smooth waters of a blue loch. A purple mountain, cloud-capped, formed a back-drop. And on the loch floated white shapes, barely visible in the distance. . . .

"Glen Ealachan," said James. "The word means 'swans'—and there they are. Mean-tempered brutes," he added. "Bite your finger off if you give them the chance. The old man adores them. There's a stupid tradition that so long as the swans swim on Loch Ealachan, the laird of Glen Ealachan will hold his ancient heritage. Dad's had it printed up in a little booklet. He sells it to tourists."

Susan nodded dumbly. She was speechless, not so much with fatigue as with a sharp attack of love at first sight. The castle was just right—not too big, not too small; built in a square, with circular towers on three corners. The towers had conical roofs, like witches' caps. On the fourth corner stood a massive battlemented keep, with arched Gothic windows. Susan wanted it, with an instant, unreasoning passion.

A neat picture-book village lay beyond the castle, and there was considerable traffic on the road that ran through the glen. Other houses were scattered about, some of them almost hidden among the trees that covered the lower hills. Only trails of blue smoke betrayed their existence. The smoke suggested fire, fire suggested cooking. . . . Susan's stomach let out a loud, insistent rumble.

"Quite," said James. "This way."

After the ordeals of the night, the path James indicated looked like duck's soup. It led through the trees and at times vanished altogether, but James never hesitated.

"One of my childhood rambles," he observed, helping Susan over a fallen log. His voice was soft; when Susan started to speak he touched his finger to her lips. "There seems to be considerable activity around the place this morning. Mairi's cottage ought to be safe; it's quite a distance from any other house.''

The cottage had no backyard. A grove of larches came right up to the back door. James surveyed the house for several minutes from behind a tree, and then led Susan in a rush to the door. It opened before he had a chance to knock. The woman who confronted them stood with her clenched fists on her ample hips. Iron-gray hair, pulled back into a bun, framed a face as weather-beaten as the surrounding rocks. She paid no attention whatever to Susan, but looked James up and down critically.

"Ye were lang in coming, Jamie. The sight gave me warning yesternicht.''

"You've no more of the sight than Prince there,'' James answered, nodding at a fuzzy black-and-white heap that lay on the kitchen floor behind the woman. An eye appeared among the fuzz. It studied James disinterestedly and then closed again.

"And who's to say Prince hasna the sight? The wee doggie has as much sense as you, laddie.''

"He looks a lot like you too,'' Susan said, unable to resist.

Mairi let out a snort of laughter.

"Aye, the lassie has the richt o' it. I ken yer reasons, Jamie, but—''

"Can't we argue inside?'' James pleaded. "We're starved, Mairi, and dead tired.''

"And fleeing frae the poliss.'' Mairi nodded in dour agreement. She stepped back from the door and motioned them in. "They were here yester even. Come in, laddie, come in; but dinna fear, there isna a mon i' the glen would betray the young laird—''

"Don't pay any attention to the way she talks,'' James said to Susan. "She picked it up from dad, while she was guiding tourists through the castle. The trippers love it; they expect all Scots to talk like Bobby Burns.

Mairi, I can think of half a dozen men who'd turn me in for a pint.''

They continued to bicker amicably while Mairi heaped the table with food. Susan ignored them. Oatmeal with thick yellow cream, eggs fried in bacon drippings, scones and homemade jam occupied her full attention. There was no coffee, but the sweet black tea was almost as good. Mairi seemed pleased at her appetite, remarking,

''There's some point to feeding a lassie that can eat like yon.''

''What we need now,'' said James, replete, ''is a wash and bed. We've been up for two nights, Mairi.''

''A basin in the kitchen is what ye'll have,'' said Mairi. ''And,'' she added, fixing James with a stern eye, ''twa beds. The one i' the loft for you, Jamie. Unless . . . the Laird save us, laddie, ye've not—''

''I've done a number of mad things in the last two days,'' said James. ''But marriage is not one of them. Mairi, you could put us side by side and not feel a twinge in your Calvinist conscience. We're both too tired.''

''Aye,'' said Mairi skeptically. ''But ye'll have two beds a' the same.''

It was late evening before Susan woke up. The slanted sunrays gave her an approximate idea of the time. She yawned and stretched, feeling about a thousand years younger than she had felt when she fell into the narrow bed. The mattress made strange rustling noises when she moved, but the linen was as soft as the finest percale, and it smelled of sunshine, fresh air, and pine.

The room was Mairi's own bedroom. The cottage was the classic but-and-ben—two rooms, with the added amenity of a loft. The bedroom was tiny and roughly furnished. White curtains blew in the breeze. A violently tinted calendar bearing the legend ''MacRae's Feed and Grain'' and the picture of a puppy nuzzling an apprehensive-looking kitten was the only ornament in the room.

Susan stretched again. The mattress rustled. The door opened and Mairi's head appeared.

"Ye maun be hungry," she said. "Hasten to yer tea."

"I think you and I are going to be good friends," said Susan approvingly.

It was her first experience with a genuine Scottish high tea, and it was almost too much for her. Ham and eggs, two kinds of cake, scones, biscuits of all varieties—the feast went on and on. James joined them, climbing down a ladder from a dark hole in the ceiling of the combined kitchen-living room, and trying, without much success, to keep the pleats of his kilt tightly wrapped around his knees. Susan stopped eating to watch.

'That's not the Erskine sett," she remarked.

"Ma husband was a MacKinnon," Mairi answered, putting another platter of bacon and eggs on the table. "The plaid an' philabeg he had frae his fayther. I wove the sark for the puir mon masel'. It would be foolish, now wouldn't it, for Jamie to run aboot the countryside in the Erskine tartan?"

"I want my jeans," James said sullenly.

"Well, ye canna hae your jeans. They're i' the wash. Sit doon an' eat, Jamie."

James obeyed, glancing suspiciously at Susan's freshly washed and ironed garments, which she had found laid out for her at the foot of the bed.

"Her clothes are clean," he said. "Why can't I—"

"Because the poliss hae a descreeption o' yer claes," said Mairi. "Ye maun change yer appearance the noo. After tea I'll juist take a wee clip wi' the scissors—"

"Oh, no," said James.

"It's a good idea," Susan said. "In those clothes, with your hair cut and your beard gone, nobody would—"

"No!"

Susan exchanged glances with Mairi.

"Aye, aye," said the latter, nodding grimly. "Juist like a' the men. Not a grain o' guid sense amang the sex. We'll leave it tae the laird to argue wi' the fule laddie."

James looked up from his plate.

"Does he know we're here?"

"Ay, he kens. I went tae the castle while ye slept. He'll be waiting for ye i' the forenicht."

"You're daft," James said. "I'm not going to stroll up to the castle in the twilight or any other time. He'll have to come here. The police must have left a man on guard—"

"Aye, they did," said Mairi, rocking placidly. "A wee bit man he is. But ye'll nae want to meet him. Na, na, ye maun gae by the tunnel. The laird has said so."

"Oh, no," James set his cup down with a crash. "Not that damned tunnel—sorry, Mairi, but it is a damned tunnel. Why, the whole thing is about to collapse. We'll be buried alive. Susan—"

He looked at Susan and threw up his hands.

"I might have known."

"A tunnel," breathed Susan rapturously. "A secret tunnel!"

The tunnel did look as if it were about to cave in. So far as Susan was concerned, this only added to the charm of the adventure, as did the candle Mairi insisted on carrying instead of James's flashlight. The light flickered weirdly over the old woman's gaunt features as she turned to warn them of obstacles in the way or to caution them to silence, which was probably unnecessary. Mairi was a frustrated romantic. She was genuinely concerned about James, but saw no reason why she should not enjoy the situation. Susan was in complete sympathy.

According to James, the tunnel had been dug for the convenience of a remote ancestor. It had proved useful on many occasions; the family had consistently dedicated itself to hopeless causes. Or, as James disgustedly put it, they never backed a winner. They had been out in the Fifteen and the Forty-Five, as well as the even more abortive Stuart failure of 1719. "Only four clans sent men to Loch Duich in 1719," said James bitterly. "Guess who. . . . We were the Claverhouse at Killiecrankie and with Montrose at Philiphaugh. It isn't only the Erskines. One of my mother's ancestors was hanged, drawn and quartered on behalf of Mary, Queen of Scots. And guess who happened to be visiting the MacDonalds at Glencoe on the night of the massacre!"

The tunnel ended in a flight of stone stairs. They went through a wooden door into the cellars of the castle. Mairi left them in the hall above, saying she would take a cup of tea with the cook while she waited; and James, squaring his shoulders and drawing a deep breath, knocked on a massive oak door.

A voice bade him enter. His hand on the knob, James turned to Susan and started to speak. Then he shrugged.

"Too late," he said. "I couldn't possibly prepare you." And he opened the door.

The laird of Glen Ealachan stood before the great stone hearth. Stags' antlers and stuffed heads and a motley collection of weaponry hung on the wall above him. He was dressed in Highland costume of such finicky perfection that it looked stagy. His sporran was of fur and considerably larger than a sporran ought to be; his socks were of the same tartan as his kilt, and the plaid draped around his stocky torso was pinned with an enormous brooch set with cairngorms. The only thing missing in the ensemble was a claymore, perhaps because the six-foot, two-handed blade was too unwieldy for his five-foot-six height. But he was adequately armed for hostilities, with a dirk in his belt and a sgian-dhu in his sock. He had a mane of white hair and bushy white eyebrows, as thick and as animated as the tails of Angora kittens.

Something else caught Susan's attention, and for a moment she wondered if her regrettable habit of seeking resemblances had not gone too far. The laird looked like her father, and that was daft, as James would say, because her father was six three in his socks and had not a gray hair in his head and looked like Paul Newman and. . . . Then she realized that the resemblance was solely one of expression. How often had she seen that same look on her father's face when she came in late from a date? But parental outrage had never been more gloweringly expressed than by the laird of Glen Ealachan as he contemplated, with agitated eyebrows, his son and heir.

But there was another resemblance. Susan frowned, trying to isolate it, while the laird greeted James in a voice that would have alerted any policeman who was less than sixty feet away.

"So ye've come at last—the last of the Erskines, a cowardly killer of auld men, dishonoring a great name, bringing my gray hairs in sorrow to the grave, and with this lassie, juist look at her, no better than she—"

"Prince Charlie," exclaimed Susan.

The laird choked, swallowed, and turned his outraged stare on her. She continued enthusiastically,

"Excuse me, sir. You're the image of Prince Charles Edward—the portrait in the National Gallery in Edinburgh."

Susan saw no reason to specify which portrait she meant. There are two of them in Scotland's National Portrait Gallery—the famous painting of the gallant young prince and another of Charles Edward at the age of fifty-five.

The laird's eyes shifted toward a mirror which hung on the wall to his left.

"Aye, weel," he said, in an accent so exaggerated that even Susan flinched, "so ye see the resemblance. It's been noted. But few hae the e'en for it. Ahem. Aye." He turned back to James, puffed out his chest like a bagpipe inflating, and took up his lecture at the precise syllable at which he had been interrupted.

". . . should be, puir lassie, wi' such a blaggard tae lead her astray. Black shame tae ye, unworthy son o' a noble house, tae think I should live tae see the day—"

"Oh, for God's sake, shut your mouth, you unspeakable old rascal," shouted his son. "What an act! What a disgusting, shameless, hammy performance! What a revolting—"

He stopped, panting with fury. For a moment the two male Erskines glared at one another, so alike in their snorting anger and their belligerent poses that Susan had to stifle a laugh. The amenities having been concluded, the pair relaxed.

"Och, Jamie, Jamie," said the laird plaintively. "What is this havers? You didn't—you wouldn't—"

He reached into his sporran and produced a large handkerchief—it was, of course, of the Erskine tartan—and blew his nose. Susan watched with fascinated interest. She knew what a Scot wore under his kilt, but she had always wondered what he carried in his sporran. She suspected, however, that she could not generalize about Scottish habits from the laird. He was unique.

"No, of course I didn't," James muttered.

"Then why didna ye gi' yerself up? That I should live tae see the day when an Erskine turned his back on—"

"There you go again," said James. He turned to Susan. "You see what he's like. You see why I couldn't explain about. . . . Dad, cut the theatrics for a minute and listen. This is serious. I didn't go to the police for two reasons. First, I didn't realize until yesterday that I

was being framed. Second. . . . Dad, are you still a
member of the Knights of the White Rose, or whatever
the hell that daft organization is called? The one Tammas belonged to?''

The laird stood transfixed as his son's meaning sank
in.

''Jamie,'' he said, in a low voice that had lost almost
all traces of Scottish accent. ''Lad, you surely didn't
think I—''

His voice trailed off into silence. James didn't respond at first; then a long, deep breath lifted his chest.

''No,'' he said. ''No. Sorry, Dad. I never really believed it, but. . . . You're so damned unpredictable!
When I heard about the sgian-dhu with our crest I had
an insane moment of doubt—wondering whether my
eyes had tricked me, somehow.''

The laird's face had softened at the beginning of this
speech, but James's tactless comments brought back the
scowl.

''Unpredictable, ye say! It's nae masel' that's being
chased by the poliss the length and breadth o' Scotland!
I niver doubted ye, Jamie,'' he went on sorrowfully,
apparently forgetting that his first speech to his son had
been a direct accusation. ''I ken weel that ye've been
taken advantage of. But how could ye think that I—''

''Now, Dad, don't play the innocent with me. You
and Tammas used to be thick as thieves, mixed up in
all sorts of daft plots—''

''Daft,'' his father repeated in an outraged voice.

''Hamilton gave it up,'' said James mysteriously.
''But some of the thieves were never identified.''

The name was meaningless to Susan, but not to the
laird. His ruddy face turned a shade redder.

''That was twenty-five years past,'' he said regretfully. ''Too long, Jamie. I'm auld now; I'll leave such
glorious deeds tae the young.''

''Never mind that. Can you understand why I was

worried? Tammas was involved in some kind of plot. I had reason to suspect you might also be involved. I had to speak to you before I took action. You honestly don't know anything about his recent activities?''

"So that's why you rushed me out of town," exclaimed Susan. "You weren't worried about me at all!"

"I owe you an apology," James said.

"I'm not sure which of us owes which an apology. In your case, concern for your father—"

"Ho!" said that gentleman, in tones of mocking irony. "Concern, d'ye say? He was hoping to catch me in some sort of foolishness so he could hold it over my head. Well, my lad, I'm sorry to disappoint you, but it won't wash. I haven't spoken with Tammas for months. We fell out, you recall, over the question of the restoration. I could not agree to overthrowing the present House. Ignoble though its origins may be, it has proved worthy of loyalty, and our own connections with the family—"

His voice had risen in volume; James had to shout to make himself heard.

"Dad, that's enough!"

"No, by God, it is damned well not enough! (I beg your pardon, young lady.) You will stop this foolishness; you will give up your improper notions about a future career; you will return to the University and apply yourself to the studies you have so consistently neglected; you will—"

"I will, will I? When I've finished serving my prison term, you mean? Can't you get it through your bony skull that I am in trouble?"

A brief lull followed this unpleasant reminder. Both Erskines seemed refreshed by the outburst, which Susan was beginning to regard as typical of their conversations.

"What's the argument about?" she asked, with genuine interest. "What is it you want him to study, sir?"

"What else could be an appropriate career for a Scot and an Erskine?" the laird demanded rhetorically. "History, of course. The glorious history of Scotland and his own distinguished house. Restoring the pride, the awareness of national honor that the foul Union of 1707 destroyed. And what does he want? Not only does he reject my ideas; he wants—he prefers—"

Outrage choked further utterance.

"What do you want?" Susan asked James.

"I want to be a policeman," he said.

"A—what?"

"Scotland Yard," said James, getting red in the face. "Detective work. Law enforcement. I mean, after all . . ."

His voice died away. Susan turned to the laird, and the two exchanged glances of perfect sympathy.

"Talk about irony," said Susan. "All my life I've been interested in Scotland. And all he's interested in is Scotland Yard. Jamie, I really don't see how you could be farther away from that goal. Especially at this moment in you life."

James sat down and hid his face in his hands.

With a courtly gesture, the laird indicated a chair.

"Sit down, Miss——"

"Please call me Susan."

"Thank you. I am honored. How on earth did a girl of your caliber become involved with my wretched son? Jamie, it is intolerable that Susan should be implicated in your sordid affairs. I insist that you clear her at once."

James opened his mouth to reply, but he was incapable of coherent speech. Taking advantage of his fury, his father proceeded,

"I know nothing of Tammas's recent activities. But I can put you in touch with someone who has that information. I had a caller this morning. He left a message for you, in case you came here."

"A caller? He wasn't a tall, dark-haired chap named Jackson? An American?"

"No, no. This fellow was a Scot. He was an associate of Tammas's; no question of that, he knew the—er—passwords, so to speak. He was most distressed at your situation. Assured me he could explain everything, and would do so, to the police, after he had spoken to you. He wouldn't leave a written message, for fear of its being intercepted. I memorized it. He will meet you in Room 212 in the Caledonian Hotel in Aldway tomorrow."

"Hmph," said James.

"That's wonderful news," Susan exclaimed. "How far is Aldway?"

"Fifteen or twenty miles, as the crow flies. It's a long walk."

"Walk," Susan repeated sadly.

"How else do you suppose we can get there? I can't very well drive out of here in Dad's car."

"We'll think of a plan," said the laird cheerfully. He flipped at the pleats of his kilt and seated himself in a big carved chair. Having conveyed the vital information, he allowed himself to relapse into broad Scots. "There's nae rush. Jamie, fetch the uisqebagh. The puir lassie needs a nip—and a rest. We'll hae a wee ceilidh, juist the three o' us. D'ye ken any Scottish songs, Susan?"

Her eyes wide, Susan watched the laird take a guitar from its case. He struck a resounding chord. It might have been meant to be an E major chord.

"I had him taught the instrument," said the laird, with a disparaging nod at his son. "But he's nae mair music in him than a lump o' stane." He threw back his head and began,

"Ye Heilands and ye Lowlands, oh where hae ye been?

You hae slain the Earl o' Moray and laid him on
the green. . . ."

With a glance at James, Susan joined in.

"He was a braw galland and he played at the
glove,
O, the bonny Earl o' Moray, he was the Queen's
love."

Susan only knew three verses of the lament. The laird
taught her a fourth. While this was going on James got
the whiskey decanter from a sideboard and poured him-
self a stiff drink. He waited till the song was over before
remarking,
"Do you suppose I could ask a question?"
The laird moved his fingers uncertainly from D sev-
enth to A.
" 'Yestreen the Queen had four maries,' " he
crooned.
"Father."
" 'The nicht she'll hae but three,' " sang Susan.
"Dad!"
" 'There was Mary Seaton and Mary Beaton,
And Mary Carmichael and me. . . .' "
James flung his glass into the fireplace.
"Now then," he said, into the silence that followed
the crash. "I will ask my question. What precisely do
the police know? I assume you talked to them?"
"Aye, aye," said the laird irritably, continuing to
strum.
Susan reached over and took the guitar away from
him. James's mounting rage didn't bother her as much
as the hideous discords. She slid her fingers into place
and began an arpeggio in a minor key.
"Whist," said the laird, beaming at her. "That's a
braw sound, lassie, we'll sing 'The Flowers o' the For-

est,' as soon as I satisfy this fule laddie. . . . Aye, the
poliss were here. They hae a picture o' you, and a description of the lassie here. They ken the claes ye're
wearing and the vehicle ye're driving. . . . Which was
news tae me, I might add; where did y'get the siller for
sich a bike?''

"Never mind that now," said James, shifting uneasily. "What about the evidence against us? Dad, we were
there. Tammas was stabbed, but not with a sgian-dhu.''

"The weapon the police found was yours," said his
father, looking grave. "They showed it to me. There's
a witness as well, some vagrant who saw you leave the
house. And some wild tale about Susan accusing Tammas. . . . Daft, gey daft, the lot o' em! Susan, lass,
would ye like tae hear the pipes?''

"You reach for those bagpipes and I'll throttle you,''
shouted James. "Dad, we cannot play and sing and
dance. We cannot talk. I've got to get the hell out of
here."

"There's nae problem. Only one wee constable frae
Edinburgh tae deal with; we'll lock him i' the dungeons
and ye can drive oot o' the glen—''

"With all the crofters standing at attention and waving flags? Dad, will you try to get it though your head
that this is not 1745 and I am not Prince Charles Edward?'' James included Susan in his scowl. "I am beginning to loathe Charles Edward Stuart. I wish he were
still alive so I could kill him. If he'd come round here
in 1746 after Culloden, I'd have turned him in and collected the reward."

"Aye," said the laird fiercely. "And I'd have stabbed
ye t' the heart masel', for yer treachery!"

James waved his arms wildly. "Why are we talking
about Charles Edward?" he demanded unreasonably.
"Times have changed. I am not going to ride out of
here on a white stallion, shouting defiance and waving
a claymore! I am not going to leave in the Land Rover

either. It's known for forty miles around. We will leave as we came, on foot; and we must leave before daylight.''

"Is there danger?" asked the laird hopefully.

"Hell, yes! The police aren't the only ones who are after us. The people who murdered Tammas and framed us are hot on our trail. One of them is an American—tall, dark, good-looking chap—"

"The Jackson you mentioned?" The old man was serious now.

"Yes. But he may use any name, and he'll have the documents to back up his story. He's extremely dangerous. Don't play any of your little games with him. Simply tell him we haven't been here, and you've no idea where we might be.''

"Very well. You'll need money, I suppose."

"I always need money."

"Very true. But in this case. . . . Wait here. I've fifty pounds in the safe in my dressing room.''

He left the room. James collapsed into a chair and glared at Susan, who was still strumming.

"Coming here was a mistake. I might have known what would happen when you and the old man got together. You're both hopeless romantics.''

"What's wrong with being a romantic? I adore your father. He's a character."

"I'll tell you what's wrong with it." James leaned forward. His hair fell over his eyes, and he brushed at it impatiently. "It's—it's impractical. The real world is a rough, tough, dirty place. You have to live in it, not in some dreamworld of your own imagination. It's bad enough to have my father talking like Harry Lauder and behaving like an aged undergraduate. Some of his tricks, when he was lecturing at Glasgow—"

"Oh!" Susan's fingers slipped into a jangling discord. She stared at James. "I remember now! Hamilton

Glasgow University, 1950. . . . The Scots who stole the Stone of Scone. Was your father . . . ?''

"They never proved it." James grinned. He looked astonishingly like his father for a moment, before he remembered that he was supposed to be registering stern disapproval. "Now do you understand why I was afraid he was a party to Tammas's latest scheme? Dad's a hopeless case; he's too old to change. But you're young. There are moments when you display some shreds of sanity. But this obsession of yours with ghosts—"

"Aha," said Susan. "You're still mad about last night. Just because I wouldn't—"

"Me, mad? Ridiculous. I am a realist. I recognize your right to reject me for rational reasons. So you don't like beards. Fine. But if you shy away from normal physical relationships because you're dreaming of the ghostly embraces of a dead—"

"You are disgusting," said Susan frigidly.

"Perhaps I am," James said, after a moment. "Strike the last remark. But my objections to your general attitude still stands. You're frittering away your life with dusty old legends that have no relation to reality, and never did."

"You are not only disgusting, you are dead wrong," Susan snapped. "The dreamers and the romantics are the people who make history—not the dull clods like you. The mystics, who founded the world's great religions; the explorers who discovered new worlds because they believed the legends the hardheaded realists jeered at; artists and poets and musicians, creating beauty out of their dreams. . . . Good Lord, you talk as if the two things were mutually exclusive. They aren't. I can enjoy the songs and legends and still manage to cope pretty well with your damned real world—as well as you do, anyway. I can't see that your performance in the past two days has been all that spectacular."

"If we're going to descend to personalities—"

"You descended first."

"Hmm. So I did. Then let me be the first to ascend from this welter of inconsequential comment. If you will kindly put down that damned guitar, I would like to discuss our future plans."

Susan complied with the request. She was still annoyed, but she had to admire James's readiness to apologize.

"I assume we'll go see that man in Aldway."

"I don't know about that. There are several loose ends I'd like to clear up. I wish we could persuade Ellie to confide in us."

"She could be quite informative, I imagine. But we can't go back to the dig; the police have probably traced us that far by now."

"I'm not so concerned about the police as I am about Jackson and his gang. They might not expect us to return to the dig. However, that isn't what I want to talk about. I've been brooding about the poem Tammas gave you. You remember the lines, of course.

'The bird, the beste, the fisch eke in the see
They lyve in fredome everich in his kynd;
And I a man, and lakkith libertee. . . .'

"Write it down," James said. "There's paper on the desk."

Susan obeyed.

"I've been thinking about it too," she said, as she wrote. "And if this is a code it's too fancy for me. Take the first letters of the words, for instance. T-B-T-B-T-F. . . ."

"What about alternate words?"

Susan shook her head.

"You can read it backward or forward or upside down. It sill doesn't make any sense."

James leaned over her shoulder, studying the lines.

"I rather expected that. Obviously you can't use a well-known quotation for a simple cipher of that sort. The message must be concealed in the reference itself—the name of the poem, perhaps. It just so happens that there's a manor house called King's Quair, not far from Inchrory."

"It's a rendezvous, then," Susan exclaimed.

"Possibly. The title of the poem gives the place. All we need is the time."

"That may have been given in another message."

"Not likely. Two messages would be unnecessarily devious. How does on communicate numbers?"

Susan frowned thoughtfully.

"The author's name? James the First. . . ."

"Insufficient. We need a date, possible a time of day as well."

"James the First," Susan muttered. "Born 1394—"

"When was the poem written?"

"I don't know. I don't think anyone knows. Sometime during his captivity, which began in 1406. His father died that same year, so you could say he became king of Scotland in—"

"Fourteen six. What's today's date?"

"June something. I've lost track."

"It's the eighth, to be precise," said James. "June eight. Eight-six."

"Fourteen-six," said Susan. "You think the rendezvous is for the fourteenth? That's the craziest—"

"So was Tammas. It's precisely the sort of fuzzy romantic message his crowd would invent. Furthermore, I suspect the naught in the date specifies the time. Noon or midnight."

"Midnight, of course."

"Of course. When I think of those poor innocents—"

He broke off, as the door began to open. "Here's Dad, I don't want him to hear any of this. It could be dangerous for—"

But the person who stood in the doorway was not the laird. It was a girl wearing a housemaid's uniform. Her sandy hair was confined under a neat white cap; her narrow face held a look of furtive triumph.

"Master Jamie," she breathed. "Oh, excuse me, sir. I didna ken. . . ."

The door closed.

"That's torn it," James groaned. "I knew I should have locked that door."

"What's the problem?" Susan asked uneasily. "She wouldn't—"

"Oh, wouldn't she? It's damned lucky for you that I'm here; you'd sit wrapped in romantic fantasies about loyal family retainers till they walked in and dropped the cuffs on your wrists. That wench has hated me since I set fire to her doll when we were kids. She also happens to be engaged to the local constable. Get ready to run, Susan."

Chapter 5

The door opened again. This time it was the laird. James snatched the wad of bills from his hand.

"She saw us," he said rapidly. "Annie Grant. Where's Mairi? We must—"

"Here," said Mairi, trotting into the room. "I was afeerd, when she came through the kitchen and ran oot. . . . Jamie, I fetched your wee knapsack and packed your necessaries. I couldna get food, not wi' yon bobbie i' the kitchen."

"In the kitchen?" Susan gasped.

"Annie didna speak wi' him," Mairi assured her. "She's tae wed Davie MacDougal i' the autumn and wants to see him take the credit. We've five minutes, nae mair."

But she did not move. Hands on her hips, sturdy legs planted squarely, she contemplated each of them in turn with shining gray eyes.

"Lock the door when we've gane, Seumas Erskine," she intoned dramatically. "Lock it, and dinna let them in. We'll gain a bit mair time if they think the bairns are still here.''

"Aye!'' The laird nodded. His eyes reflected the gleam in Mairi's. He glanced at the claymore that hung above the hearth. It looked as if it hadn't been polished or sharpened for centuries; Susan hoped it was too dull to do more than dent the unfortunate Davie. The same idea occurred to James. He exclaimed urgently,

"For God's sake, Dad, don't do anything violent! Keep them out, if you can, but don't—''

"God save ye, my son,'' interrupted the laird, wringing James's limp hand. "And ye, ma bonnie lassie—''

He threw his arms around Susan and hugged her. Susan hugged him back. He was certainly a theatrical old man, but the emotions guiding his acts were perfectly genuine.

"I'll take care of Jamie,'' she said, her voice muffled in the voluminous folds of the laird's plaid. "Don't worry, we'll be fine.''

"A fayther's blessing on ye, lassie,'' the laird said in a choked voice. "God go—''

James plucked Susan from his father's embrace.

"You nauseate me,'' he snarled. "All of you. Mairi—''

Mairi, who had been watching the scene with moist eyes and a quivering chin, started violently.

"Och, aye,'' she agreed. "We maun make haste.''

Once Mairi got moving she was quick enough; they went back through the tunnel at top speed and ran down the hillside, through the tumbled rocks that concealed the tunnel's entrance. They stopped at her cottage only long enough to collect Susan's knapsack. Mairi stuffed it and James's pack with such odds and ends of food as she could collect in a hurry, while James danced up and down in a frenzy of impatience.

"That's splendid,'' he said, snatching his knapsack. "Splendid, splendid. Let's be off, Susan.''

Mairi flung her arms around him.

"God gae wi' ye, laddie," she exclaimed. " 's rioghal mo dhream . . .' "

Since James was at that moment trying to get his arms through the straps of his pack, the ensemble was somewhat reminiscent of Laocoon and his sons entwined with serpents. He extricated himself with tight-lipped efficiency.

"You are a gem of a woman, Mairi," he said. "But if you try to embrace me again, or quote inappropriate Gaelic slogans at me, I'll scream for the police myself."

II

They spent the night in a cave some five miles north of the glen. Susan was delighted with the cave. It brought back fond memories of Bonnie Prince Charlie, who had spent considerable time hiding out in caves. But she decided it would not be politic to mention this to James.

Having slept through most of the day, Susan was not particularly sleepy, although her legs ached from climbing. Stretching them luxuriously, she tried to engage James in conversation.

"I love your father."

"You would."

"Why are you so mean to him?"

"*I* mean to *him*? He's living in the wrong century. He's trying to run my bloody life for me. I'm twenty-four, for God's sake. I wouldn't mind so much if he'd hit on some sensible career; but no, he wants me to be a combination Celtic bard and antique Highland laird. The market for that type is strictly limited. And—well, you saw him; he's the most god-awful old ham who ever lived."

Susan laughed.

"I suppose he is amusing, if you don't have to live with him," James admitted glumly.

"He's adorable. Oh, Jamie, I wish we could have seen him beating off the bobbies. Do you suppose he used the claymore?"

"Undoubtedly. He's lived the part so long he believes it himself."

"That's unfair! He's backing you up in every possible way, from money to unquestioning belief in your innocence. I know fathers who would be chewing the carpet if their son had gotten into a mess like this. And we have him to thank if we find that man who can explain. . . . We are going to Aldway, aren't we?"

"I don't know."

"Why not, for heaven's sake? If that man can clear us—"

"I don't know how you've survived till the age of— what? Twenty? You are incredibly naïve, woman. How do you know that message isn't a trap?"

"The man wasn't Jackson—"

"You don't suppose Jackson is working alone, do you? He knows we're on to him; he wouldn't appear himself. There's something about that message that doesn't feel quite right. It's too vague. If the anonymous savior can clear us, why doesn't he do so? I tell you, I don't like the sound of it."

"You have a point," Susan admitted. "Then you don't want to go to Aldway?"

"Yes, I do."

"But if it's a trap—"

"Then we'll spring it—and hopefully hoist our friend by his own petard. Thank God for Shakespeare," James added meanly. "A poet who wasn't a Scot."

III

Aldway was a tourist town, and the tourists were all of one kind—fishermen. The town was crowded with them, all wearing flies in their hats and downcast expressions; for the sun shone benevolently down on the quaint village and sunlight, as everyone knows, is anathema to the angler.

Susan felt as conspicuous as a Martian amid this crowd. She was in worse case than James, whose well-worn kilt and homespun shirt were in keeping with their surroundings. The long hike had reduced her jeans and T-shirt to the state they had been in before Mairi washed them, and her knapsack contained only a single change of clothing—another pair of jeans and a shirt, hopelessly wrinkled and equally recognizable.

She felt increasingly uneasy as they sauntered along the village street, trying to look as if they intended to go fishing. She suspected they were not notably successful.

"This is insane," she mumbled. "At least we ought to disguise ourselves."

"How? I'm not much good at theatrics. That's my father's forte."

"I can think of one obvious method," said Susan, glancing at him out of the corner of her eye.

They had already had an acrimonious discussion on this point. Among the items Mairi had packed was a razor. Discovering this, Susan had exclaimed approvingly, and James had flown into a rage. Susan wondered if he was clinging to the beard to spite her, after her insulting comment; certainly his insistence on the conspicuous appendage was beginning to seem like an obsession.

This was not the time or the place for further debate, she decided, and fell silent, scampering along to keep up with James's long strides.

The hotel was a sprawling three-story structure. The approach to it was crowded. James headed straight for the front door.

"You're going to walk right in?" Susan asked.

"Can you think of any other way of getting in? We'd look a trifle suspicious climbing in windows in broad daylight."

Above the ground floor the hotel was quiet enough. They located room 212 at the end of one of the wings. Standing before the closed door they exchanged glances. James made a grimace whose import Susan understood perfectly; then he lifted his hand and knocked.

The man inside had been waiting for them. The door opened immediately.

"Come in, come in. Don't stand in the corridor."

The first sight of him relieved Susan's worst worry. The man was not Jackson. Of medium height, compactly built, he had fair hair and a face of the type that is sometimes described as pleasantly homely. His eyes were striking: long-lashed, of an unusual golden brown, they narrowed, echoing the smile on his full-lipped mouth. It was the sort of face Susan trusted instinctively. She smiled back. Maybe this was the beginning of the end of their troubles.

The room was low-ceilinged and of good size. It contained a double bed, a miscellany of cheap furniture, and a view, out of the window, of mountains and blue sky.

"My name's Farragut," said the man, closing the door. "No need to ask who you are. What about a nip, eh? Imagine you could use one."

"We could use an explanation," said James.

Farragut chuckled. His low, well-modulated voice defined his social class, and his clothing confirmed it—beautifully cut tweeds and a V-necked cashmere sweater. His tie was dark, with some sort of insignia in gold and scarlet. Susan wondered whether it was a regimental tie. She had read about regimental ties in books.

"Don't blame you for feeling that way, old chap," said Farragut. "You'll get your explanation, never fear. I'm taking you to see someone who can explain far better than I. We can wait till we get there before we have that drink, if you like. In your position I'd be in a bit of a rush myself. Shall we—"

"Who is this mysterious person you want us to see?" James demanded.

"A lady, old boy." Farragut's face grew serious. "A very distinguished lady. I'm only her humble servant. Can't take the responsibility of breaking the news myself."

He started for the door. James stepped in front of him. He was twisting his hands nervously together.

"I say, now," he stuttered. "You can understand my position, can't you? I mean, I'm not going anywhere with you without more information. I mean, I don't even know who you are. That is to say, I can't even be sure Farragut is your real name."

"Quite, quite," Farragut said. "I'm sure this will convince you."

He reached casually for his inner coat pocket.

James left the ground in a spectacular leap. His left shoe connected with Farragut's chin and Farragut went reeling back. His head smacked against the low eaves of the ceiling. He doubled up and fell. James's exploit ended less elegantly than it had begun. He lost his balance and fell heavily to the floor. Crockery rattled.

"Holy cow," gasped Susan, reverting to a childhood expletive in the extremity of her astonishment. "Where did you learn how to do that?"

"Hope the room underneath isn't occupied at the moment." James raised himself to a sitting position. He winced. "Where do you suppose I learned it? Karate is very useful to a police officer. I've been taking private lessons. Unfortunately, I missed last week's session. . . ." He rose stiffly to his feet and rubbed his hip. "I never did that before," he said, staring at Farragut's crumpled body. "Not to hurt anybody. . . ."

"I—I think you killed him," Susan whispered.

James bent over the body.

"No," he announced, in relieved tones. "He may have to wear a neck brace for a bit, but he's breathing. Perhaps it's just as well I did miss last week's session. Tie him up, Susan."

"Who, me?" Susan's back was already against the wall or she would have retreated even farther. "Uh-uh."

"What a heroine you are," James muttered. He yanked Farragut's tie loose and began to bind the limp wrists.

"Why did you hit him?" Susan asked.

James rolled the unconscious man onto his back and began investigating his pockets. The first item he brought out for Susan's inspection was a gun.

"That's what he was reaching for. It certainly would have convinced us to go with him. Find some rope or something, can't you?"

In the wardrobe Susan found a rack of ties, which James accepted.

"Quite a dandy," he grunted, winding a handsome Italian silk item around Farragut's ankles and knotting two others together to bind his knees. By the time he had finished, Farragut was wound around with neckties. James stuffed a washcloth in his mouth and fastened it with the last of the ties, a tweedy knit.

"Neat but not gaudy," he said, surveying his work with modest pride. "Now let's see what we have here."

What he had was the contents of Farragut's pockets. They included a well-stuffed wallet, which James calmly divested of its contents. There was a conspicuous absence of identification in the wallet and in Farragut's luggage, a handsome matched set.

"That's it. Let's go," James said.

"Aren't you going to question him?"

"Him?" James gestured. Susan saw that Farragut's eyes were open. He had not moved, and he appeared not only helpless but rather ludicrous. Yet the expression in the steady amber eyes made a chill run through Susan.

"I wouldn't bother questioning him with anything less drastic than a set of thumbscrews," James said. "Farragut, the only reason I don't use your own weapon on you is that I don't care to have a real murder on my record. But if you get in my way again you may not be so lucky."

It was an empty threat, and they all knew it. Farragut's very eyeballs sneered.

"We can get out the window," Susan said, glancing through that aperture. "There's a shed or something below—not a long drop."

"I'll wager that's how we would have left the room later tonight," James said, "if we had refused to buy Farragut's story of a mysterious lady waiting to interview us—in the middle of a grouse moor, perhaps? Some quiet and remote spot where gunshots wouldn't attract attention. He couldn't risk shooting us here. We'd have been knocked out, or tied up, or both, then dropped out the window after dark. Which suggests that Farragut may be expecting friends to drop in later on. Sorry we can't wait to meet them, old chap. No, Susan, not the window. We were seen coming in, we may as well go out the same way. Er—keep your nose clean, Farragut."

"That was a silly thing to say," Susan remarked, as James locked the door on the outside and pocketed the key.

"I had to say something. Brrr. That man gives me the cauld grue."

"Me too. Let's hurry."

"Don't hurry, try to appear casual. I doubt that Farragut will call for help. Publicity is bad news in his racket. He can work himself free in an hour or two."

"So what do we do now?"

"We get as far away from here as we can in an hour or two," James answered. "When Farragut does get loose I don't want to be within twenty miles of him."

"Maybe you should have. . . ."

"Oh, unquestionably I should have," James agreed gloomily. "I do wish I weren't so damned law-abiding."

An hour later they were deep in the woods. Susan had always thought of Scotland as a small country. She was beginning to believe it was far too large for comfort, and that most of it was covered with mountains. Walking was difficult, and was further complicated by James's insistence that they should not be seen.

Finally they struck a stretch of level moorland and walked along side by side.

"That little episode was a real fiasco," Susan remarked.

"Oh, I don't know. We've identified another member of the opposition, and we have a gun—whatever good that may do us."

"He had also identified us. James, I don't mean to nag, but don't you think we ought—"

"Yes, damn it. I hate to agree, but I suppose it's time we changed our appearance. Only how do we do it?"

Susan was silent.

James groaned. "Susan, you don't understand. I simply cannot shave."

Susan stopped. Putting both hands on his arm, she looked up into his face.

"Jamie, I don't know how to say this, but. . . . We've

shared some wild adventures, right? We're friends, right? I mean, people don't even *notice* physical appearance. The thing that counts is personality, character. . . ."

James listened interestedly.

"What a beautiful philosophy. But you're on the wrong track. I am not deformed. It's worse than that."

Susan stamped her foot. "It couldn't be worse. Anyhow, what alternative do you have?"

James sighed. "What about you?"

"There are a lot of things women can do. But I will need some different clothes. It wouldn't be smart to buy them, I guess."

"No." James started walking again. "Nor can we check into a hotel as ourselves and check out as two different people. What we need is a house whose owners are off on holiday. Preferably a long holiday."

"What a marvelous idea," Susan exclaimed tactfully. She was too wise to crow over her success; but now that she had won, she was conscious of a vast curiosity. What unimaginable horror could be concealed under James's beard.

It was almost midnight before they found their empty house. It was on the outskirts of a sizable town. They had to kill time waiting for dark, which was late in coming, but James refused to take the chance of being seen on the streets. They were too close to Aldway. Anyway, he argued, the easiest way of finding an unoccupied house was to locate one that had no lights on.

"In the States people leave the lights on to deter burglars," Susan said. "We even have automatic switches that turn them on and off at certain times."

"We, too, are in the modern age," James snapped. "But no Scot is going to waste electricity when he isn't there."

The outer suburbs of the town consisted of row upon

row of drab little houses, postwar atrocities that made
Susan think better of American subdivisions, which at
least tried to simulate individuality. But these houses
had one advantage over the normal American suburb.
The yards were all fenced. They woke up two dogs
before they found their goal, but the animals couldn't
chase them.

They had to break a window to get into the house of
their choice. Susan waited outside while James recon-
noitered. He appeared after a moment and helped her
over the sill.

"It's perfect," he whispered. "But we'll have to leave
before morning."

"Why?"

James clapped his hand over her mouth just in time
to stop a scream. Something warm and sinuous was
twining itself around her ankle.

"Someone—a neighbor—must come in to feed the
cat and let it out," James said. "Since we don't know
the schedule we can't take any chances."

Susan bent over and picked up the cat. It spat and
sank its teeth into her hand. She dropped it.

"No time for playing," James said severely. "Just
don't tread on its tail."

James locked himself in the bathroom while Susan
took his flashlight and investigated the bedrooms, hoping to find a dress she could wear. The cat went with
her. It was a sleek, fat, gray tabby wearing a rhine-
stone-studded collar, and it was friendly enough so long
as she didn't try to pick it up. In fact, it was a nuisance,
purring and sitting down on her feet whenever she stood
still.

"Lucky you aren't a dog," Susan murmured,
scratching it under the chin. "Although I've known
some dogs who wouldn't be any more critical of burglars than you are. . . . Is it a good boy, then? Does it
miss its folks?"

Hearing a sympathetic voice, the cat flung itself onto its back and writhed kittenishly.

Susan rubbed its stomach. It bit her playfully, then rose and trotted to the head of the stairs, where it paused and looked at her suggestively.

"You don't need to be fed," Susan told it. "You're too fat now."

The bathroom door opened a crack. "For God's sake, who are you talking to?" James hissed.

"The cat."

"Well, stop it and get moving. I would get involved with a woman who talks to cats."

"It's better than talking to yourself," Susan retorted; but the door had closed.

A she had come to suspect from the cat's spoiled behavior, the house was occupied by an older couple whose children, if any, had departed. To judge by her clothing the woman was about Susan's height and thirty pounds heavier. Her taste was atrocious. Finally, in a back bedroom that smelled stale and unoccupied, Susan found a chest of drawers containing some old clothes, carefully wrapped and packed in mothballs. They had been outgrown by the owner, but were too precious to throw away.

When James emerged from the bathroom he was confronted by a dark figure. He reeled back, holding his nose.

"My God, you smell frightful!"

"I can't help it. Maybe a good roll in some pine needles will help. How do you like the effect?"

"I can't see it. Wait a sec, I'll risk a light. . . . Hmm. Isn't it a bit too quaint and peasanty? Fetching little aprons and laced bodices aren't being much worn this year. I deduce that you discovered the lady's fancy-dress costume. Not a bad idea; it may be some time before she realizes it's missing. . . . Susan. Susan, don't look at me like that. I tried to warn you."

"Oh, my," said Susan. "Oh, my."

He was different, there was no question of that. He was unrecognizable. She wouldn't have known him except for his voice and his clothing. As she had already noticed, James's lean hips and long legs looked marvelous in a kilt. The removal of a foot or so of hair had done wonders for his looks. But the features now fully revealed by the removal of the beard struck her dumb. He wasn't deformed. His face was rather handsome, in an unobtrusive sort of way. Susan had always considered it a handsome face. She knew it well. She had seen it in countless photographs, in newspapers and magazines, even on postcards. . . .

"I feel as if I ought to curtsy," she said weakly. "Or kiss your hand."

"A simple bow will suffice," said James grimly. "Now you see why. . . . I don't know whether I can go through with this, Susan. The poor devil has troubles enough as it is. If word reaches the press that he has been cavorting around the Highlands in the company of an unidentified young person of the female sex. . . ."

"But, Jamie, it's fantastic! Don't you see how we can use this?"

"Oh, no. Never! Not under any circumstances whatever. Impersonation is bad form. It is also illegal."

"Well." Susan abandoned this line of argument. James would grasp at it readily enough if he were backed into a corner. She was still bemused by the resemblance. It wasn't really that exact; if the two men stood side by side it would probably be easy to tell the real article from the counterfeit. But it was close enough to be decidedly embarrassing—and potentially useful.

"I can't believe it," she said. "How did it happen?"

"Don't let your vulgar imagination run away with you," James said coldly. "The families are connected. . . ."

"How? Bonnie Prince Charlie was on the loose in the Highlands for a long time, and his reputation with the ladies—"

"You are obsessed with that feckless fool," James said through his teeth. "If I thought he was one of my forebears I'd shoot myself."

"Then there was that story about James the First, of England," Susan went on dreamily. "The bones of the infant found in a hidden recess in Edinburgh Castle, wrapped in rotting cloth of gold. . . . If the son of Mary, Queen of Scots was stillborn, and the child of the Countess of Mar was substituted for it. . . . She was an Erskine, I believe. And the present Royal House is descended from that child. . . ."

"Oh, do shut up," James growled. "I knew I'd regret this. Hurry and do whatever you need to do. And don't leave a mess; I'd rather the occupants didn't know anyone had been here."

"What about the broken window?"

"I'll leave a rock in the midst of the broken glass in the kitchen. With luck they'll blame it on some undisciplined but basically honest youth. Oh, and Susan . . ."

"Yes?"

"You aren't planning to—I mean, will you cut your hair?"

"I was considering it."

"Girls with long brown hair are common," James said rapidly. "And Farragut will be expecting us to change our looks. That is, we might fool them by not doing what they think we would do because we think—"

"I'll think about it," said Susan, and shut the door in his face.

When she came out, some time later, James was waiting. He was visibly pleased to see that she had braided her hair instead of cutting it. The thick plait hung over her shoulder, and Susan had pinned the shorter strands firmly down with bobby pins.

"Your face looks different," James said, eyeing her critically. "What did you do?"

"Makeup—blusher, eye shadow, liner. Makes my eyes look smaller and lighter, broadens my nose."

The cat followed them back to the kitchen, where it discovered the open window with a low yowl of surprise and pleasure. It went out in a single effortless leap. Moments later, Susan heard a high tomcat challenge rise over the rooftops of the sleeping town.

IV

They spent the rest of the night in a cave on the mountainside. Susan was beginning to lose her enthusiasm for caves. She said so, adding disagreeably, "If we have to spend so much time in caves, you might at least pick a good one. I think a skunk used to live here."

"It is rather small. But there are no skunks hereabouts. I'm afraid you're responsible for the aroma, love. I don't think I can stand being in here with you and those clothes."

"They are rather overpowering in confined quarters," Susan admitted.

"Why don't you hang your dress outside and let it air?"

"Hmmm," said Susan.

"Don't be so stuffy. Hand it over. I can't see you, it's too dark. I'll drape the dress on a bush. It's such a nice night I'm tempted to sleep outside."

He took the garments Susan handed him and vanished, crouching to get through the low opening. She wrapped Mairi's cloak around her and followed him out. It *was* a nice night, and whatever James might say, the cave smelled of other things besides mothballs.

After the frowsty closeness of the cave, the night air was intoxicating—pine-scented, and cold enough to bring goose bumps out on Susan's shoulders. She squatted down on a bed of pine needles near the mouth of the cave, pulled the cloak closer, and breathed deeply.

James had draped her skirt and blouse over the branches of a tree. He had also removed his shirt, and was carefully arranging it on another branch—so it wouldn't get wrinkled? Susan grinned. He was about as subtle as a sledgehammer. If he thought the removal of the beard would remove her inhibitions, he was mistaken.

There was a sound, not far away, among the trees; only an owl, muttering to itself, but it brought James around in a quick turn, to stare in that direction. Susan caught her breath. The moon had set, but the northern skies, brilliant with stars, had a luminosity that let her see quite clearly. James's lean body, in its archaic costume, was frozen in a pose of animal grace, the heavy folds of the kilt settling back into position, the dark hair lifted to show the firm mouth and strong jaw. He had a beautiful body, lightly muscled, without an ounce of superfluous flesh.

Susan struggled with herself as James came toward her, the folds of his long plaid draped casually over one shoulder. He stretched out beside her, supporting himself by one elbow.

Susan gulped. "Aren't you cold?" she asked.

"No. Quite the contrary. Are you?"

"No. Yes."

"Then why don't you pull that cloak up around your shoulders?"

"It scratches," said Susan.

James turned on his side.

"This is wool too; but it's old and soft."

He arranged the plaid around her. Susan was silent; she knew her voice would squeak if she thanked him.

"I'm glad you didn't cut your hair," James said softly. "Don't these pins give you a headache?"

He drew them out. The loosened tendrils curled around Susan's face. James's long fingers cupped the back of her head, supporting it until it came to rest on the bed of pine needles.

"Wait a minute," Susan said.

At least that was what she had meant to say. She spoke his name instead; and that was all she had time to say before his lips stopped her voice.

Susan thought: this is unfair. Using my own fantasies against me. Kilts and plaids and love under the stars. "My plaidie to the angry earth, I'll shelter thee. . . ." And she thought: Whoever implied that Scots were clumsy lovers? And then she stopped thinking.

She didn't stop talking, though; in the intervals between kisses she murmured appropriate words, endearments, snatches of poetry—and his name over and over. He was talking too. Through the roar of her pulsing blood Susan caught snatches of Burns and Stevenson, and a few of the lines that are not reprinted in high-school anthologies of poetry.

Then, suddenly, James stiffened and straightened. Leaning on both elbows, his face inches from hers, he shouted, "What did you say?"

"What?" Susan stammered. "What?"

"What did you call me?"

"Darling?" said Susan, and put her arms around him. James rolled over and sat up, breaking her hold.

"You called me Charlie," he said furiously.

"I did not! Jamie, darling—I couldn't. . . . Did I?"

It had been a long day. Susan couldn't help herself. She began to laugh.

Her reaction was fifty percent hysterics, but James

was too furious to realize—and too furious to care if he had realized. He got to his feet in a single lithe movement and stood glaring down at Susan, his hands on his hips.

"I don't expect a great deal," he said, snapping his teeth between practically every word. "I don't claim to be the greatest lover since Don Juan. But I do expect my women to keep my identity in mind while I'm—"

He cut the word off short, but it was too late. Susan's laughter stopped.

"Your women," she exclaimed. "You conceited male chauvinist Scot! How many women? I suppose you keep a list. Well, you won't add me to it! Go away, get lost. I don't ever want to see you again!"

Snatching up the cloak, she crawled into the cave. James did not follow her.

By morning she was calm, and slightly repentant. If she really had called him Charlie. . . . It was bad enough to conjure up the shade of the romantic Stuart prince; but James's peculiar circumstances added insult to injury. No man likes to think he succeeds in amatory exercises only because he reminds the lady of another man. Susan's feeling of guilt was intensified by the gray light that came in through the mouth of the cave, and a sound that was unmistakably that of dripping water.

She crawled out to find that it was not actually raining, although the effect was almost as damp. They were surrounded by a genuine Scottish mist, so thick she couldn't see anything six feet away. James was squatting morosely by a tiny fire. It smoked badly, but he had managed to heat some water in an empty tin can.

"Tea?" he inquired.

"Yes, please," said Susan.

So the incident of the night was to be buried in oblivion. It was probably the best thing to do, although she felt as if she ought to apologize. James was extremely wet. His hair clung to his head and his shirt clung to his body. The effect was disturbing. Susan concentrated on her tea, which was not very hot.

"Where are we going today?" she asked brightly.

"Suppose we call on Ellie."

"All that way, in all this wet?"

"Och, it will be a fine day," said James grimly. "When the mist clears."

The mist did clear as they went down the mountain. They followed a path into a wide, well-populated glen and headed for the nearest restaurant. James walked with his head drawn in like a turtle's, and his shoulders hunched; and Susan remembered the fatal resemblance.

"Should we risk it?" she asked.

"We'll have to, sooner or later," James grumbled. "At this moment I don't give a damn if I am recognized. I'm hungry. I need something hot. I think I caught cold last night."

He looked reproachfully at Susan.

She had to admit that a hot breakfast, on the lavish scale of Scotland, did wonders for her morale. No one seemed to recognize James. He kept his hand in front of his mouth, coughing occasionally to lend verisimilitude. They had agreed that James would do the talking, for fear that Susan's accent might remind someone of the American girl who was wanted "to assist the police in their investigations," so she sat squinting shyly at her hands whenever the waitress came by.

After breakfast they bought Susan a guitar in a hock shop. Her "borrowed" costume was a generalized peasant dress. The full skirt and laced bodice might have belonged to any nation, and as Susan pointed out, it was no more eccentric than many other outfits worn by traveling students that summer. That guitar added the final touch to the parts they were playing—students of folklore, wandering from one village festival to the next in search of songs and local color.

They walked for a few miles, letting the sun dry their damp clothes, and then caught a bus, without arousing any particular notice. By afternoon they had worked their way, by circuitous routes, to the neighborhood of Blair Atholl.

"Right back where we started," Susan said. They were sitting on a bench in a park eating sandwiches. Susan strummed the guitar experimentally. It had been badly out of tune, and she had been working on it on and off all day.

"I need a new E string," she remarked.

"Don't play E."

"You don't know anything about music, do you?"

Food usually restored James's good humor. He crumpled the wax paper into a neat ball and pitched it into a nearby waste basket.

"Anything you can sing I can sing." In a saccharine falsetto, he caroled, " 'I have heard the mavis singing, His love song to-o-o the morn; I have seen the dewdrop clinging. . . .' "

Susan joined in. They worked their way through "Mary of Argyle," "The Wife of Usher's Well," and "The Flowers of the Forest," by which time they had collected a small crowd.

"Aren't they just too cute for words?" exclaimed an unmistakably Virginian voice. "A Scottish laddie and lassie singin' their way through the country, like ol' troubadours. Could you sing 'The Skye Boat Song,' honey? One of mah ancestors was with Bonnie Prince Charlie."

To Susan's surprise, James promptly obliged. The malicious gleam in his eye and his overly broad accent warned her that he was up to something. When the song

was ended he passed the hat. They collected almost two
pounds, one of them from the Virginia lady.

"That was a low trick," Susan said, after they had
taken their leave of the audience.

"Thrift, thrift, my good Horatio," said James, in a
high good humor. "Never turn up your nose at good
siller. We'll need it. I'm going to buy some bikes."

"It's uphill all the way, if I remember correctly."

"Well, can you think of any other way of getting
there? It's too far to walk; I'm a bit wary of the local
bus, and anyhow we've probably missed the last
one."

Susan's memory had not played her false. It *was* uphill all the way. But they reached the turn-off to the dig
on schedule—James's schedule. As he pointed out, they
had to arrive before dark, when the workers would re-
tire to the inn for supper, and for the inevitable paper
work that accompanies an archaeological expedition. If
they wanted a private conversation with Ellie they would
have to lie in wait for her among the ruins and hope to
catch her alone.

They left the bikes hidden among the trees and
crept along like Indian scouts out of Fenimore Coo-
per; at least James's idea of woodcraft seemed to de-
rive from that source. He kept muttering words like
"Hist!" and " 'Ware!" They made a wide circle in
order to avoid the inn; the detour was, naturally,
straight up and down most of the way. But finally,
perspiring, scratched, and out of breath, they lay on
a ledge looking down on the site from the north. It
was very picturesque in the mellow late sunlight. The
ruins were more extensive than Susan had realized,
and from the height she could get a better idea of the
arrangement of the remaining fragments than she had
been able to do before.

"You know," she remarked to James, "that long
broken stretch south of the keep looks almost like

cloisters. Could there have been an abbey way up here?''

"There could be anything way up here. Including Jackson and a whole brigade of bobbies. Do you see Ellie?''

They were high enough up so that the toiling figures below looked like dolls. Ewen's red hair stood out like a blob of fresh paint. Peter's peculiar stoop was unmistakable, and so was Ellie's diminutive figure, although she wore the same drab trousers and khaki shirt as the men.

Susan pointed her out and then added, her professional instincts at high pitch, "They're still surveying the site. I'm surprised they haven't made more progress.''

"What's that gadget Peter is carrying?'' James asked. "Looks like an oversized banjo.''

"That's what they call it—a banjo." Susan sat up, so interested that she forgot she might be seen. James reminded her with a big hand on the back of her neck, and she subsided. "It's a soil-conductivity meter," she went on. "They used it at Cadbury—the place that's been identified as Camelot. It works sort of like radar, registers differences in the conductivity of the soil. You can spot metal, and even trenches and postholes. I didn't know Campbell planned to use one here. Oh, damn, I wish I were down there!''

"Pray, then," said James. "Or cross your fingers, or do whatever you like to bring us luck. If things work out, you can get back to your beloved ruins in a matter of days. You know, I'm tempted to trot on down and face them. Ewen helped us before.''

"There's someone new down there," Susan said, peering. "Looks too young to be Campbell; but we couldn't trust him. Or Ellie, or her boyfriend. You socked him on the jaw, remember?''

"That wasn't the only place I socked him," James

muttered. "He may indeed feel hostile. And there's Campbell to consider. He's the chap I particularly want to avoid. Middle-aged professors with reputations are not inclined to sympathize with fugitives. Do you see him anywhere about?"

"I don't see anybody who could be Campbell, no."

"Well, no use putting it off. Follow the leader."

Eventually they were crouched behind a stretch of stone wall not far from where Ellie was working. Notebook in hand, she was recording the figures called out to her by Dugald, who was moving around with a steel measuring tape and a level.

"They must be planning to sink a trial trench there," Susan whispered.

"Do forget your job for a while, can't you? We'll have to wait till Dugald leaves."

They had to wait for almost an hour. Finally Dugald called out to Ellie, "Get us a beer, will you, luv? It's warm out here."

"Right, luv," Ellie answered. She put down her notebook and started walking toward the inn.

James jerked his head at Susan and started off on a parallel course. The fragments of stonework converted the area into a perfect playground for skulkers. Ellie was out of Dugald's sight almost at once, descending into a hollow ringed with stones. James pounced.

Ellie was a foot shorter than he, and fifty pounds lighter; he had no trouble handling her. Clapping one hand over her mouth, he tucked her under the other arm and carried her into the grove of trees where Susan was waiting.

The girl was quiet, staring at James with bulging eyes, until she saw Susan. Then her eyes widened even more and she began to squirm. Taken aback by the frantic quality of her struggles, and handicapped by his upper-class instincts, James almost lost hold of her. It was not until Susan clipped her across the jaw that she subsided into a gasping, shaking heap.

James looked critically at his rescuer.

"I've no patience with her," Susan snapped, answering the implied reproach. "Now listen, Ellie, you keep your mouth shut except to answer questions, and you answer them correctly. He may be too much of a gentleman to slug you, but I'm not."

Ellie sat up and pushed her glasses back into position. She looked even frailer and more mothlike. Susan felt a qualm of pity, which she ruthlessly stamped down. Ellie's first comment made the job easy.

"You murderers," she gasped. "You leave me alone or I'll scream. The police were here yesterday—no, I mean, there's a policeman at the inn now, and—"

"Hold on a second," James said irritably. "We're the ones who are supposed to be threatening you, not the other way round. There are no police here. No one is going to rescue you. You answer our questions and you won't be in any danger."

Ellie drew herself up. "You can tear me limb from limb," she cried. "I won't talk. You'll never find it through me."

"Find what?" Susan demanded.

"Oh, don't pretend you don't know! You've killed a harmless old man to get it. You can kill me, too; go ahead. I'll never speak. I'd rather die than see it fall into your hands."

The "murderers" looked blankly at one another. The interrogation wasn't going at all the way they had planned. Verbal intimidation was the only kind they were prepared to use, and James was visibly distressed at having to do that much. It was evident that Ellie was not to be intimidated by threats, and Susan was inclined to suspect that she would remain silent even under stronger methods. She had the look of a fanatic as she huddled on the ground staring up at them, her eyes blazing and her small mouth set in a line of triumphant martyrdom. Only what was she so fanatical about? What was the mysterious "it" that she was prepared to defend with her life?

In addition to being too tough for them, Ellie was also too smart. Her eyes narrowed thoughtfully as she looked at the crestfallen faces of her kidnappers. Then she threw her head back and let out a piercing scream.

Susan pounced, but too late; Ellie got out several more ear-shattering yells. Footsteps came pounding through the trees. Susan considered socking Ellie, just on general principles, and then decided against it. She rose to her feet in time to see Ewen come rushing to the rescue, brandishing a spade like a club. He stopped short at the sight of James and Susan.

"Ellie's not hurt," James said quickly. "We only wanted to talk to her. Give us a chance, can't you?" He smiled ingratiatingly.

Ewen's face turned scarlet. "You bloody killer!" he shouted. He raised the spade and struck.

The blow was aimed at James's head. He got his arm up just in time; instead of splitting his skull the heavy tool knocked him flat. He fell on his back. Ewen struck again, aiming straight at James's upturned face.

Susan hit him with her full hundred and ten pounds. Contrary to the poet's claim, it is not purity of heart that strengthens a combatant, but the reverse; Susan was boiling with fear and anger, and the impetus of her charge was enough to throw Ewen off balance. The spade split the ground inches from James's right ear. Ewen stumbled. Still in the grip of a red berserker rage, Susan caught up a handy rock and brought it down on Ewen's head. She didn't wait to see him fall, but turned on Ellie, her fists clenched. Ellie took one look at her face and fainted. Erect on the field of battle, which was strewn with the bodies of the fallen, Susan heard a voice that had to be her own declaiming hoarsely in Gaelic. It was the only Gaelic she knew, and she had never expected to find herself in a situation to which it would apply—the old war cry of the Camerons, "Sons of the hounds, come here and get meat!"

Chapter 6

A sound from somewhere in the vicinity of her left foot brought Susan out of her fit. It was a horrible, choking sound like a death rattle, and it sobered her instantly. She was afraid to look down to see from which throat the hideous noise had come. If she had hit Ewen harder than she intended . . .

Drunk or sober, maddened or calm, she was not chiefly concerned with Ewen. Slowly she turned.

James had risen to his knees. His eyes were as round as coins and his eyebrows had disappeared under the fringe of damp hair on his forehead. His right hand was clamped tightly around his left elbow; above his fingers a reddening flap of sleeve hung loose.

Again he tried to speak. He cleared his throat and finally managed to croak, "What was that you said?"

"Never mind. We've got to get away."

"You said—"

"James, the others will be here any second. We've got to—"

"Where did you learn Gaelic?" James got to his feet,

145

very slowly. "Your accent is terrible," he added, swaying.

Susan stamped her foot. "This is no time for philological criticism. Can you run?"

"I can try. Is Ewen . . . ?"

"I forgot about him." Susan knelt.

"You—forgot—" James said stupidly.

"He's okay." Susan stood up. "He's lucky to have such thick hair." A querulous mutter from Ewen confirmed her diagnosis. "He'll be awake in a minute," Susan went on. "And I think I hear inquiring voices somewhere in the distance, but rapidly approaching. Honestly, Jamie, I don't think you're cut out to be a policeman. You have no sense of self-preservation. I suppose now you want me to give Ellie first aid. She just fainted, that's all."

"I don't blame her," James said. "If you had seen your face—"

"Come on! Let's go!" Susan put her arm around him. Staggering and intertwined like participants in a three-legged race, they ran. And ran. And ran. Not until the voices had faded and half a mountainside lay between them and the dig did Susan stop. They stood beside a small burn whose water sang and tumbled over peaty brown stones. James sat down suddenly and put his head on his knees.

"I need a drink," he said.

"There's water in the burn."

"Not the sort of drink I had in mind." James lifted his head. His face was ashen, but he managed a faint smile when he saw Susan's expression.

"Don't look so sick. What's the trouble—reaction setting in?"

Susan sat down next to him. "I guess so. I feel funny. Jamie, I don't know what came over me. I never did anything like that before."

"Where did you get the Gaelic?"

It was Susan's turn to put her head on her knees.

"I memorized it, ages ago, just for fun," she mumbled. "I'd forgotten it, until. . . . I think I'm going to throw up."

"No, you aren't." James's fingers stroked the back of her neck. "Take a deep breath, you'll be okay. You saved my life, you know. I think I owe the romantics of this world an apology. If you hadn't gotten carried away, Ewen would have smashed my face in. I have certain objections to my face, but I'd hate to go around without it."

"He asked for it, didn't he?" Susan felt better. "But I'm glad I didn't hurt him badly. What do you suppose made him act like that?"

"I presume Ellie and Jackson convinced him that we really are murderers. He found us threatening Ellie, and his basic instincts took over."

"He acted like a savage," Susan said, shivering. "Like one of those damned Picts Campbell is so crazy about. . . . I'm okay now, Jamie. Let's see that arm."

The injury wasn't as bad as she had feared, but it was bad enough. James's sleeve was covered with blood from a deep cut, and the muscles around it were swelling. Susan washed it in the stream and bound it up, using strips torn from her apron. The rest of the fabric made a serviceable sling.

"You need a doctor," she said uneasily. "That cut ought to be disinfected."

"I've got a few first-aid supplies in the knapsack." James got stiffly to his feet. "Lucky it's my left arm. And lucky the blade hit a glancing blow."

"I don't see anything lucky about it. The whole thing was a disaster."

"We learned one thing. There is a treasure."

"The famous 'it' Ellie kept muttering about. Yes, I guess that bears out your theory. But it doesn't help us much. You weren't thinking of doing a little illicit digging of your own, were you?''

"The idea tempts me. But it would be idiotic. The site is large and they don't seem to know where 'it' is themselves.''

"They—some of them—may know, though,'' Susan said. She knew James was talking to keep his mind off the pain. Since he had disdained the help of her arm, the only thing she could do for him was to keep the conversation going.

"What do you mean?'' James asked.

"The expedition seems to be legitimate. Campbell is a big name in the field, and the students act like normal archaeology students. Campbell selected the site, looking for his rotten old Picts. Somebody else got wind of the treasure—found a clue Campbell missed—and is using the expedition as a cover, planning to steal the treasure if and when it is finally located. This somebody contacted Jackson, who is a professional crook. The amateur could be one of Campbell's own students—''

"Or an outsider who had forged false credentials to win a place on the expedition staff.''

"I don't like that theory. I'm the only outsider.''

"Oh, I don't blame them for being suspicious of us,'' James agreed. His voice and face were under perfect control, but he was supporting the injured arm with his right hand. Susan looked at him anxiously.

"Are you all right?''

"Perfectly.''

"All right, then,'' Susan said. "We return to the burning question of what this mysterious 'it' could be. An honest-to-God Pictish treasure would be worth a lot of money on the illegal antiquities market—enough money to attract the interest of a man like Jackson. I suppose crooks specialize these days, like everybody else. Maybe Jackson is a well-known antiquities burglar. If so, he'd know enough about the subject to recognize a clue for himself. Only where is the clue?''

''You have that book of Campbell's still, don't you? We might have another look at that.''

''In our copious free time,'' Susan agreed wryly. ''It won't work, James. Campbell is an expert. It's ridiculous to think an amateur like Jackson, or even a student, would spot a clue that Campbell had missed. The vital lead must have come from another source. Maybe that's how old Tammas got involved. He knew a lot about Scottish legends and traditions, you say. Ellie must be a member of Tammas's group. If she told her buddies of the White Rose about the dig, and one of them remembered something about the site—some old story or fragment of legend . . .''

''It's possible,'' James agreed. ''But it's pure theory, Susan. We're damnably short on facts.''

''I know. I keep thinking we're overlooking something. Something important.''

''Do you? I have the same feeling. God knows we've not had time for calm meditation. . . . The bikes should be just ahead.''

Susan didn't ask how he proposed to ride. She didn't have time. James grabbed her and dragged her down onto a large plant of the thistle variety. Bristling with prickles, Susan clamped her teeth shut and swallowed her groans.

''What is it?'' she whispered.

''Someone's there.''

They had been traveling parallel to the road, on a slope about ten feet above its surface. Susan's eyes were dazzled by diffused sunlight sifting through the branches of the stunted trees. A breeze stirred the lighter branches and shook the needles of a spruce.

Then she saw a movement that could not have been caused by the wind—a slight agitation of a bushy plant that was only partially visible through the trees. She could not identify the plant; it was a violent, virulent green, with broad leaves.

James's hand, still on her arm, tightened till the fingers dug into her flesh. Between the bright-green leaves another color showed—a smoother, flatter black than the shadows under the bush. The crimson rays of the setting sun touched the patch of color and it shone like a blackbird's wing.

"Jackson," she breathed. "How did he—"

"Sssh." James shaped the sound with his lips. Feeling carefully on the ground at his feet, he picked up a rock and threw it.

Jackson was a victim of overconfidence. No doubt he assumed his concealment was so good they would stumble into his arms. He took off after the crash of the stone, which sounded promisingly like the stumble of a clumsy foot. As soon as the sleek black head turned away from them, James began to run. Susan followed.

It was almost an hour later before James conceded that, for the moment at least, they had eluded pursuit. They were traversing a patch of boggy ground crisscrossed by streams, and both were soaked to the knees.

"What did you say about luck?" Susan inquired. She pulled her foot out of a patch of mud which closed with a horrible sucking sound.

"I retract the statement. We've lost all our gear—food, clothes, bikes, Farragut's gun, even your guitar. Thank God I had the money in my sporran."

"We've got to get out of this," Susan gasped, as another boggy patch dragged her foot down. "Ugh! I keep thinking about quicksand, and the Hound of the Baskervilles. There ought to be a village or something around here."

"We can't risk being spotted so close to the dig," James said. "You'll have to settle for another cave tonight."

Susan stopped, with one foot in a stream, and looked at him squarely.

"Jamie, don't be childish. I'm worried sick about your arm. The chances are a hundred to one that it will be infected. We don't even have iodine. And we're getting nowhere fast. Jackson is hot on our trail with God knows how many allies. We need help, and there's only one logical place to look for it."

"I'm not such a fool as you think," James said quietly. "I thought of going to the police some time ago—when Ewen came at me with that spade, to be precise. But there's a difficulty."

"What difficulty? They won't believe our story, but at least we'll be safe."

"That's not the difficulty. If we could get to Edinburgh, or even to a good-sized town, and turn ourselves in at a police station, I'd agree. But it's awfully easy to hire a uniform. Many of the local constables don't even wear them. How are we to know whom we're surrendering to?"

"They can't be everywhere," Susan said, but her objection was weak. She had not thought of this problem.

"We have no idea of the size of the organization we're fighting. Jackson is an American, Farragut is English or Scottish; that suggests an international group. And don't forget the casual bystanders like Ewen. Whether they are part of Jackson's group or not, they are clearly prejudiced against us. I don't want to encounter any more maddened Highlanders with deadly weapons. I can't always count on you to rescue me."

"Then what can we do?"

"I don't know," said James candidly. "If our wild theories are correct, there will be a meeting at King's Quair in a few days. We may learn something there—if we can get there."

"We've got to find someplace to hole up in the meantime," Susan said. "Or some way of getting to the police. There's only one safe place I can think of."

James nodded wearily.

"We may as well head for the family homestead. At worst, we might ring the Chief Constable from there and demand a personal escort. But I wouldn't gamble a great deal on our chances of getting there. That's one place they will certainly have staked out."

Susan's submerged foot was getting numb. The water was icy. As the sun sank lower, a chill breeze arose. James was shivering, despite his efforts to conceal it.

"Let's go, then," Susan said, trying to sound cheerful. "It's a long way."

To her relief they soon left the boggy area and began to climb. Her relief was short-lived; James's strength was rapidly running out. He was climbing one-handed, which is not a safe procedure under any circumstances, and he was increasingly unsteady in his movements. Unobtrusively Susan kept to one side and slightly below him, although she knew she didn't stand a chance of holding him if he should fall. Standing on a narrow ledge on a steep slope, she watched his good hand fumble before it slid over the projecting rock that was its next hold. There was a streak of blood across the back of his fingers, and his nails were torn and bloody. She knew then what she had to do.

They reached the top of the ridge and saw a valley below. Houses clustered around a circular loch. Lights were beginning to come on in the windows. Susan glanced at James, who stood beside her. His eyes were closed, and he was rocking slowly back and forth.

"We may as well stop here," she said gently. "There's nothing any better for miles. Maybe in the morning I can go down and get some food."

James didn't object to either suggestion. He let her guide him into a hollow at the base of a tree, where the massive roots had dug a space, and subsided without opening his eyes. He was asleep almost at once. In the fading light Susan bent over him. She was afraid to touch the bandage, but his face was warm under her light fingers.

She waited for half an hour, while the dark crept in around them. James was breathing heavily, and his temperature had risen. Susan rose carefully to her feet and looked for the path she had seen earlier.

It was a path she would never have attempted in darkness if she had had any choice, but she went down it without giving its dangers a thought, except for an irritated "damn!" when her foot slipped. She had to cross a pasture to get to the road. Unmistakable evidence indicated that it was normally occupied by sheep.

The road soon turned into a village street. Susan walked down it, followed by furious barking, but no one came out to see who was intruding. She was looking for a particular kind of house, and praying that a village of this size would have what she needed. She was in luck. The house was some distance from the main huddle of the village; the brass plate on the neat white gate had been freshly polished. It glittered in the starlight.

The gate was securely fastened. Susan didn't waste time trying to unlatch it. She climbed the fence. As her foot touched the ground, a small dark shape darted at her. A ghastly shriek climbed the scale and a bundle of spikes sank into her ankle.

The door of the house opened. Light spilled out across the graveled path. A voice called,

"Come in, whoever you are."

"I can't," Susan groaned. "I'm caught by this infernal—"

It was a Siamese cat, the largest and darkest Susan had ever seen. It had released its tooth-and-claw grip when the voice spoke, and now sat crouched at Susan's feet. Its tail lashed like a black whip, and enormous eyes, reddened by the reflection, glared at Susan.

"Beelzebub," said the voice.

The cat moved back six inches. It continued to lash its tail. Susan thought of kicking it, but reconsidered, for a number of excellent reasons. She started up the path, limping. The cat fell in behind her like a sentry. As she approached the open door, she saw that a hand-carved sign hung over it. She was familiar with the quaint British custom of giving pretentious names to retirement cottages, but the name of this one sent a shiver down her back. It read "Endor."

As soon as she had entered, the door closed quietly behind her. Susan would not have been at all surprised to learn that the cat had done the job; it appeared to be capable of more complex acts, and the only human inhabitants of the room were seated in a semicircle around the fire.

There were three of them, all women, all elderly. All were knitting. One was tall and thin, one was short and fat, and the third was a frail, hunched bundle of bones that looked as if they would fall apart if the shawls enclosing them were unwrapped.

Endor is right.

Susan wasn't conscious of having spoken aloud, but one of the women—the fat one—looked up and spoke.

"Yes, we thought it appropriate. Beelzebub has a diabolical personality, and we three. . . . But I will spare you the obvious. What is it you want, young woman, and what are you doing here?"

"No better than she should be," grumbled the thin woman, without taking her eyes from her wad of blue knitting. "Send her away, Frances."

"I was looking for the doctor," Susan began. "Is he—"

"We are the doctor," said the woman called Frances.

"Or, to be more specific, we are all three doctors. Do you require a heart specialist, a dermatologist, or a surgeon? I trust it is not the last; Amelia''—she nodded at the bundle of shawls—''is the surgeon, and I would personally hesitate to trust my organs to her operations at present.''

Before Susan could express her complete agreement the bundle stirred.

"Who asked for your opinion?'' inquired a thin, malevolent voice. ''You always were jealous, Frances. Just because I was prettier than you.''

The uncanny effect was heightened by the fact that no face was visible among the clothes, but gradually a rounded shape heaved up out of the bundle. Covered with a bright-red knitted cap, it appeared to be a head. It jerked and heaved until a face came into view. Susan stepped back. Wrinkled and spotted like that of a mummy, the horrid countenance held two bright black eyes, lashless and deep-set, that fastened unwinkingly on Susan's face. She felt like a bird hypnotized by a snake.

"Ahem,'' said Amelia, after at time. ''Yes. Give the girl a nip of whiskey, Annabelle. Can't you see she's faintish? Don't blame her. I'd faint too, confronted with three such hideous old women.''

She emitted a sound like a dry sticks cracking.

However they might insult her, the oldest sister was obviously the boss. The thin woman rose obediently and poured whiskey into a glass. Susan dropped limply into a chair.

"You're very kind,'' she said.

"Kind!'' The elderly mummy's eyes snapped. ''It's acid that runs through our veins, child, not the milk of human kindness. I'm curious, that's all. You're an exotic bird to come in out of the Highland night. Drink your whiskey like a lady, and then you can tell us what you want.''

The needles clicked as the three went back to their work. Susan wondered how the eldest sister could see; her head had retreated down into the shawls like that of turtle. She took a cautious sip of the amber liquid and felt its smoothness slide down her throat, spreading warmth through her limbs. Her wits began to come back to her. Covertly she studied the room.

It was a small room, jam-packed with bric-a-brac. Apparently the three sisters had highly individualized tastes, and none of them was prepared to sacrifice her share of the space. A large table, covered with a hand-woven spread in soft colors of beige, brown, and green, was littered with garden tools, balls of yarn and— Susan's eyes widened—a motorcyclist's helmet. Two very modern canvas-sling chairs were occupied respectively by Beelzebub and a huge stuffed pink bear, of the sort that is given as a prize at carnivals. Leaning against the wall was a rake, a cricket bat, and a long, peculiar string instrument. Books and magazines were strewn around. They were a motley collection, including *Principles of Anatomy, The Prisoner of Zenda,* and a recent issue of *Woman's Own,* with a photograph of the Queen on the cover. The first faint ghost of an idea stirred wispily in Susan's brain. Ignoring the other pictures that covered the walls like the displays of the Pitti Palace, her eyes went straight to the one that held the place of honor over the mantel. It was a huge colored portrait of the royal family.

The preposterous plan took shape, born of desperation and sired by fantasy. Susan put down her empty glass and spoke.

Annabelle—the tall, thin sister—came up the mountain with her. Susan could never have managed without her; James was only three-quarters conscious, and guiding him down the path in the dark would have been impossible without someone who knew every pebble on the hillside. The old woman's arms were as strong as a man's. Susan decided that the cricket bat and the gardening tools must belong to her. She had already learned that the cyclist's helmet belonged to Frances, who was the only practicing physician among the three. The village had had no doctor of its own, and Frances had been more or less drafted into general practice after the sisters had retired to Scotland.

Susan had learned this, and other information, as Annabelle led her up the mountain. For all their apparent sophistication the sisters were romantics, and Susan's story had been almost as good as *The Prisoner of Zenda*. The poor young couple, snatching a few weeks of happiness before the boy's titled parents forced him into a match of convenience. . . . Susan wondered whether any parent, these days, succeeded in forcing any child into any sort of marriage, much less one of convenience. But it didn't matter. The ladies had bought the story, hook, line, and sinker, including the part where James had rescued her from a lustful farmer with a shovel. She had to explain the wound somehow, and she assumed the ladies had enough medical knowledge to identify the type of weapon with fair accuracy. It was a perfectly ridiculous story. The ladies had loved it. Susan had not given them the coup de grace. It would be much more effective if they simply saw James's face.

James was on his feet when they reached the cottage. He walked through the door and across the room, straight into the wall. His face pressed against it, he declaimed, with perfect accent and rhythm,

"The stait of man dois change and vary,
 Now sound, now seik, now blith, now sary,
 Now dans and mery, now like to dee. . . ."

and sank gently to the floor.

A thrill of terror, part real, part pure superstition, ran up Susan's spine. It was an ill-omened verse—the old classic of Dunbar's, with its grim refrain, *"Timor mortis conturbat me."* The fear of death. . . . Forgetting plots, plans and the silent spectators, she dropped down beside James and cradled his head against her breast. Then the quality of the silence struck her. She looked up.

Annabelle and Frances were standing. They were staring at James. His head had fallen back over Susan's arm and his features were mercilessly exposed.

Susan held her breath. Would it work? How could it possibly work? They couldn't be such innocents. . . .

Creak. Crack. With a snapping symphony of stiffened joints old Amelia unfolded, in sections, like a tripod. Slowly and painfully she tottered up until she was standing as straight as a woman her age could stand. The expressions on all three faces were identical. Susan knew she had done it. She pulled James's face against her breast and bowed her head over his. There were tears in her eyes, but she would have had a hard time deciding whether they were tears of relief or shame or pure amusement.

James had an infected throat. That was what had caused the fever. The gash on his arm was beginning to fester, but as Susan should have realized, it had not had time enough to reduce him to his state of collapse. Pumped full of antibiotics, he was considerably better the next day, and so embarrassed at his weakness that he was impossible to talk to.

Susan visited him long enough to indicate, in a few well-chosen words, the basis of the old ladies' illusion, and then left. Annabelle was teaching her to play the sitar.

On the following morning she decided to beard James again. They couldn't stay here forever; it was hard to keep their presence a secret from the other villagers, and she was running out of romantic-plot episodes. There was a further danger. She had sneaked out of her room the first night and short-circuited the old ladies' radio, but sooner or later they were bound to hear of the activities of James's alter ego, cutting ribbons or escorting a young lady of impeccable family and ancient lineage to a social function hundreds of miles away. The sisters might swallow the idea of a double, but their capacity for gulping down improbabilities must be limited. And there were other problems.

"What chance does Jackson have of tracking us here?" she asked. James was sitting up in bed. He had received her with affable condescension. The awed respect with which he was treated seemed to be going to his head a little.

"Not much. But we can't sit here forever. I think we ought to leave tonight."

"How's the arm?"

"A little stiff, but useful." James flexed it, then looked at her conspiratorially and lowered his voice. "How did you bring it off? They really believe—"

"We are lovers," said Susan. "Your titled family will not allow us to wed. I didn't mention *any* names, Jamie."

"Titled family!" James grinned. "Oh, well; might as well be hanged for a sheep as a lamb."

"They can't pin a thing on us," Susan assured him. "I don't think impersonation is a crime unless you try to swindle somebody. Can we help it if three naïve elderly ladies think—"

"Well, we could have helped it, you know. They've been awfully good. I feel a little . . ."

"So do I. But it had to be done. I feel even sorrier for your double."

"I don't like to think about it," James said, with

feeling. "So we'll take our departure tonight. The ladies will accept our desire to remain inconspicuous. The question is, whither do we go?"

"The meeting at King's Quair is day after tomorrow," Susan said.

"If there is a meeting."

They stared at one another in silence for a moment. Then James shrugged.

"It must be the medication they've given me. I feel frightfully courageous and full of optimism again. Shall we risk it?"

"By all means," said Susan. "You know, Jamie, I don't think it's the medicine. I think your true colors are beginning to show. All that poetry you've been quoting, while you were delirious and—uh—delirious. . . . You are your father's son, after all."

"You needn't be insulting," said James.

They took a solemn, formal leave of the three sisters just before midnight. James looked like a prince as he bowed over the ladies' trembling hands—not simultaneously, of course, but one after the other.

"We ought to give them a good show," he had remarked, passing his hand over his freshly shaved chin. "It's the least we can do."

And he did it well. Tall and straight in his freshly pressed kilt, the plaid draped across his chest, the ancient silver brooch gleaming, he made even Susan's blood run faster. But when he straightened up after saluting Amelia's withered hand, his eyes met hers; and for a moment he stood motionless, staring as if some silent message were passing between them.

"I'm immensely grateful," he said.

"Time is passing," said Frances. "If you don't mind, your—that is, Mr. James—we should be going now."

Frances had insisted that they take her motorbike. It was an old one, she was thinking of trading it in anyway. . . . It was impossible to refuse the offer and equally impossible to offer to pay for the vehicle. James was visibly moved. Susan only hoped he would be able to restrain his finer instincts and keep his mouth shut. He managed to do so until they stood in the quiet cul-de-sac where the bike was waiting. Then the old woman bent her arthritic knees in a curtsy and reached for James's hand. Susan was thankful that Frances couldn't see his face.

"Hurry," she hissed, before James could weaken.

They pushed the bike along between them until they were a mile or so out of town; the villagers knew the characteristic sound of the motor and might wonder who had been taken sick in the night. James was silent for a long time. Finally he said,

"I feel the most unutterable swine."

"How do you think I feel?"

"I think you're enjoying yourself enormously. You're as bad as my father. No. You're worse than my father. Running amok with rocks and inventing nauseating stores—"

"That's gratitude," exclaimed Susan, stung to the quick. "I wasn't going to rub it in; but I would like to point out that we have been saved from disaster twice in a row by what you nastily refer to as my Bonnie Prince Charlie romanticism."

"Just because we were lucky enough to encounter three other romantics—"

"Ewen wasn't a romantic."

"That depends on how one defines the word," James said drily. "Oh, hell, let's not argue. I didn't mean to snap at you. I suppose you feel bad about deceiving the ladies too."

"Yes, I do. Only I wonder if we really did fool Miss Amelia."

"So do I. She's a marvelous old witch, isn't she? And

she's perfectly capable of helping us for the sheer dev-
iltry of it. But the others bought the whole bit.''

''We'll make it up to them.''

''How?''

''Tell them the real story, someday. They'll get an
enormous charge out of it.''

''There's a thought.'' James sounded more cheerful.
''It won't be as good as yours, though.''

''How do you know? We're not at the end of it yet.''

Chapter 7

Philosophers have had many things to say about the dangers of overconfidence. Susan was not familiar with these works, or she might have remembered them during the next few hours; but it is probable that even familiarity with the classics would not have dulled her high spirits. The change in their situation was dramatic. Forty-eight hours earlier she had been standing ankle deep in a bog, lost, pursued by villains, and without so much as a spare handkerchief to her name, as she watched James's temperature rise. And here they were roaring along a nice smooth road at sixty miles an hour, clean, full, and rested. Their knapsacks were packed with goodies, packs and food alike having been supplied by the ladies. Frances had with difficulty been restrained from packing a bottle of champagne. Susan's spirits bubbled over. She began to sing.

" '. . . ere the king's crown go down, there are crowns to be broke!

Then each cavalier who loves honor and me
Let him follow the bonnets of Bonnie Dundee!' ''

James hunched his shoulders and increased speed.

Susan claimed, later, that their troubles stemmed from this mistake. The aged bike wasn't up to such rough treatment. James sneered. The bike was a wreck, and would have collapsed anyhow. At any event, morning found them having elevenses in a dreary café on the outskirts of a small town and staring disconsolately at the garage across the street where the bike was undergoing expensive repairs.

"What are you in such a hurry about?" Susan asked. "We've got two days, almost."

"I just wish this had happened in a large city," James grumbled. "We're too conspicuous here. And we're too damned close to Balmoral. You realize, don't you, that our disguises are no longer of any use? Ewen and Ellie saw us; they can tell the police I'm beardless. For all we know, our new descriptions have been circulated all over the country. I was out of commission for two whole days."

"There's nothing about us in the paper." Susan indicated the Aberdeen newspaper they had bought.

"That makes me even more uneasy. You needn't suppose they've abandoned the search. They've probably got some lead they don't want to publicize."

"You sure are a cheerful fellow traveler."

"I feel cut off," James said. "I almost wish something would happen, so we would know where we stood."

He got his wish.

It was the bike that proved to be their undoing. When they went back to the garage, James stood with his back turned, pretending to examine an advertising poster, while Susan dealt with the mechanic. They had followed this procedure when delivering the machine. The mechanic was bending over the bike when they came in, and Susan's heart sank when she saw that pieces of the machine were still strewn about.

"Can't you fix it?" she asked.

The mechanic backed away from her. One sight of his face told Susan all she needed to know; but it was too late to run. From the office stepped a tall, dignified form clad in blue.

"Now, then," it said. "Let's have a look at your papers, if you please."

Susan turned. The mechanic stood blocking the exit, brandishing a spanner.

"Aye, I told ye," he said triumphantly. "It's the auld doctor's bike, right enough. They stole it."

"No, no, she gave it to us," Susan said. "Loaned it, I mean. Call her; just call her and ask."

"She means we should ring up the doctor," the mechanic explained to the constable. " 'Tis an American idi-om."

"American," said the constable. "Aye. I suspected from your descr-r-ription." He pulled a piece of paper from his pocket, and took his time about reading it. "Aye. It's them. Nae doot aboot it. Come along, you two."

"Where are you taking us?" Susan asked despondently.

"Weel, noo." The constable pushed his cap back and scratched his head. "Wi' twa sich desperate creeminals, I dinna ken if our bit preeson is strang enough. Ye'll help me to guard them, Davie Burnett, until the gentleman from the International Poliss can come for them."

"Gentleman," said Susan. "What gentleman?"

James was still standing with his back to the conference. Susan glared at him. Why didn't he do something? She saw his shoulders hunch when she asked the question to which she already knew the answer.

"Dinna play the innocent," said the constable sternly. "International creeminals ye are, with Interpol itself after ye. He gave me the descr-r-ription himself, the gentleman did. An American like yersel'. Nae doot ye've committed mony a crime back in Chicago, where the hoodlums live. Ta think that a lassie so young could be so wicked!"

James turned. "Constable," he said. "Come here, if you please."

His voice had changed. Slow, deep-pitched, the University accent slightly exaggerated, it held a tone of command that moved the constable two steps forward. Then he stopped, glancing at his collaborator for support.

"Dinna heed him," cried the stalwart, waving his spanner. "He'll have a pistol, nae doot, or be one o' those judo experts. . . ."

James laughed. It was a triumph of acting; only Susan heard the quaver in his voice.

"I assure you, Constable, you are in no danger from me," he said lightly. "You may stay at a safe distance. I shall come to you."

He moved forward, one step at a time. His stride was so regal that Susan could almost hear the strains of "Pomp and Circumstance." The constable stared. James had not taken many steps before the man's jaw started to sag. His sandy eyebrows rose slowly up till they almost touched his hairline. Suddenly he snapped to attention, saluting so smartly that his hand smacked against his forehead.

"Sir!" he exclaimed. "Sir!"

"That will do, Constable," James sketched a return salute. His half-smile was a masterpiece of friendly condescension. "You understand why I prefer not to show you my credentials. Will you be good enough to instruct this good fellow to complete the repairs on my machine?"

"Sir!" said the constable.

The mechanic was more articulate. He had crept cautiously toward them until he could get a good look. The spanner dropped from his hand and rang on the concrete.

"The guid Laird bless us," he gasped. "It's his—"

"No names," said James, raising his hand and looking down his nose. "No names, please, my friend. I am, so to speak, incognito. I know I can trust your discretion."

"Sir!" said the constable.

The mechanic, recovering himself, glanced at Susan. A small superior smile curved his lips.

"Aye," he said. "I understand. Weel, weel, we're all human; a lad needs a bit o'relaxation now and then."

"A lad needs a method of transportation as well," said James, allowing a slight frown to mar the gracious mien of his noble brow.

The constable was still frozen in salute.

"At ease, Constable," James said, nodding.

"Sir!" said the constable. He turned a desperate scowl on his former ally. "What are ye dawdling for, Davie Burnett? Get on wi' it. His—the gentleman is in a hurry."

"And you, perhaps, are in a hurry to call the efficient gentleman from Interpol," said James.

His Highness had graciously permitted himself a joke. The constable laughed.

But James's smile vanished when the man said, "Aye, weel, it's a fule I've made o' masel' this day. The gentleman will be fair angry when he arrives and finds I've made an error."

"Oh," said James faintly. "You—you rang him earlier."

"Aye." The constable peered at him "Ye'll no be wantin' to see him, sir?"

"No," James said candidly. He glanced at Susan.

"I knew she'd send someone after you!" said Susan. All three men gave her startled looks. James swallowed.

"Can't she understand you're an adult?" Susan went on, warming to her theme. "Everybody else gets a vacation now and then, but you can't even go away for a few days without your ma——"

"Susan," shouted James. The constable looked shocked, but the mechanic gave Susan a broad grin.

"They're all alike, these mums," he said consolingly. "Dinna fash yersel', lassie, I'll hae the pair o'ye oot and gane before the poliss can get here."

He was as good as his word. As soon as they were out of town James turned off the road into the first track that would take the bike. Susan endured the bone-shaking ride without comment; she understood the necessity for it. Jackson was on his way; if they stayed on the main road they might meet him. The very idea turned her cold. And James didn't have to point out the corollary. They had fooled the two locals, but Jackson would be under no illusion as to their identity, and their proximity. He might wangle a description of the motor-bike out of the constable. The net was closing, and there was no way of knowing how many hands were drawing it in. Obviously Jackson had credentials good enough to deceive a country cop. He could create allies even where he had none of his own.

The glen was of good size, and so beautiful Susan was impressed in spite of her preoccupation with more imminent problems. The burn that ran through it was almost big enough to be called a river; arched stone bridges crossed it at intervals. The hills closed in on all sides, the foothills wooded with green, the higher peaks beyond laced with purple shadows and white waterfalls. There were some deciduous trees, but most were pines, scenting the air with freshness. The fields were thick with green crops, the farmhouses low and huddled.

On a deserted stretch of track James ran the bike onto the side and stopped.

"You aren't going to like this," he said.

"I know, I know; we'll have to abandon the bike. Well, anyhow, Frances will get it back. I'm sure she needs it."

"I don't intend that she will get it back." James pushed the bike among the trees. "If Jackson finds it, he'll know where to start looking for us."

They left the machine in a clump of bushes, and James smoothed over the scar its entry had made. The wheels had left no track on the rocky ground.

"We've got thirty-five miles to go," he said, tossing one of the knapsacks over his shoulder. "Let's get started. Oh, and Susan—"

"Yes?"

"Don't count on this face to get us out of trouble hereafter. I've done enough damage with it."

"I suppose it would be risky, now that Jackson knows what you look like," Susan agreed regretfully. "But it was handy."

James snorted.

"Handy, indeed. I believe you revel in this sort of thing for its own sake. Your comments back there were quite unnecessary. When I think what you have done to that poor devil's reputation—"

"At least my contribution made him sound human and sympathetic," Susan retorted. "You talked like the most god-awful prig! I'll bet he never talked like that in his life. 'At ease, Constable!' "

"That will do," said James. "And if you refer once more to romantics and dreamers and makers of history, I'll leave you in the bush with the bike."

Under different circumstances Susan would have enjoyed the following hours. The arduous cross-country travel of the past few days had hardened her, and the country they passed through was lovely. Following the rivers, they managed to avoid difficult climbing. The clear, uncontaminated mountain streams furnished drinking water, and the ladies had packed enough food for a regiment. The area was thick with castles—ruined castles, their fanged walls perched on crags; small, homey castles, still inhabited, on the shores of deep-blue lochs; large, impressive castles, whose gray stone battlements were circled by lovely gardens. Burns and lochs and castles and moors; the glimpse of a graceful dun shape—a stag—moving on delicate leisured hooves through a shadowed clearing, until the wind brought their scent to his dilated nostrils and he took off in a great leap; larks tossing high in the blue heavens; plover and grouse and other birds Susan had never seen before. For long periods she was able to forget that they were not hiking for pleasure.

Dusk had gathered in before they stopped and stretched out in the shelter of a rock overhang that was not quite a cave. Susan was tired; wrapped in an old cloak of Annabelle's, she was just drifting off when James sat up.

"What—" she began.

"Sssh." James's voice was a thin thread of sound. "Look there."

He must have heard some sound her city-bred ears had not caught, for the beam of the flashlight cut cleanly through the dark and caught the animal unawares. Susan had a fantastic, flashing glimpse of a sinuous tawny body and long ringed tail, of pricked ears and twitching whiskers. The fat, fuzzy paws were outsized, like those of a kitten. Then the big cat lifted its lip in a silent snarl and was gone.

"A wildcat," James said. "One doesn't see them often. Nothing to be alarmed about; he'd go underground to avoid us if he could. The only predator that looks for a fight is man."

Susan had never slept so soundly. Once, much later,

she was awakened; the long, yearning howl echoed eerily through the night, but it did not last long. Smiling sleepily, Susan rolled over and drifted off again. It was nice to know that something, out there in the night, had found what it was looking for.

II

The following day they made good time, but found it increasingly difficult to avoid being seen. They were coming into lower, more inhabited country that was on the edge of the tourist trails, and the roads they skirted with some effort had quite a lot of traffic. Still, they managed to keep on schedule. It was not long past noon when they followed a side road into a small glen and took to the slopes. Part of it was open country, covered with coarse stands of bracken and gorse, but there were enough trees to provide adequate concealment. After some search they found a secluded spot above the village that was their destination. They settled down for a well-deserved rest and ate the remainder of the bread and cheese the ladies had packed.

The village was a snug, prosperous-looking place, with stone houses fronting a narrow main street. The shops seemed to be doing a good business. Then Susan's eyes focused on the nearer view; they had situated themselves as close to the house as possible.

It stood, as was proper, smugly aloof in its own park a mile or two from the village. It was not a castle, but a fortified country house of the seventeenth century, with little stone turrets jutting out from the whitewashed walls. Smoke rose from one of the high brick chimneys. Much of the house and grounds was hidden by shrubbery, but they had a good view of the front entrance. The ornate wrought-iron gates were closed. An open stretch of graveled space separated the gates

from the main road. To one side stood a small structure
like a sentry box.

"Hell," James said in a disappointed voice. "He's
opened the family mansion to the public. Doesn't look
like an appropriate locale for a bunch of dastardly plot-
ters, does it?"

Susan had to admit that it didn't. She had expected
King's Quair to be run down and sinister, with crumbling walls and weedy terraces and an air of brooding
decay. However . . .

"It's not bad cover for a meeting," she pointed out.
"People could come—and not go. No one would notice
except the gatekeeper, and he'd be one of the gang."

"I don't know," James said doubtfully. "Our theories are awfully wild, Susan. What if we're all wrong?"

"It's the only clue we've got left. We may as well
stay around for a while and see if anything develops. I
need a rest, anyhow. I couldn't walk another block if a
tiger were after me."

"I think I might manage a brisk trot if Jackson were
after me," James said.

"Stop shedding gloom and disillusionment. What do
you know about this place?"

James dusted bred crumbs off his hands and stretched
out.

"It's owned by a Gordon—one of the lesser branches.
Minor gentry, like ourselves. I think I've heard Dad
mention the old man. He's probably dead now."

"Aha," said Susan.

"Not all my father's acquaintances are as mad as he
is," James retorted. "I know nothing about the younger
Gordon's political opinions. Of course, if he is offering
our conspirators a den in which to conspire, we can
make some reasonably good deductions about those
opinions. We may also deduce he's not overburdened
with worldly goods, or he wouldn't be selling tickets to
the public. Beyond that I refuse to conjecture."

He let his head fall back and closed his eyes.

"Are you going to sleep?" Susan demanded indignantly.

"I might. Keep an eye on things, will you?"

Since there was nothing else to do, Susan kept an eye on things. It was a procedure lacking in excitement. She was beginning to share James's doubts about the validity of their reasoning, and the doubts increased when, at around two o'clock, a man emerged from a smaller doorway next to the main gates and busied himself around the booth, opening a shutter and arranging articles on the counter. Business was not brisk. It was almost three o'clock before the first car pulled into the parking space. A family party—man, woman, and three children—approached the ticket booth and then went into the grounds through the small door. James began to snore.

At three thirty, the sound of his snores and the warmth of the sun began to weigh down Susan's eyelids. She poked James.

"Your turn," she announced, as he grumbled protestingly. "Twelve people and two dogs so far. You can at least wake up and talk to me."

At four thirty-five more people had visited the manor, and most of them had come out. The average length of stay was an hour; Susan timed it, for want of anything better to do. Her hopes sank down with the setting sun.

Then James sat upright with a hiss of breath. Another car had joined the ones in the parking area—a bright-red, low-slung sports car, with its top down.

"Look!"

"It's a red car," said Susan intelligently.

"A red Aston Martin, you ignorant wench. They are relatively uncommon. The last time I saw one was in front of the hotel in Aldway."

It took Susan several seconds to understand.

"But what makes you think the one you saw was Farragut's car?"

"I don't think; I know. Look at the driver."

The man behind the wheel did not get out of the car. They were too far away to distinguish his features, but the leonine head with its thatch of thick, fair hair was distinctive.

"Wow," said Susan.

After exchanging a few words with the driver, the attendant approached the gates and opened them. The Aston Martin drove through and the gates were closed.

"A favored visitor," said James. His eyes were bright with excitement. "That does it. Our far-out theory is confirmed."

"Mmm-hmmm."

"Why so depressed?"

"He scares me as much as Jackson," Susan said.

"Me, too. Come on."

"You're not going in there now! It's broad daylight."

"Precisely. I want to scout the lay of the land while it's still light. If we start prowling in the dark, we're certain to fall over something. And there may be a dog."

The only hopeful aspect of the situation was that the area around the house was thickly wooded. They were able to find cover until they got right up to the wall. They followed its circuit away from the entrance.

There was no dog; nor was the wall much protection. At the rear of the house, away from the public area, it was in poor repair. In several places there were gaps big enough for a person to squeeze through. They could see the stableyard and outbuildings. The cobblestoned yard was thickly overgrown with rank weeds and the stables had not held horses for years. The weeds had been crushed by two cars. One was the red Aston Martin. The other was an old Mercedes, which deserved better treatment than it had received.

"That must be Gordon's," James muttered.

"Haven't you seen enough?"

"I think so. We'll wait till dark before we actually break in. I should think they would close up shop at five or six."

The rest of the day both dragged and sped by. With one part of her mind Susan ached for action; it was nerve-racking to wait, when she did not feel at all safe from discovery. But she was not looking forward to entering the house.

As darkness fell, there were signs of activity in the house. Lights came on in several windows, and there was the smell of cooking. Susan started to salivate. It had been a long time since lunch, and they had finished the last of their supplies. James was unsympathetic, probably because he was as hungry as she.

"Can't you think of anything but food? When this sort of thing happens in books, the characters don't sit about eating all the time; they're too busy."

"Much you know about it," Susan said disagreeably. "James Bond eats all the time. He thinks he's a gourmet or something. He gives people karate chops if they shake his martinis ten times instead of twelve. Not that I blame him. I mean, being chased and scared and beaten up uses up a lot of energy. If I ever write a suspense story, I'll have my people eating lots."

"Do shut up," said James swallowing.

It was quite dark when the back door of the house opened. A woman's form could be seen silhouetted against the light, before she turned it out. She was a stocky, sturdy figure dressed in drab clothes, and Susan guessed she must be a servant who came by the day, to "do" for the lord of the manor. She took a bicycle from one of the empty stables, switched on her lamp, and rode away.

"Now," said James. "They'll be sitting by the fire

swilling brandy and talking. Now's the time, when they're fed and happy and, hopefully, off guard.''

It was almost too easy. They walked through the gap in the wall, crossed the courtyard, and approached the back door.

They knew the door was locked because they had seen the woman turn the key. James proceeded to check the back windows. Standing on tiptoe, Susan peered in. She could see nothing, not even a crack of light.

"Locked," said James.

"Nobody's in there. Do we break a window?"

"Might as well."

The decrepit condition of the part of the house that was not on show made entry relatively easy. The window-panes hung in crumbled strips of putty, wedged against rattling by wads of paper. James produced a pocket knife and scratched at the putty until he was able to remove one of the panes and unlock the window. He boosted Susan over the sill and followed her. His flashlight showed a large kitchen with a rusty sink and an antique refrigerator, and cracking linoleum whose pattern had been worn off to a uniform brown. Every object in the room appeared to be at least forty years old, with one exception. Posed demurely in the center of the kitchen table, watching them with wide golden eyes, was a ginger Persian kitten. Its tail was coiled neatly around its front paws, and as the light reached it, it greeted them with a delighted meow.

"This is getting to be ridiculous," James said angrily. "I never knew there were so many damned cats in the whole damned country."

"It's not a damned cat," Susan said. The kitten had jumped down from the table, purring loudly. It bumped its head against James's ankles. "See how friendly it is. Poor thing, it's probably lonesome, locked up in here."

"We have no time to entertain bored cats," James

said, moving away from the kitten. It let out a low moan of distress. Susan bent to stroke it, but it skittered away from her, propped itself against James's foot, and gazed up at him with a look of infantile infatuation.

"It loves you," Susan said.

James told the cat what he thought of it. Fortunately it was too young to understand the words. Purring insanely, it began to bite the flaps of his brogues.

"Oh, damn it," James said helplessly. "Maybe if we ignore it. . . ."

After considerable maneuvering they managed to get outside the kitchen door without their attendant. But the moment James closed the door, a wail of feline despair rose to high heaven.

"My God," James gasped. "That will fetch our friends. It sounds as if it's being skinned. What's wrong with it?"

Susan opened the door. The wailing stopped; the kitten shot through a crack that looked far too narrow to admit its furry fatness. Before either of the exasperated humans could move, the small bundle crouched and leaped. Its claws caught the hem of James's kilt; it swarmed up him, swinging giddily on the folds of the plaid, and sat down on his shoulder.

Without moving the rest of his body James slowly turned his head. His eyes were wild. The kitten stared back at him. Its eyes were slitted in adoration. Coquettishly it tickled his cheek with its whiskers and then settled, paws dug into the plaid, long tail hanging down behind.

Susan had both hands over her mouth; she was shaking with laughter. James turned his outraged stare on her. After a moment the corners of his mouth twitched.

"What am I going to do with this?" he asked in a low voice.

"We can't leave it here. It will yell."

"Hmph," said James. "Now, then, Susan, just follow me. And keep quiet. Not a word from now on."

He started off along the corridor. The kitten's tail
waved like an orange plume.

Their external explorations during the day had given
them a rough idea of the layout of the house. Two wings
had been added to the older central block. They were
in one of these wings, which contained the service
rooms and servants' quarters. The conspirators might
be meeting anywhere—in the library or the master's
study, or even in the cellars, if they were romantically
inclined. The entire house would have to be searched.
It was a risky business, especially since they didn't
know how many people might be in the house. Belat-
edly, it occurred to Susan that one of them ought to
have watched the front of the house to see if any other
familiar faces appeared. No other cars had driven into
the courtyard, but that didn't prove anything; people
might come by bus or taxi, or on foot.

The conventional green baize door separated the servants' regions from the main living quarters. When
James opened it a crack, Susan saw that the public part
of the house was in striking contrast to the back part.
Paintings, molded ceilings, handsome oriental carpets
could be seen in the entrance hall and the drawing room
that opened off it. A single light burned in the hall. The
strips of carpeting that protected the handsome floor
from the feet of the humble were still in place. The
house was uncannily quiet. It had an uninhabited, museum atmosphere.

In order to reach the drawing room or the stairs, they
had to cross the hall. There was nowhere to hide in its
vast space; it was exposed to the front door and the
stairs, as well as to the open rooms on the right and
left. After a long appraisal of the situation, James
headed for a yawning opening under the main stairs. A
strip of carpeting led to this doorway; apparently the

cellars were part of the tour. They went down the stairs, looking for a less conspicuous way of reaching the upper floors. There had to be several staircases in a house of this size.

Bare bulbs, set in wire cages in the ceiling, shed a dim light. After a time Susan understood why the cellars were part of the tourist attraction. Indeed, they must be the *pièce de resistance*. How much of the setup was genuinely antique and how much was clever stage setting she did not know, but in the gloomy light the effect was quite impressive. The corridors were stone faced; their floors looked as if they had been cut into the rock under the house. The rooms opening off them had been fitted up as medieval dungeons. Rusty manacles dangled from the walls; Susan bit back a yelp as one door opened to display a skeleton dangling from a set of chains. Closer examination showed the skeleton to be plastic.

The last room on the corridor was a torture chamber, and if the instruments weren't genuine they were excellent imitations. The ropes of the rack dangled, the Iron Maiden grinned sickly. On the slimy stone-flagged floor a huge brazier, stained with fire, held sets of pincers, probes, and other unpleasant instruments.

"Let's get out of here," Susan whispered.

"Gordon appears to be a macabre soul," James agreed. He reached up to stroke the kitten, which had closed its eyes and appeared to be half asleep.

A second corridor, blocked by a door bearing a notice that barred the public from that area, led to more prosaic rooms—wine cellars containing only a melancholy dust, storage areas, and a tool room, with scraps of wood and the usual household tools—screwdrivers, wrenches, hammers. . . .

The tools reminded Susan of a scene she had almost forgotten—Tammas's veined and mottled hands, empty on the dusty floor as they seemed to grope for the objects they had grasped in the last spasm. The hammer and the stone. . . .

Susan gasped. They were ascending another flight of stairs, having seen all there was to see in the cellars. James was ahead. She grabbed at him.

"James! I've just thought of something. I think I've got it. The meaning of—"

"Sssh!" James's hand closed over her mouth. Then she heard the sound too—footsteps, slow and steady, across the hall beyond the closed door at the head of the stairs.

It might have been Susan's overheated imagination, but she could have sworn the steps stopped outside the door. The heavy steps were those of a man. They went on, if they had actually paused at all. Before they had quite died into silence, James moved.

"Jamie, didn't you hear me? I think I know—"

"Not now. Later. Follow him."

Dangerous as this might sound, it was a sensible suggestion. The meeting might be taking place anywhere in the big, rambling house, and the longer they wandered aimlessly, the greater the chances of discovery. So Susan closed her mouth and followed. The revelation could wait. She was sure she was right, though. As she tiptoed behind James, trying not to make a sound, she searched her fact-packed mind for confirmation, and found plenty of it.

The door at the head of the stairs opened onto a hallway, less elegant than the front of the house but not so shabby as the kitchen area. It too was dimly lighted by a low-wattage bulb. The stairs continued on up. From the floor above Susan heard the footsteps. So the rendezvous was in one of the bedchambers on the upper floor. It seemed to Susan that might make their task easier. There are closets and cupboards and bathrooms adjoining bedrooms.

When they peered cautiously into the upper corridor,

there was no sign of the person whose footsteps they had followed, but they no longer needed a guide. A door at the far end was slightly ajar, and a murmur of voices could be heard. Susan eyed the long corridor without approval. It was carpeted, which was good; but it was very long and very bare. An occasional table was the only furniture. Closed doors lined the walls—possible hiding places, and also possible sources of ambush.

James's twisted mouth and raised eyebrows indicated that he shared her qualms, but that there was nothing to be done about them. One after the other, tiptoeing like comedians in a silent film, they proceeded. The kitten, bobbing up and down to the rhythm of James's stride, added the final touch of comedy. James tried the door next to the one from which the voices issued. It opened. It squeaked. The voices stopped.

The room they had planned to enter was quite dark. Anything might be in there. But to Susan the dangers she knew not of were preferable to the dangerous people in the adjoining room. She ducked into the dark. James was right behind her. He paused only long enough to deposit his furry admirer gently on the floor. It wailed forlornly. James closed the door; the squeak of the hinges blended with the kitten's complaint.

Ear pressed against the panel, Susan heard an unfamiliar voice remark, "It's the damned cat. Martha must have left the door ajar. If I've told her once—"

"No, don't kick it." This voice was feminine, and familiar. "It's a beautiful kitty. . . . Come here, kitty. You aren't very friendly, are you? Don't be afraid, I won't hurt you."

They heard the kitten mumble protestingly as Ellie caught it, and then the sound of the door closing.

Susan let her breath out slowly. They were in a bedroom. Moonlight, filtering through foliage outside the mullioned windows, allowed her to make out the shape

of the high-canopied bed and a few other pieces of furniture. From the size of the room she deduced that it
must be one of the major bedchambers, with a study or
sitting room adjoining. There was a connecting door; a
small square of light indicated the location of the keyhole. Like everything else in the house, it was old and
considerably larger than a modern keyhole would have
been.

James stooped and applied his eye to the aperture.
After a moment he rose and took hold of the door handle. Again Susan held her breath. It was a chancy thing
to do, but they had to risk it if they hoped to overhear
the conversation next door.

A hairline crack of light appeared and slowly widened. There was no sound this time, thanks to James's
caution. He stopped when the crack was less than an
inch wide, but it was enough. Susan put her eye to it.

Opening the door had not been as chancy as it
seemed. There were three people in the room, but they
were all seated with their backs to the door, facing a
fireplace in which a low fire burned fitfully. The chairs
were massive, high-backed affairs; Susan could only see
the top of Ellie's brown head. The chair to her right was
occupied by Farragut. The firelight exaggerated the size
of his features; his chin protruded like Mussolini's, although he was smiling as he watched Ellie. Susan assumed the girl was stroking the cat, although she heard
no sound of purring; perhaps the animal was sulking
over the disappearance of James.

The third person was a man she had never seen before. His profile was sharply outlined against the dark
paneling, and once again Susan fancied she saw a resemblance to someone whose portrait she had seen—
some villain or other. It was not an attractive face, with
its long, beaky nose, no chin to speak of, and a thin,
cruel mouth. He was wearing Highland garb, the som-

ber blue-and-green Gordon tartan, with its narrow yellow stripe, identified him as the owner of the house.

"Stop playing wi' the cat, Ellie, and let's get down to business," he said irritably. His voice was high-pitched and whiny. "There's a lot to discuss."

"We cannot begin without Jackson," Farragut said in his even, precise voice.

"I don't know why not. He's been small help to us, letting two bairns escape him time after time."

"Those two children managed to elude me as well," Farragut said. "They are not what they seem, and I, for one, will not rest easily until I know who is behind them."

Ellie leaned forward and turned toward him. Her glasses sparkled in the firelight.

"Why are you so sure anyone is behind them?" she asked timidly. "I've begun to wonder, lately, whether we might not be mistaken—"

Gordon swore. "No, no, they're too canny to be innocents."

"They know too much," Farragut agreed. "I think we must speed up operations and try to finish ahead of schedule."

"How can we?" Ellie asked. "There's another week's work on the crypt—"

"You've located the crypt, then?" Gordon leaned forward, eagerly.

"Oh, yes, there was no difficulty about that," Farragut replied. "It's only a question now of removing the fill. Not only did the roof collapse, but sections of the wall as well. Some of the stones are damned heavy. However, I think we can do the job in eight hours if we concentrate on it and don't waste time with recording and photographing and that sort of thing. But we must get rid of the staff while we do it. And we shall need a plausible excuse."

There was a brief silence, while Farragut presumably

considered excuses, Ellie stroked the silent cat, and
Gordon sat bolt upright in his chair, staring at the fire.
His face had an odd, set expression. Suddenly he burst
out,

"That I should live to see the day! Bless the Lord
that he has spared me to see it, the day when the thirst
o' our brethren, night and day sobbing and groaning for
the bread o' life, shall be assuaged! Oh Lord . . ."

Susan shivered as she heard the ranting phrases—an
insane mixture of quotations from Knox and the more
rabid Reformation preachers. The man was a religious
fanatic. Was that the distorted form his patriotism had
taken? Even the noblest emotions can be distorted by
sick minds—the love of God into religious bigotry,
mother love into smothering, clinging destructiveness,
passion into lust and jealousy and the demand for total
possession. Gordon seemed to her the most terrifying
of the group. Ellie was watching him with wide eyes,
her thin lips slightly parted.

"That's enough, Gordon," Farragut said sharply.

The tirade faltered. Gordon rubbed his eyes.

"Aye, but the Laird must be served," he muttered.

"Certainly. And so must certain of your personal re-
quirements." Farragut's voice was dry. "Where is
Jackson? I want to get on with this."

"Here," said Jackson.

But the voice did not come from the next room.

Susan spun around. The door of the bedroom had
opened. The light in the hall shone on Jackson's sleek
black head and glinted off the gun in his hand.

"Surprise," said Jackson, grinning at them. "Not a
bad try, kids. I rather thought you'd be along, though.
That's why I've been making the rounds every half hour.
When I found the missing windowpane I waited in the
room at the top of the stairs. Figured you would get up
here eventually."

He gestured them out into the hall, bowing to Susan

with a nasty parody of courtesy. The other three conspirators boiled out of the study. Farragut was the only one who did not seem surprised—which didn't prove that he had known of their presence. He was the sort of man who hated to display emotion, but something flared in his amber eyes as he looked at James.

"Well, young fellow, I believe you've made a mistake at long last. I'm not at all a vindictive person; I rather hate to see you end this way."

Ellie gave him a startled look. She was cuddling the cat, which watched the activities of the humans with narrowed eyes. The tip of its tail began to twitch.

"But you don't mean to—" Ellie began.

"What we mean to do doesn't concern you," Jackson broke in. "Gordon. We'll take them downstairs."

"No!" Ellie's voice rose. "You said there wouldn't be—I don't care what they've done, you can't—"

"Shut up!" Jackson's temper, which Susan knew all too well, had not improved since she last met him. "And get rid of that damned animal," he added, grabbing at it. "I hate cats."

Ellie turned raising her shoulder, and Jackson's clawed fingers slid away from the kitten's back. They must have pressed painfully, though; the animal let out a howl of rage and lashed out. Jackson swore and sucked at his hand. The kitten jumped from Ellie's arms and streaked off. It tossed an equally profane comment back as it ran.

"This is ridiculous," Farragut said contemptuously. "Get them out of her. And find out—"

"I'll find out," Jackson said.

He jabbed James with the gun.

"Ellie," Susan said quickly. "You're all wrong, you know. We didn't kill Tammas. These men—"

Jackson slapped her. She reeled against James, who caught her around the waist.

"Don't, Susan," he said. "This isn't going to do any good."

Gordon led the way down the stairs. Jackson followed with his gun in James's back.

"Where?" Jackson asked the owner of the house, when they had reached the cellars.

Gordon opened a door. The Iron Maiden smiled a sickly greeting.

Chapter 8

As James insisted later, he was fairly sure Jackson wouldn't shoot. Nevertheless, his action was foolhardy. He wasn't being logical, he was angry and frustrated and determined not to submit without putting up a fight. The fight didn't get off the ground. As he lunged, Jackson stepped back and clipped him neatly across the head with the gun barrel.

"Relax," he said, waving the gun at Susan.

"I didn't move," Susan said bitterly. "You rat," she added, looking down at James's huddled body.

"Tie her up," Jackson ordered.

Gordon reached for Susan. She stepped back into the torture chamber. She preferred to face the grisly instruments rather than let Gordon's long white hands touch her; but she wondered why he had chosen this particular room. Surely it was accidental. Gordon couldn't intend. . . . Her mind recoiled from the very idea. But the look on Gordon's face was not reassuring. The man wasn't right in the head. If his religious beliefs followed those of Knox and the other fanatics he had quoted, he might not object to torturing enemies and other infidels. Had not Knox called the cold-blooded murder of Archbishop Beaton a "Godly act?"

Gordon backed her against the wall and clamped a set of rusty manacles around her wrists. Susan got a close look at his eyes. Her flesh crawled. If Gordon wasn't crazy, he was so close it made no difference. Jackson had dragged James's limp body into the room. He glanced around, his forehead creased with annoyance.

"My God, what a place. Find some rope, will you? And a chair. I can't squat on the floor while I question him."

"Put him there," Gordon said, in a strange cracked voice. His hand pointed at the rack.

Jackson straightened up, eyeing his associate with his head cocked on one side.

"You can't do that," Susan said. "He's crazy, can't you see?"

"Nothing will happen to your boyfriend if you cooperate," Jackson said, rubbing his chin thoughtfully. "I'm not exactly up to date on this particular apparatus, though."

It was a grisly echo of the wit that had attracted Susan on their first meeting. She started to answer, but Gordon cut in.

"I know how," he said softly. "I know. Put him up on the table. I'll do the rest."

Susan felt light-headed, as if she were drugged or feverish. This couldn't be happening. The past few days had taught her to accept the reality of violence, but only in its contemporary form—guns and knives and blows. Not this. This was sick.

James was still unconscious. He didn't stir as they stripped him to the waist and lifted him onto the table. Blood streaked one side of his face from a cut on his temple.

For the first time in her life Susan regretted her knowledge of history. She wished she hadn't bragged so loudly to James; this was almost like a judgment, forcing her to acknowledge that the glamorous legends she cherished had their dark and ugly side. Torture had been a legitimate part of the judicial process throughout the Middle Ages; even in Elizabethan England a turn of the rack was an approved method of wringing confessions out of reluctant suspects. Susan knew far more than she wanted to know about the rack. Its operation was horribly simple. The victim lay flat on a table, his feet and his outstretched arms fastened to ropes that went around revolving drums. As the operator turned a crank the ropes wound up, pulling the victim's body out as far as it would go—and beyond. If continued, the rack dislocated every joint in the body.

James groaned as Jackson pulled his feet into position, and Jackson stepped back, covering James with the gun. Gordon had already tied James's wrists. Now he scuttled to the foot of the table and fastened his ankles to the ropes.

"Wake him up," Gordon said urgently. "Make sure he's awake."

Susan tried to speak. Her tongue felt as if it were glued to the roof of her mouth. Gordon unbuckled his sporran and brought out a flat bottle. He tipped some of the contents into James's mouth, spilling a good deal in his enthusiasm. James coughed and moved his head. The reek of whiskey momentarily overcame the other stenches of the room.

"Don't do that," Susan shouted, finding her voice at last. "He could choke."

"No Scot ever choked to death on whiskey," Jackson said. He seemed to be deriving an ironic amusement from the situation, but the look he gave Gordon was as inimical as the one he turned on James, whose eyes were now open. They rolled up and down and around, and then widened in disbelief as he realized what was going on.

"What the hell—" he began.

"I'll talk," Susan stammered. "What do you want to know? Whatever it is, I'll tell you, just don't—"

"Talk, then," Jackson said.

Gordon touched his arm.

"Let's try it out," he said in a whisper. "Just a wee twist . . ."

"This is ridiculous," said James. He licked his lips. "Criminal waste of good whiskey, too. What do you think you're doing, Jackson?"

"I've never met such a bunch of blabbermouths," Jackson exclaimed. "You all talk and talk, and you don't say a damned thing that makes any sense. That includes you," he added, scowling at Gordon, whose hands were fluttering around the crank of the rack. "I've dealt with screwballs in my time, but this crowd is something else. All right, Susan, you know what I want. Speak up like a good girl, and there'll be no trouble."

"What do you want to know?" Susan asked.

"Who are you working for? What put you on to this? And who else knows about it?"

"That's the important question," said James, from his Procrustean bed. "You don't suppose we would be fools enough to run head long into this meeting without leaving word with someone, do you? If we don't show up, unharmed, by tomorrow morning, there will be a crowd of curious people on your trail."

"Naturally you'd say that," Jackson remarked. He had put his gun away; now he seated himself on the foot of the rack. The planks cracked ominously, and he shook his head in disgust. "What a place. I don't know how the hell I ever got into this mess. . . . You'll have to prove to me that you're speaking the truth, Erskine, otherwise I'll let my drooling friend here play with his toy. With whom did you leave your message? The police? You appear to be rather young to be police spies, but they're using all sorts of material these days. I would be more inclined to believe you left word with your father or a friend. Speak up.''

James took a deep breath.

"The police," he said.

It was a mistake. Susan knew it as soon as he spoke, but she understood his motives; he didn't want to send Jackson after his father or any other innocent party. But Jackson wasn't about to buy that answer. He had mentioned the police as a decoy, to see if his victims would fall for it.

Jackson smiled broadly. "No, no," he said, like a professor admonishing a dull student. "The police don't operate that way, my boy. It's only amateurs who leave cryptic messages to be opened at dawn. You are amateurs, aren't you? You haven't done badly, but then you've been lucky, too. How did you get on to us?"

James opened is mouth, and left it open; it was clear that he was running out of ideas. Susan couldn't blame him. His position was not conducive to clear thinking. The half-healed scar on his arm had cracked open and a trickle of blood was forming a small pool on the splintered wood near his shoulder.

Jackson's eyes narrowed. "I wonder," he said slowly. "I wonder if we were wrong. How much do you know, really? A pair of bright kids could have figured out that idiotic message of Tammas's; I was afraid some such thing would happen. Why the damned fools didn't use the telephone I'll never know. Amateurs always enjoy unnecessary mystification. It seemed harmless at the time. It was sheer bad luck for us that Susan was the one to intercept the message. Then, by killing the old fool, I made matters worse, didn't I? I had to do it, of course; he was becoming dangerous. I thought the murder would hold you two up for a while, but you lucked out there too, and naturally you wanted to find out who

had framed you. And that's it, isn't it? You don't really
know a damned thing, except what you've managed to
pick up from us.''

James turned his head and looked at Susan with naked appeal in his eyes. The exchange of glances was as
specific as words, they understood one another so well;
but Susan was as confused as James. Was it safer to
admit ignorance or claim greater knowledge than they
had? Jackson would probably kill them when he had
learned what he wanted to know. How could they postpone that undesirable event? Susan had no hope of rescue or of advantage from delay, but nobody wants to
die sooner than he has to.

She was still wrestling with the problem when Gordon spoke.

''Just a wee twist,'' he said conversationally. ''To
find oot what they know.''

Without waiting for a reply, he turned the crank. With
a stiff, cracking sound the ropes went taut.

James turned his head away. Susan couldn't see his
face, but she saw the muscles in his arms stand out,
saw his breast arch and the oozing cut open so that the
blood streamed out. She screamed. Gordon started and
released the handle. Perspiration streamed down his
face. He stared at Susan, blinking like a man awakened
abruptly from deep sleep.

''I'll tell you,'' Susan began to babble. ''We do
know. We know all about it. We know what you're
looking for and where it is, we . . . our group. Yes,
our group, they're the ones we warned, if they don't
hear from us they'll go and get it. You can hold us
hostage. We'll send them a message, tell them to leave
you alone, if you promise to let us go.''

''Now you're talking sense,'' Jackson said approvingly. He glanced at James. ''You awake, Erskine? Yes,
I see you are. Must be an interesting experience. Obviously not fun. Let's not do it again, shall we?''

James turned his head back. He had bitten into his lower lip.

"Susan," he said thickly. "What are you talking about?"

"We'll have to tell them, Jamie," Susan said. "I can't stand any more."

"*You* can't stand any more?" said James. "If I can, you can. I forbid you to speak. Shut up. It's ours. You can't give it to them."

Susan's eyes overflowed. He didn't have the faintest idea what she was talking about, but he was playing up to her like a Spartan. He was wonderful. And she had hurt his feelings—jeered at his ideas. . . . She sent up a silent, heartfelt supplication: If we ever get out of this, I'll never mention Prince Charles Edward Stuart again, not to a living soul. Just let me save Jamie. Compared to him Charles Edward was a jerk.

"There you go again," Jackson said impatiently. "Wasting time. Convince me, Susan. Convince me, or—"

"I'll convince you." Susan drew a deep breath. She wished she could wipe her face, the salt tears stung and itched. But she wasn't going to cry anymore. She was going to outfox Jackson, and for that she needed every ounce of intelligence she could muster.

"You were right, Jackson," she said. "We got into this by accident, but we're smarter than you give us credit for. And we do have an organization behind us. James has a lot of friends, some of them in high places. You've lost track of us for days at a time, haven't you? What do you think we were doing during those days, running aimlessly around Scotland? No! We were enlisting allies. Some of them are already at the dig. They're waiting for you to find it. Then they'll jump you."

"I see," Jackson said. "All right, Susan, I'll buy it so far. But you still haven't told me anything specific.

A girl with an imagination like yours could invent that story in her sleep. Tell me what we're looking for, and I'll believe the rest of your story.''

"Tammas gave us the clue." Susan looked at James, who had turned his head at a painful angle and was watching her intently. She could only imagine the struggle it cost him to keep his abused body from clouding his mind, but his eyes were alert and waiting. Some quality in her voice had warned him that she had a key card to play, and he was ready to play up to her, if she could give him the information without letting Jackson know that it was a recent inspiration instead of part of a long-range plan. James's original idea had been right. They had to convince Jackson that someone else knew about the treasure, and would act unless they were alive to restrain him.

"The quotation wasn't the only clue Tammas gave us," she went on. "When we found him, his dead hands were clutching at two objects he had selected from the clutter in his room. A hammer and a rock. Or, to be more accurate, a hammer and . . . a stone.''

She had been almost certain she was right, but a wave of relief swamped her when she saw, by the narrowing of Jackson's eyes, that he understood her emphasis on that last meaningful word.

"A stone,'' she went on, with growing assurance. "And a hammer.

"Back in 1328, the throne of Scotland was up for grabs. There were two claimants. One was named Balliol, the other Bruce. Scotland was split by the struggle; the lords called in Edward of England to settle the argument. Edward picked Balliol. He wanted Scotland for himself, and he knew Balliol was a weak man, who would submit to English domination in return for Edward's support. But the Scots wouldn't put up with English overlords. They rebelled. Edward came north. Year after year he came. He laid the country waste, but whenever he turned his back, the Scots rose again. Edward won a nickname that way. The called him the Hammer of the Scots.''

It was dull, dry history; but none of her listeners interrupted. They knew what she was leading up to. Even James knew now; she had seen the quick, shaken movement of his chest as the truth dawned on him.

"Bruce won eventually," she went on, deliberately drawing out the story, taking a perverse pleasure in the fascinated interest of her audience. "Robert the Bruce, Scotland's greatest hero. But before the final victory of Bannockburn, before William Wallace fought and died for Scottish independence, Edward the Hammer came north on one of his bloody campaigns. It was a successful campaign, for Edward. He left Scotland in October, and with him he took cartloads of plunder. The Sacred Black Rood of Saint Margaret, with its fragment of the True Cross, the archives and documents of Scotland—and a stone. The Stone of Scone, on which Scottish monarchs had been crowned for centuries. The stone he took is in Westminster Abbey now, under the throne of England.

"An old tradition claimed that the sacred stone had been brought from Tara in Ireland. The Scots came from Ireland originally, and when Kenneth MacAlpine defeated the Picts, to become the first king of Scots and Picts, the capital was moved to Scone with its sacred stone. But geologists have examined the stone in Westminster. It is Lower Old Red Sandstone, quarried in a region close to Scone. Not in Ireland.

"There has always been a rumor that Edward got the wrong stone," Susan said. "A legend, that loyal Scots hid the most sacred object of all before the Hammer's army reached Scone. And that makes sense. It makes sense that they would hide it in a remote glen, safe from the hated English, until Scotland had a king again. But when Bruce got the throne he wasn't the beloved hero legend later made of him. There were other factions, other pretenders. It was a hard, bloody period. People died of disease and were killed in battle. So the last of the men who had hidden the true Stone died, without passing on the secret. Except, perhaps, as a legend in certain families. . . .''

"Mine," Gordon said suddenly. "It is mine. The Stone, the heritage. The crown. My ancestors were kings of Dalriada. My mothers' mothers were princesses of the Picts. My forebears hid the Stone, leaving only an old song to tell the truth. But I understood the song! I knew—it is mine, only mine. . . .''

"When Professor Campbell decided to dig at that site, he must have researched the old traditions about it," Susan said. "Tammas was an authority on Scottish legends; he was once a respected scholar, it would be natural for Campbell to talk to him. Gordon and Tammas were friends too; their interests are similar. So Tammas realized what Campbell might find. He got his Knights of the White Rose, or whatever they are called, involved. No wonder they were thrilled. The true Stone—how could a rabid Nationalist let it go to England? That's where it would go if Campbell's excavations were carried out in the official manner."

"Right," James said. He was fighting to keep his voice calm, but his eyes were shining with incredulous excitement. "The Stone was buried—hidden—in secret, with the intention of reclaiming it one day. That's the legal definition of treasure trove, and unless the heirs of the original owner can be traced, treasure trove belongs to the crown—although the finder must be paid the full assessed value. But it wouldn't do you any good to find it legally, would it, Jackson? Even if you could dispossess the archaeologists before they located the treasure, there is that little matter of the heir. Because the legal heir of the sacred Stone is the monarch, who is descended from the kings of England and Scotland. I doubt that the finder would get a penny.''

"That's not all, though," Susan said quickly. "There is something else hidden besides the Stone. Otherwise you wouldn't be involved." She nodded at Jackson, who was listening with an enigmatic expression on his handsome face. "I'll admit we don't know how you got into this," she added candidly. "But we know why. The Stone wouldn't interest you. Its value is purely emotional. There must be other, more marketable treasures in the same cache, and it isn't difficult to figure out what they might be. If I remember my guidebook correctly, the Honours of Scotland are older than the English regalia, which was melted down during the Commonwealth and replaced in the seventeenth century. But the oldest object in the Scottish collection is the crown, which is traditionally supposed to be Bruce's. It has been remodeled; but even if it can be proved to go back as far as Bruce, what happened to the earlier Honours? Where are the crowns of the Pictish kings, the ceremonial swords of Malcolm and MacBeth? Why did Bruce have to have a brand-new crown? Because the old one had been hidden in the crypt of an ancient sanctuary; and it has been there now for over six hundred years.''

Jackson nodded.

"You've proved your point," he said. "You are a bright pair. It's a pity. . . .''

"Never mind the threats," James said coolly. "We know; and so do others. Let us send a message and they will leave you alone until you've had time to remove the treasure.''

"Very well," Jackson said, after the briefest hesitation. "Where do I send the message?''

"Oh, no." James smiled crookedly. "I don't like to be offensive, Jackson, but I don't really trust you. You release Susan. She'll carry the message to the proper place. I'll remain as hostage.''

"No," Susan said.

"No," Jackson agreed. "You've convinced me that you know what you're talking about, but that doesn't mean I trust you any more than you trust me. What's to prevent Susan from going to the police or arranging a neat little ambush? Look at it this way. We've no reason to kill you; we simply want you out of our hair for the next few days. We'll lock you up in a nice comfortable cell, with plenty of food and water, and release you after we've finished our job. Now you do see that that makes sense, don't you?''

"No," James said.

"We're all being very negative today," Jackson complained. "Give me the name of your contact and we'll make you comfortable.''

"He'll speak," Gordon said, coming to life again. He was acting like a badly constructed robot that jerked into action, said its programmed piece, and then subsided until the next touch of the button. There was a trace of froth at the corners of his mouth.

"Aye, he'll speak," Gordon mumbled. "When his limbs are stretched and torn asunder . . . .''

Carried away, he snatched at the handle and gave it a sudden vicious twist. There was one moment Susan never forgot, when James's body lifted in a taut arc of pain. Then the rope broke.

The scene turned suddenly from high melodrama to howling farce. Thrown off balance, Gordon tumbled onto his back, his feet kicking like those of an overturned beetle. Jackson swore. Susan giggled hysterically and James, limp but conscious, rolled a malevolent eye in her direction.

"This is too goddamned much," Jackson concluded, after several other forceful comments. "Of all the stupid, inefficient, unnecessary. . . . Here." He picked up

James's torn shirt and tossed it to Gordon, who had gotten to his feet. "Tear that up and tie his hands, will you, and stop horsing around! I'm afraid to leave you long enough to look for a rope, for God's sake! And if I did find one in this museum, it would probably fall apart. All right, Susan, let's have a name. Right this bloody minute, or I'll beat your boyfriend to a bloody pulp. I doubt that any friends of yours will inconvenience us, but I dislike being made a fool of by a pair of juveniles. The name of your contact."

"James Dunbar," said Susan steadily. "He's a lit student at Edinburgh, a friend of Jamie's. He lives in Blackfriars Wynd."

"All right. I'll check it out. And God help you if you're lying to me." Jackson spun around. "Aren't you through yet, Gordon? You half-witted idiot, tie his hands to the crossbars, or he'll be out of that in five minutes! Come on, let's get out of here."

He herded Gordon out of the room. The heavy door slammed. Susan heard the sound of a bar being dropped into place.

There was a short silence.

"Literature student," said James finally. "James Dunbar. *The Lament for the Makers. 'Timor mortis conturbat me. . . .'* "

"It disturbs me too," said Susan. Her voice cracked. "Oh, Jamie, are you hurt?"

"That is probably the most foolish question you've ever asked," said James, bleeding in three places. "I feel as if someone had gone over me with a club. May I suggest that instead of asking irrelevant questions you try to get out of those absurd chains? Not that you don't look rather seductive hung up that way, if one's tastes happen to run to the sadistic. . . ."

"How do I get loose?" Susan asked.

"I'll wager a good hearty heave will do it. The place is falling apart, hadn't you noticed? Imagine having the rack give way, just when you're throwing your back into it. What a blow to the ego.''

Susan gave an experimental pull and was rewarded by a creaking, yielding sensation. The rusty metal bit into her wrists. She twisted her fingers around the chains and jerked. The whole apparatus came out of the wall, along with a crumbling shower of mortar that got in Susan's eyes. She dropped onto her knees.

"Very nice," said James approvingly. "Now come over here and untie me."

"I'm going to need plastic surgery on my knees if I—I mean, when I get out of this.''

Wincing, she got to her feet and limped toward the rack.

"You look rather seductive yourself," she remarked, leaning over James and hitting him in the nose with the chains that dangled from her wrists. "Oops, I'm sorry. I mean, all that bare muscle. . . . Oh, Jamie, I was so scared. Could I faint? Just a little?"

"No. You could kiss me, though. I'm helpless to resist.''

As Susan had learned earlier, osculation was one of James's more highly developed skills. He surpassed himself on this occasion; when Susan straightened up she was weak in the knees.

"Not bad," said James judicially. "I could do better, though, if I had the use of my arms."

The clumsily knotted cloth gave way easily. Gordon had been in a hurry. James snapped the ropes on his feet with a jerk, remarking, "That should be a lesson to us. Always keep your torture chambers in good repair. ''

For all his levity, he moved very carefully. When he slid down off the table he had to grab at its edge to keep from falling. Susan saw that he was shivering.

"Here," she said, picking up his plaid. "I'm afraid

you shirt is kaput. Gordon used the sleeves to tie you up."

"He would," said James bitterly. "The man is mad as a hatter. Fancy ruining a perfectly good shirt that way."

He put his arms around Susan as she draped the plaid over his hunched shoulders; for a few moments they stood in silence, her cheek against his chest, his lips on her tumbled hair. Then James sighed.

"Enough of dalliance. Susan, that was absolutely brilliant of you. I'm converted. Never again will I sneer at ancient history. I'll even buy you a framed portrait of Bonnie Prince Charlie to hang over the bed."

"I guess I had that coming," Susan said, without moving. She had never heard a more heavenly sound than the steady thump of James's heart under her cheek. "But I don't ever want to see his face again. I'm through with legends."

"Not me. Your legends just saved our necks. I should have seen it myself. How could I be so dense? And to come out with it like that, at precisely the strategic moment—"

"I only thought of it a little while ago. On the stairs, remember, when I tried to tell you? Things happened so fast after that I didn't have a chance. I almost couldn't believe it myself; but I had to say something, I couldn't watch them . . ."

"Torture me?" James's voice quivered with incongruous amusement. "It's too damned ridiculous, Susan. I shall dine out on that experience for years to come. How many men can claim to have been racked? I mean, it gives one a certain cachet—"

"And how many girls can brag about having been chained to a dungeon wall?" Susan withdrew and wiped her nose surreptitiously on the back of her hand. The chains banged into James's chest.

"We'd better get those off," he said.

"I think the door is barred from the outside."

"One step at a time."

But first he secured his plaid in place with the silver
brooch. Then he took up one of the blunt instruments
that were lying around—their purpose being only too
plain from their design—and pried the links of the chain
apart. Susan was left with red-rusted bracelets on both
wrists. They were unbecoming and uncomfortable, but
an improvement over the chains.

"Now," said James. "The door."

But here their luck came to an end. The door was in
bad repair too, but a six-inch thick slap of oak and
hinges the size of soup plates have to decay quite a lot
before they are no longer functional. Breathing hard,
James stepped back and glared at the obstacle.

"I think our best hope is to unscrew the hinges. See
if you can find anything we can use as a tool."

"That will take forever! They're probably on their
way to the dig right now."

"Dearest love, I am not worrying about the damned
treasure. Not at the moment. I am worrying about us."

"We could wait till they come back and then jump
them," Susan suggested. "Hit them on the head. There
are plenty of things to hit them with."

"They would probably break," James said, with a
disparaging glance at pincers, thumbscrews, and what-
have-you. "Anyhow, it's too risky. Suppose they don't
come back?"

"Oh, no!"

"It's not a bad way of disposing of us," James
mused, rubbing his bristly chin. "Not bad at all. We're
fugitives. We might hide in such a place. Gordon could
claim that he had locked the place up in the routine
manner after visiting hours. Then, if he should depart
on a lengthy trip, and tell the cook not to bother coming
round. . . . No one would hear us, banging about down
here."

"That's gruesome," Susan said.

"So is Gordon. So is Jackson. And so, in his way, is the enigmatic Farragut. I wonder how he got involved with this gang? He's not a daft enthusiast of a criminal type."

He was working on one of the rusted bolts as he spoke, and making singularly little impression. The makeshift tool did not grip well.

The door opened. James was caught off balance; he fell over. Flat on his back, he stared unbelievingly at Ellie, who stood in the doorway.

"Quiet," she said unnecessarily. "Don't make a sound. Just come along. Hurry."

James got up. "Where to?" he inquired suspiciously.

"Anywhere. Out of here. They're going to kill you!" Her voice rose hysterically. She clapped her hands over her mouth. Her pale eyes rolled.

"I suspected as much," James said. "Why the change of heart, Ellie?"

"I didn't know they were like this," Ellie mumbled. "He said Jackson was a friend, a distinguished scholar—that we needed his help. I never liked him, but I didn't know till tonight that he. . . . He's no scholar! He hit you. The cat didn't like him either. And Mr. Gordon, he's . . . strange. You two don't look like murderers. I couldn't believe. . . ."

"Okay," James said, realizing that the pitiful, incoherent explanation might go on indefinitely. "You're right, Ellie. We are not murderers. Jackson killed Tammas. He's the wolf among all you lambs. He and Farragut."

"Farragut?" Ellie's eyes widened. "But he—"

She spun around.

"I thought I heard something," she gasped. "Hurry, please hurry; there's no time to talk."

They followed the girl along the narrow corridor and up the stairs into the dark kitchen.

"They are leaving any second," Ellie whispered. "All of them. They were going to leave you here to starve, or die of thirst. Jackson said that if he discovered you had tricked him he would come back and—and—"

"What about you?" James asked. "If they find out you set us free—"

"They won't find out. Not for a long time, at any rate. If you leave very quietly . . ."

"Oh, no," said James. "I'm not going to skulk away into the night, on foot and wanted by the police, while that crowd steals the Stone. I am tired of hiking and hiding. You're coming with us, Ellie, and we're leaving in a blaze of glory."

He caught the girl by the wrist as she started to back away from him.

"You don't trust me," she gasped. "And I'm not so sure about you any longer. Maybe I should—"

James's fist caught her on the chin.

"She was going to scream," he said to Susan, catching the frail body as it crumpled. "The girl is a nervous wreck. Small wonder. Open the door, Susan."

He tossed Ellie over one shoulder and carried her out. The moon had set and starlight shone faintly on the polished fenders of the Aston Martin, the chrome of the old Mercedes. James dumped Ellie into the back of the Mercedes.

"Why not the red car?" Susan asked. "It looks faster."

"It is." James looked admiringly at the sleek lines of the Aston Martin. "But it's not roomy enough. I don't want Ellie on my lap, she's too unpredictable. Get in the rear seat with her and—uh—calm her if she gets hysterical."

Susan obeyed.

"No keys," she remarked, glancing at the dashboard.

"Naturally not. It's all right, I can start it. I'd better put the Aston Martin out of commission first."

"Are you going to throw rocks in it?"

James gave her an indignant look.

"Mutilate a beauty like this? Certainly not. I'll just remove one or two essential parts. . . . Now then, Susan, brace yourself. I intend to cover the distance between here and the front gates in approximately nineteen seconds."

"The gates!" Susan exclaimed. "They'll be closed—"

"Undoubtedly. I only hope they aren't chained."

"What if they are?"

"In that case," said James, "We do what we've been doing so expertly for days. We run."

Chapter 9

The gates were not locked. They were extremely heavy, however; it took the combined strength of James and Susan, spurred on by irate shouts from the direction of the house, to shove them open. The old car's engine had not been tuned for years, and it made enough noise to waken the dead. The speed and unexpectedness of their escape had caught the opposition by surprise. No one had yet appeared when they got back into the car and headed across the parking area with gravel spurting up like water from under the back wheels. James made a racing turn onto the highway and put his foot down.

They had passed through the sleeping village and were several miles along the road before Susan spoke.

"Maybe we shouldn't have taken the car. Gordon can call the police and say we stole it."

"We did steal it," James said. "But Gordon won't report the theft. They need eight hours. Remember the conversation we overheard? Your brilliant deductions have changed the entire picture, Susan. We now have proof of our wild story, and we know where the proof is to be found. Farragut mentioned a crypt. There was an abbey or church on the site of the ruins, and the treasure was buried in its crypt. If we were picked up by the police, we might be able to convince them to have a look in the ruins before Farragut and Jackson could finish their work. They can't risk that. Nor can we; there is an equally good chance that the police might simply lock us up and throw away the key. And once the treasure has been removed, our proof is gone."

"Then what can we do?" Susan leaned forward, her chin resting on the back of the seat.

"Only one thing to do. Get to the dig as quickly as possible. Locate the treasure ourselves—"

"With Ewen and the others trying to beat our brains in?"

"With Ewen and the others helping us. Don't forget we have Ellie on our side now . . . I think. Suppose we march in openly, with our hands in the air. They can't massacre us out of hand if we surrender voluntarily. Then we demand to be taken to their leader. We keep forgetting about Campbell; he's never around when he's wanted. But he is the key figure now. If we can convince him that the treasure may be there, he'll investigate. Then if Gordon and the others turn up, that will substantiate our story. I don't see how we can lose—if we can reach the site before the crooks get there."

His arguments were convincing, and Susan's spirits began to rise. Success seemed almost in their grasp.

James began to sing—weird snatches of ballads, old Highland love songs and weird antique Reliques out of Percy's collection. Symbolically, dawn began to break. The pale streaks of light surprised Susan. She hadn't realized so much time had passed.

Then she remembered Ellie, and turned. She was relieved to see that the girl was conscious, although the fixed regard with which Ellie was watching her made her uncomfortable.

"Are you okay?" she asked politely.

"He hit me," said Ellie.

Susan sighed. Ellie seemed to place an inordinate importance on people's hitting people, as though it were a vital indication of character.

"He did it for your own good," she explained, somewhat mendaciously. "He was afraid you wouldn't come with us, and it was very dangerous for you, if they suspected you had helped us escape. I forgot to thank you, Ellie. You have done Scotland a great service tonight!"

Ellie's expression did not change. "Where are we?" she asked.

"I was rather hoping you could tell me that," said James.

"Damn it, Jamie," Susan exclaimed. "You haven't got us lost, have you?"

"If I have, it's the first time," James pointed out in an injured voice.

Ellie leaned forward and looked out the window. Susan was pained to observe that there was a lump on her small chin.

"You'll have to go back," she said, after a moment. "You took the wrong turning. We must go east."

"East? But we're heading west and south."

"The best road is G Seventeen," Ellie said. "It connects with this road two miles back."

"Okay." James backed and turned.

They had gone about five miles when Susan began to get uneasy. Ellie hadn't spoken, or removed her fixed stare from Susan's face. They were going through a pass from one glen to another; the central Highlands consist almost entirely of glens separated by mountains of varying heights, and at this ungodly hour the road was deserted. High slopes, covered with trees, rose on either side, and the inevitable burn ran merrily along the side of the road.

"How did you get into this situation, Susan?" Ellie asked suddenly. "Or is that your real name?"

"Of course it's my real name. I'm an archaeology student. Professor Campbell let me join the dig. Tammas gave me the clue—"

"Right," said Ellie. "That does it. Stop here, James. If that is *your* name."

"What do you mean, stop?" James demanded.

"I think," said Susan slowly, "that you'd better, Jamie."

Ellie had a gun. It was a small gun; even so, Susan couldn't imagine where she had hidden it. It was now pointed at Susan, who did not like the way the muzzle wavered. Ellie didn't appear to be accustomed to using a weapon, but at these close quarters she could hardly miss.

James shot a glance over his shoulder and came close to running off the road. He slammed on the brakes and came to a crashing halt six inches from a tree. Then he turned, his arm over the back of the seat.

"What the hell are you doing? I thought you were on our side."

"I don't think you are on *my* side," Ellie said. "Open the door, James. Then slide over to the other seat."

Mumbling profanely, James obeyed. Ellie got out.

"I'm going to the police," she said. "I'm confused. I don't understand who is doing what; but I don't trust you any more than I do the rest of them. Stay right where you are. I shall be watching, and if either of you gets out of the car, I'll—I'll shoot."

"Now, Ellie," James began.

Ellie fired. Susan flinched and closed her eyes, but the shot came nowhere near her. A hiss and a gentle subsistence followed. When Susan opened her eyes she saw Ellie running up the hill, fleet-footed as a doe. She vanished among the trees.

"Oh, hell," said James. "That was a tire."

After the tire had been changed they turned back in the direction they had been going before Ellie "corrected" them. Susan had found a map, and James was able to locate their position with more or less certainty. If his interpretation was correct, they had gone some distance out of their way. The detour and the flat had wasted over an hour.

"And that," said James grimly, "we cannot spare. Perhaps my optimism was premature. I hate to admit it, Susan, but I am beginning to feel a trifle tired."

He climbed in behind the wheel. Susan looked up from the map, which she had been studying in hopes of finding a shortcut. It was the first time she had really gotten a good look at him in broad daylight.

"We may be short on time, but we'll have to spare a little more," she said, trying not to sound as worried as she felt. "You look terrible, Jamie. You're covered with blood; if a traffic cop got a look at you, he'd run us in just on general principles. Oh, Jamie, darling, does it hurt much?"

James had been bowed over the wheel. He straightened up and grinned feebly. "Yes. Would you like to kiss it and make it well?"

"You're not as bad off as I thought," Susan said, pushing him away. "You don't need kisses, you need first aid and food. Do you realize we haven't eaten since yesterday? No wonder you're that funny shade of green. We'll stop in the next town. I'd offer to drive, but I'm not used to the left-hand bit."

The town was only a few miles beyond the point where Ellie had had them turn back. Apparently she knew the area, if they did not. In a suburban street they found a self-service shop, and James waited in the car while Susan went shopping. She came back with an armload of delicatessen and some first-aid supplies. While James wolfed down cold meat and bread, she worked on his various wounds, clucking sympathetically as she did so. James seemed to enjoy the sympathy as much as he did the food. He looked much better by the time she had finished.

"That's the best I can do," Susan said. "Let's go."

James didn't move. Arms folded across the wheel, he stared pensively out the window.

"I wonder if we're going about this the right way. We've been running so fast we haven't had time to think."

"I'm open to suggestions," Susan said, through a mouthful of food.

"I've got an idea." James opened the door and got out. "Back in a minute."

"Jamie, should you . . ."

He waved reassuringly at her and strode off. Susan watched him go. He certainly was a bizarre sight for a quiet Scottish village in the cool of the morning. Half naked, his plaid slung rakishly over the grease stains and dust that streaked his chest, bandaged fore and aft, he was half a head taller than anyone else on the street. Amid the prams and primly clad matrons shopping with their string bags, he was as exotic as a Hindu in turban and robes. And the face. . . . Susan had forgotten about the face. Choking with laughter, alarm, and salami, she watched him until he vanished into a small shop whose nature she could not make out from where she sat.

He came out sooner than she expected, carrying nothing she could see; but the sporran bulged. He waved at Susan and then went into a telephone kiosk that stood on the corner. Susan entertained herself by speculating on whom he was calling, but she was increasingly uneasy. Several passers-by had stared, and one woman lingered by the kiosk, eyeing James through the glass.

Finally James came out of the telephone booth. He saluted the inquisitive lady, who stepped back as if he had aimed a blow at her, and then swaggered back to the car, the pleats of his kilt swinging.

"What are you doing?" Susan demanded. "You might just as well walk up to them and tell them you're Erskine, the Edinburgh murderer."

"Precisely," James started the car and made a debonair U-turn. "I've decided that what we need now is publicity. The more of it, the better. It's quite possible that Farragut and Jackson are ahead of us now. We may need allies."

"But what—"

"Wait, wait. It will all be made clear at the proper time." He began to whistle.

Traffic grew heavier; they were approaching the center of town. Susan's taut nerves tightened even more when they reached the marketplace, where an ancient stone cross stood in the middle of an irregular paved area. Today was market day. Wooden stalls crowded the pavement; pedestrians carrying baskets and bags rambled about. Traffic had slowed to a crawl. James stopped the car, bringing the traffic to a complete halt. An irritable driver leaned on his horn.

James got out of the car. Susan was paralyzed with horror. She decided that he had finally lost his mind. It was no wonder, after all he had been through, but. . . . A policeman pushed toward them.

"You canna stop here," he shouted over the heads of the crowd. "Sir! Move on—"

Then he got a good look at James. He let out a bleat of consternation.

James had taken an object from his sporran.

"Hoy," he shouted, waving it above his head. "Hoots, avast, *attenzione*!"

The object was small and round. A short string or wire protruded from it. Amid a fascinated universal silence, James struck a match and applied it to the end of the string. With a neat underhanded swing he heaved the smoking object at the crowd. It scattered. James jumped into the car and propelled it through the gap. The bomb went off.

It emitted a cloud of black smoke and an indescribably evil stench. Susan caught a whiff of it as they roared through the marketplace and into a side street. Looking back, she heard the screams of terror change to screams of outrage, and saw a mob fill the street. Fists were shaken. A maddened, hysterical voice was shouting in Gaelic.

They were out of town and heading rapidly southwest before Susan could bring herself to speak.

"Was there any point to that?" she inquired. "Aside from general adolescent joie de vivre, I mean?"

"Joie de vivre, my foot," James said. "Use your head, woman."

"If you're trying to attract attention, you succeeded," Susan admitted. "Do you think they'll follow us all the way to the dig?"

"So long as the constable got our number, I don't care who follows us."

"I see. Whom did you telephone?"

"Oh, lots of people. Dad . . . the Edinburgh police . . . a pal of mine who's fishing near Aberdeen . . . the Hereditary High Constable . . ."

"The Hereditary . . . wow!" Susan was impressed. "If you know somebody that important, why did we run away in the first place?"

James took a deep breath. "One: I don't know him; my father does. My father knows everybody. Most of them hate him. Two: The HHC doesn't live in Edinburgh. He's got a country place not far from here. Three: If he were King of England and head of the Commonwealth, he still couldn't get me out of a murder rap. Four: He only has jurisdiction over crimes of assault and riot committed within four miles of the sovereign's person."

"I don't suppose she was at—"

"No, she was not! And it wouldn't make any difference if she was."

"Those are all good reasons, Susan said. "Whom else did you call?"

"The Director of the Royal Scottish Museum, the American Consul-General . . ."

Susan began to laugh. "Jamie, you're crazy," she said admiringly. "I hope you didn't tell your father the whole truth. If you mentioned the Stone—"

"I'm not that crazy. I merely hinted at mysterious ancient treasures."

"Did you by any chance telephone the folks at Balmoral Castle?" Susan asked.

James's face fell. "Damn! I knew I forgot someone."

James let off another bomb in Blair Atholl and had the satisfaction of hitting a traffic policeman neatly in the chest. The infuriated, reeking constable pursued them for a mile on a stolen bicycle before giving up the chase.

The delight this episode induced faded as they neared the site. James's grin relapsed into sobriety, and his marching songs died away.

"Suppose you wait in the car while I reconnoiter," he said, without looking at Susan. "You can direct the pursuit. They might miss the turn-off."

"No. And don't think of clipping me on the jaw, the way you did Ellie."

"I was rather hoping you'd say that. We'll leave the car by the turn-off. Just as well to go in on foot anyhow."

The sun was high when they started along the track. Susan was feeling quite sober now. She glanced up at the cloud-streaked blue sky and realized that the weather, at least, had performed magnificently for them. And she wondered whether this was the last morning sky she would ever see. They were taking a chance, going in this way. For all his stiff upper lip, James was in no condition for a fight, and if the gang had already reached the site, they were in trouble. It was questionable as to whether they could enlist the support of Ewen and the others without Ellie to support them. And there was a possibility that even those dubious assistants might not be at the site. Farragut had said something about sending them away.

She reminded James of this, and he nodded soberly.

"I thought of that myself. But I'm counting on Campbell. I can't believe he would abandon the site completely. Once excavation has begun, there is always a risk of looting by the locals. The gang might succeed in luring a majority of the staff away on one pretext or another, but one or two of them ought to be around. No doubt Jackson plans to put them out of action. We might just find ourselves rescuing Ewen from a fate worse than death."

"I don't think Jackson is that sort of—"

"Losing his precious antiquities would hurt Ewen worse than death," James explained. "And don't forget Campbell. If we could rescue him, we'd be heroes. No problem about proving our bona fides then."

"You're getting light-headed. We don't know what we'll find up there."

"I know. All we can do is take matters as they come. Above all, don't rush into anything."

"You don't need to warn me about that," Susan said with feeling.

They took to the hills and worked their way along to the heights behind and above the site. At first Susan thought they were too late. The ruins appeared to be absolutely deserted. Had the miscreants already come and gone, taking their loot with them and leaving . . . ? Susan's stomach contracted. She rather liked Ewen, in spite of his hasty habits with shovels. She hoped he wasn't lying dead down below.

The staff had worked hard since their last visit. It did not take Susan long to identify the spot they had concentrated on. A large stretch of it gaped open to the sky, and with a thrill she recognized the massive unfinished granite blocks of a substructure—the crypt. Her trained eye picked out at least two different periods, marked by changes in the masonry. There was a section of roofing preserved—the roof of the crypt, and the floor of the church above. She would not care to work under the precariously balanced slabs, but someone was doing just that. Watching, she saw a familiar bright head emerge, followed in due course by the rest of Ewen. He climbed up out of the hole and started walking toward the inn.

"I see how they figured it," Susan said. "Look at the orientation. The church faced east. So the altar must be *there*. That's where the relics would have been placed, in the most sacred part of the church. There must be a hidden alcove, bricked up, covered with masonry. . . ."

"Never mind that. Let's have a chat with Ewen."

"You can't do that. You haven't even got—"

James was already on his way.

They caught up with Ewen before he reached the inn. He stopped short at the sight of them.

"Damnation!" he exclaimed. "You two never give up, do you? Thought you'd catch me off guard. Well, I don't need a shovel to deal with the likes of you!"

Folding his fingers into fists, he started toward James, who fumbled in his handy sporran.

"Hands up," he said, pointing a gun at Ewen.

Susan stared. One look told her the painful truth. The gun was a toy, no doubt purchased in the same novelty shop where James had procured his stink bombs. She only hoped Ewen would be too angry to notice.

"You won't get away with this," Ewen said, snorting with rage.

"All I want to do is talk," James insisted. "Just listen to me for five minutes, can't you?"

"I can hardly do anything else. A cold-blooded killer like you wouldn't hesitate—"

"I am not a killer," James said tightly. "I haven't killed anyone."

"No? What would you have done to Ellie that day if I hadn't interfered?"

"You damned fool, Ellie is one of the gang. Do you realize what those bastards are up to?"

"The only gang I know is you," Ewen said, his forehead corrugating. "Talk sense, will you?"

"I don't think either one of you is making much sense," Susan intervened. "James and I are not murderers, Ewen. Tammas was killed by Jackson—the man from Interpol, only he isn't really a policeman, he's a crook. Tammas and Ellie and some other enthusiasts found out about the treasure and planned to steal it, but they didn't mean any harm, not really. The trouble started when Jackson got into the act. He wants to sell the treasure on the illicit antiquities market. And if you don't help us, he'll succeed. Please, Ewen, you've got to believe me!"

"I don't know what the hell you're talking about," Ewen said. "What is this treasure you keep babbling about?"

He sounded genuinely bewildered, and somewhat less aggressive.

"The Stone," James said impatiently. "The sacred Stone. It's up there in that crypt you've been excavating, along with God knows what other treats."

"The Stone," Ewen repeated slowly. "That wouldn't be the Stone of Scone you're talking about?"

"Yes."

Ewen smiled. At least his mouth opened, showing teeth; his forehead acquired even more wrinkles.

"But, old chap," he said soothingly. "That's in Westminster Abbey, you know. Bloody shame, I agree; but that's where it is."

"Oh, Christ," James said furiously. "I know that's where it is. Only it isn't. I mean, the one that's in London is not the real Stone. The real Stone is here, so it can't be in London."

"Yes, of course," Ewen said. "That follows quite logically. If the real Stone is here, it can't be in Westminster Abbey. If it's not in Westminster Abbey it must be somewhere; why not here? Marvelous thinking! Now you just give old Ewen that gun and we'll run up and find your Stone."

"He thinks we're crazy," Susan said conversationally.

Ewen had begun to advance, one cautious step at a time. His hand was outstretched and he was crooning softly, "Must be here; can't be there. If it isn't there—"

James backed up as Ewen advanced. He was still pointing the gun.

"It's true," Susan said. "He's telling the truth, Ewen. James, why don't you give him the gun? We aren't getting anywhere this way."

James shook his head. His jaw was set stubbornly.

"Get back, Ewen. So help me, I'll shoot if you—"

He stumbled over a tree root. He recovered his balance immediately, but the damage had been done; his finger had contracted on the trigger. From the muzzle of the gun came a popping sound, plus a small red flag, on which the word "Bang!" was printed in neat black letters.

"Damn," said James furiously. He flung the gun onto the ground. It bounced twice before settling, with the red flag at an angle. "Damn, damn, damn!"

Ewen's mouth twitched. His nose twitched. The

wrinkles in his forehead smoothed out. He burst into a
roar of laughter. He laughed till his face was as red as
his hair, slapping his knees and gasping. James stood
with arms folded, wearing a frown of majestic dignity.

"Oh, God," Ewen wheezed, after some time. "You
poor fool, I'm almost ready to believe you. About Tammas's death, that is. You just aren't the murdering type.
But I'm afraid I can't buy your treasure. This dig has
been a dead loss so far; we haven't found a trace of
Picts, just some local sanctuary dating from the eleventh century."

"But that's why the Stone—"

"No, no." Ewen shook his head. "Let's not get back
onto that subject, please. Look here, you two, I was
somewhat stirred up last time you came round; the re-
ports of Tammas's death had reached us and I thought
you had done the poor chap in. Filthy, cold-blooded
killing an old man like that. Now I'm not so sure.
Maybe you aren't responsible. I shan't judge you—"

"That's damned decent of you," James snarled.

"But you've got to turn yourselves in," Ewen went
on. "Can't have people like you running loose, babbling about Stones and treasures and so on. This isn't
Russia, you know; they won't beat you and brainwash
you, they'll just tuck you up in a nice peaceful cell until
you—"

"The police should be arriving before long," James
said.

Ewen cocked a skeptical eye at him.

"That's splendid. Why don't we go and have a drink
while we wait for them?"

"Because they aren't the only ones who will be
here," James shouted. "I'm surprised Jackson hasn't
arrived before this. Look here, Ewen, if you don't believe us, call Professor Campbell. Perhaps he's not as
stupid as his staff. Where is the chap, anyhow? Doesn't
he ever visit his precious dig?"

"Oh, yes," said a voice behind him. "I'm here, Mr. Erskine."

Susan turned. She knew the voice. Her stomach had sunk down into her worn shoes even before she saw the man who had spoken.

He stood watching them, a smile on his face. He was dressed like an archaeologist out of a film, in crisply pressed khaki shirt and trousers. A brown paisley scarf filled in the neck of the shirt, and his thick fair hair shone in the sunlight. Sartorial elegance was his trademark, in both his incarnations—Campbell, the distinguished professor, and Farragut, the conspirator.

Chapter 10

"Splendid, Ewen," said Campbell-Farragut, nodding approvingly at his assistant. "I overheard the entire conversation. It is evident that these unfortunate young people are in urgent need of medical assistance. Judge not lest ye be judged, eh? We cannot condemn our fellowman for sinning when a slight readjustment of brain cells or a trivial chemical imbalance may reduce us to the same state. I really am so glad—"

The insufferable voice was too much for James. With an inarticulate howl of rage he jumped Campbell. His reflexes were in bad shape; Campbell stepped nimbly to one side and tripped James up. He fell heavily and lay still.

Susan sat down on the ground beside him. She was numb. No wonder the legitimate archaeologists, like Ewen and Ellie, had been so hostile. Campbell was their leader and mentor, a scholar of impeccable reputation; they would accept any story he chose to tell them. Ellie's change of heart that morning was understandable now. She, Susan, had claimed to be an archaeology student hired by Campbell, and yet she had failed to recognize her own boss. It was her word against Campbell's, and she honestly couldn't blame Ellie for calling down a plague on both their houses.

James rolled over. He started to get up, and then thought better of it. Susan had to agree that there seemed no particular point in moving. They were done for. Campbell was in the plot up to his neck. Evidently money meant more to him than did scholarly prestige. Which most people would consider quite sensible.

"That's right," Campbell said cheerfully. "Just relax. I think, Ewen, we had better lock them up in the shed there. Then you can take them into the town. Peter and the others had better go along; the poor young people aren't responsible, but both of them are exceedingly dangerous. Their car must be about somewhere, I'll just see if I can locate it."

"You devil," Susan exclaimed. "You really are ingenious! You were looking for an excuse to get rid of the staff, and damned if we didn't hand you one."

"Language, language, young lady." Campbell looked disapproving. "Come along now, don't make matters harder for yourselves."

No one spoke as they marched toward the shed. James stumbled as he walked, his shoulders bowed, and let himself be urged into the temporary prison without difficulty.

The floor of the hut was of packed earth. There was nothing in it except a strong smell of sheep. Streaks of sunlight penetrated the interior through cracks between the stones where the mortar had flaked away. The place swam in a dusty gloom, but it was light enough to see fairly well—if there had been anything to see.

Susan sat down on the floor. James dropped down beside her and put his head in her lap.

"That feels good," he mumbled.

"I'm glad. It may be the last 'good' you'll ever feel. Aren't we going to try to break out of here?"

"No use."

"Maybe they aren't going to kill us. Ewen isn't one of the gang. If he takes us to the police station . . ."

"Hmm-mmm." James's head moved in negation. "Didn't you follow that jolly little plan? The bastard had the gall to explain it right in front of us. He'll locate the car. And when we depart there will be an indiscernible but significant defect in that car. Brakes, steering . . . there are many possibilities."

"Good Lord! He'd wipe out the whole expedition staff, just to get us?"

"We may not all be killed," said James lazily. "I don't know, I may be mistaken. Perhaps Farragut—Campbell, that is—is willing to take his chances. What can we prove, after all? Once the treasure is gone we haven't a prayer of convincing anyone it was ever there. An empty cavity? Robbed in antiquity, my lads! But I am not going to relax in that Mercedes."

"Can't we persuade Ewen to look the car over?"

"I thought of that. But I doubt that he'd believe me. His credulity level seems rather low where we're concerned. Perhaps it's just as well he doesn't believe us. Gordon and Jackson must be somewhere about, and we know Jackson has no qualms about killing. Ewen is rather emotional. I can picture him charging Jackson, screaming Gaelic war cries—"

" 'Sons of the hounds, come here and get meat!' Only," Susan added, "Ewen would be the meat."

"Quite. Our only hope now is to stall for time."

"Your reinforcements? Jamie, do you really think . . . ?"

"My credulity level is rather low too," James admitted. "There is only one point I would like to make, Susan. Let's endeavor to survive, all right? I mean, these characters annoy me, but I'm not ready to die for the sacred Stone, or anything foolish like that."

"Quite," said Susan emphatically.

They had scarcely finished this exchange before they heard voices outside. Someone started to unfasten the door. Susan's heart sank. Illogically, she had expected they would have more time. But of course Campbell had to move quickly. If the police arrived he would be forced to hand over his captives, and there would be no excuse for dismissing the unwitting staff members.

Susan looked at James.

"No," he said, reading her thoughts. "We don't fight. Not now. There may be a chance later."

The door opened. Ewen stood in the doorway.

"All right, you two," he said, nodding toward the great outdoors.

The prisoners obeyed, trying to look meek and beaten—and succeeding quite well. The Mercedes stood near the shed, and Ewen herded them toward it.

"It will be rather crowded," Farragut said. "The young lady will have to sit on her friend's lap. That will cramp his style a bit, eh? Dugald on one side of them, Alex on the other. Ewen will drive, Peter next to him. Yes, that will do admirably."

They arranged themselves accordingly. Alex was the only one of the group whom Susan had not met before. He was slight and boyish-looking, with curly dark hair and long eyelashes, but the arms bared by the rolled-up sleeves of his shirt were hard with muscle. Perched self-consciously on James's knees, Susan felt totally surrounded. Peter, who was sitting beside Ewen on the front seat, turned to look at the prisoners with the cool curiosity of a scientist examining a particularly nasty germ.

"You may as well stay the night in town," Campbell said casually, as Ewen started the car. "The police will want statements. I'll be in in the morning, tell them that."

"Righto," said Ewen.

James put his arm around Susan; she leaned back against him, careless of the interested eyes of the others. Why fight? All they could hope was that the car had not been tampered with. Through the open window she saw the flanks of the hills flow by. Nothing moved except the smaller branches, stirred by the wind. So much for James's hope of reinforcements. . . .

The car bumped uncomfortably along the track. Ewen was going rather too fast. They swung around a curve and headed for the main road. Susan's hasty breakfast began to churn in her stomach. If only they could persuade Ewen to check the car! She leaned forward. The man next to her—Alex—put a hand on her arm.

The car stopped on the verge where the track met the road. Ewen turned, his arm over the back of the seat.

"Okay," he said briskly. "Tell us more about your bloody treasure."

At first Susan thought she hadn't heard correctly. Her eyes blurred.

"You mean—you mean you believe us?"

Ewen shook his head. He looked very sober, and Susan realized how difficult it must be for him to admit the possibility of a flaw in his leader.

"I don't believe you, no. But there are a few peculiarities in the situation. Enough to cast a certain doubt."

"There are traditions about the Stone," said Alex, speaking for the first time. "Folklore is one of my specialties. When Ewen told us your wild yarn, I had to admit that it might make sense. And Peter—"

". . . has been doing his homework," said Peter precisely. "This site could not possibly be a Pictish town. I've been down to bedrock in several carefully selected areas, working on my own, and everything indicates an original occupation in the eighth century, followed by—"

"Enough," said Ewen. "We get the idea, Peter.

There's no sign of the whitewashed stones Campbell told us about. He's been behaving oddly. For one thing, he's been absent from the dig a good deal of the time. I've worked with him before, and as a rule he hovers like a hawk. And how did he know you had a car? You might have had bikes, or taken a bus. I'm still not convinced, mind, but a reasonable doubt has been established.''

James fell back limply against the seat.

"Thank God," he said devoutly. "We'll convince you, all right. Campbell knew we had a car because we—well, to be quite candid, we stole it from one of his chums. Look here, I think the easiest way of proving our story is to get back to the site. The lads will be hard at work as soon as they are sure you've left. We'll catch them in the act."

"Jamie, I don't like this," Susan said. "We'd be crazy to go charging in there now. You don't know how many of them there are—"

"Would you believe three?" James asked. "We've been as mistaken about them as they were about us, Susan; everybody seeing gangs all over the landscape. We were idiots not to suspect Campbell from the start. He selected the site, and he had the expert knowledge to interpret the clues he found. Something alerted him to the existence of what we have vaguely referred to as the treasure. Searching for more information, he looked up Tammas and his crowd. Gordon was a member of that group, and Gordon, unlike the others, was taken into Campbell's confidence. Maybe Campbell had to tell him the whole truth because he held the missing pieces of the puzzle—those family traditions he kept raving about. Or maybe Campbell realized that Gordon was mad enough to go along with his nefarious plans. Tammas would not have done so. He'd enter into a scheme to rescue Scottish treasures from the Sassenachs, yes; and that was probably how Campbell put it

to him. But Campbell is neither a patriot nor an altruist.
I don't know how he got in touch with Jackson; maybe
he had had dealings with him before, or had heard of
him through professional connections. It doesn't matter. He did contact Jackson, and Jackson was interested.
They don't need a gang. They've been using unwitting
persons, such as Ellie and the rest of you chaps, to do
their preliminary work. Once the treasure is located,
Jackson will sell it and they'll split the profits.''

"Even if there are only three of them, they're armed
and dangerous," Susan argued.

"Right. So we go in under cover, and scout the lay
of the land before we strike. All right?" James asked.

His audience, who had been following the debate in
absorbed silence, nodded as one man. They might not
be logically convinced, but by this time they were emo-
tionally involved, and, like all Scots, were rather looking forward to a fight. Susan's heart sank as she
contemplated their rapt faces. They knew Campbell
only as the conventional professor, and they didn't know
Jackson at all. They were like lambs being led to the
slaughter. And James was as bad as they were, with
less excuse, because he had faced the terrible threesome
already.

"Why can't we wait for the police?" she asked pit-
eously.

No one heard her. They were already scrambling out
of the car. There was nothing for Susan to do but bring
up the rear. She knew how Cassandra must have felt,
making inspired predictions nobody paid any attention
to. There was a further danger James apparently hadn't
considered. The gang might decide to wait until dark
before removing the treasure. If their newfound allies
sat around all afternoon watching the dig and saw nothing more sinister than Campbell calmly smoking his
pipe, they would start wondering whether they had been

had, and then she and James would be right back where
they had started.

All in all, the prospects did not look very bright.
Susan turned for a last despairing look along the
track. No cars, no policemen, no Hereditary Constables. . . . A gray squirrel sat up on its haunches, folded
its paws across its breast, and started after the retreating
procession.

"No," Susan told it. "You're no help at all."

Their first look at the site, from the old familiar post
up on the hill, confirmed her worst fears. It lay open
and deserted under the benevolent sun of midafternoon.
No one was visible, not even Campbell. Then they
heard sounds from the cavity of the crypt. Someone
was inside, working. The sounds were those of a chisel
on stone.

Susan looked apprehensively at Ewen. There was
Campbell, working away like a good little archaeologist, and nary a villain in sight. But Ewen seemed to
interpret the situation differently. His forehead wore the
now familiar wrinkles as he stared down at the pit.

"He's no business in there alone," he said. "We
agreed the place needs shoring up before we go on."

"Aye," said Alex slowly. Peter nodded.

"Let us gae doon and attack him," Dugald said.

"No, wait," Ewen said. "I'm still not sure. . . .
Where are the others, Erskine? You said they'd be hard
at work. And where is the van in which they mean to
carry the Stone away? That's a flaw in your argument,
you know; they could hardly hope to drive a van in and
out of here without being noticed by one of the crofters."

"They don't mind being noticed," James said.
"What does a closed van prove? Anyway, they don't
need a van. They aren't interested in the Stone; at least
Jackson and Campbell aren't. There's something down
there that is far more marketable than a chunk of rock.

Think, you brilliant scholars; what else would our loyal ancestors have hidden from the bloody English? It needn't be bulky; it might fit easily into the boot of a car.''

"Let us gae doon," Dugald repeated. His hands were balled into fists and his eyes glowed.

"Wait," Susan exclaimed. "You're going off half-cocked, on the basis of a lot of wild theories. You can't be sure there are only three of them. We don't know where Jackson is—"

"I can't resist that cue," Jackson said. He stepped out from behind a rock.

"Well, now," said Ewen, his eyes on the gun in Jackson's hand. "Well, now. You've convinced me, Erskine.''

"Rush him," said Alex. "He canna kill the lot of us—"

"No," Jackson agreed. "One will be sufficient." The gun moved around the group and centered on Susan's midriff. "Come here, Susan."

Following Jackson's orders, they moved down the hill toward the crypt. Jackson held Susan's arm and the muzzle of the gun bored into her back. As they reached level ground Campbell emerged from the excavation. He was not looking quite so trim. White dust smeared his trousers and hands. A scowl marked the intellectual serenity of his brow when he saw the group trudging toward him.

"Good God, not again!" he exclaimed. "Jackson, couldn't you—"

"No," Jackson said. "It's your fault. I told you we were being too easy on these fool kids."

"They do seem to be hard to get rid of," Campbell agreed. "Well, Jackson, I shall allow you to overrule me. Enough is enough. What about my loyal staff?"

"Not so loyal," Ewen said, glaring at him. "You took us for a pack of gullible fools, didn't you."

"No use trying to convince you of my innocence now," Campbell admitted. "I don't suppose any of you are susceptible to bribery? You've chosen a very poorly paid profession, gentlemen; it took me some years to come to that realization. Perhaps you are more precocious?"

The sullen faces around him were answer enough. He shrugged.

"They'll all have to go, I'm afraid," he remarked to Jackson.

"How do you plan to go about it?" Peter inquired curiously. "Massacres are a bit out of date, you know. We haven't indulged in that sort of thing for several hundred years, not since the Campbells—"

"Always the Campbells," Dugald growled. "Massacring MacDonalds at Glencoe, slaughtering fellow Scots at Culloden; Covenanters, Hanoverians—"

"Forget the insults," Campbell said, getting a little red. He turned, in response to a sound from the black hole behind him. Gordon came crawling out, covered with stone dust and blinking in the sunlight.

"What's the delay?" he demanded in his fussy, high-pitched voice. "We're almost through the wall; this is not the time. . . . Ah, Lord, who's that?"

"I've come back to haunt you," James said. "You and your bloody rack! You ought to be locked up, you maniac."

Gordon shrank back.

"It's Erskine," he cried. "Am I never to be rid of him? Oh, God, I didna mean—"

"Shut up," said Campbell, looking at Jackson. The exchange of glances did not bode well for Gordon. After all, Susan thought sadly, what's one more corpse? She and James would be blamed for the carnage; Jackson could shoot the other witnesses and then arrange to have her and James mashed under the stone of a collapsed crypt, or killed in a car crash, or any one of a number of alternatives. She sighed, and looked wistfully at the peaceful vista—gray crumbling stone and green meadows, sunlight sparkling on the waters of the burn. . . . Then her eyes widened.

"Look!" she cried out, forgetting the gun in her back. "Jamie, look!"

From among the trees, along the rocky track, an insane cavalcade poured. It looked like a cavalry charge, perhaps because it was led by a screaming figure on a big white horse. The figure was that of a small man wearing Highland garb; the ends of his plaid streamed out behind him and he was waving a sword over his head. Behind him came a more orthodox collection of jeeps, motorcycles, and cars. It was like a parade, and the villagers who had joined it to gape and shout added to the festive air.

"Whooppee!" Susan shouted. "Hurray! It's our reinforcements!"

She was thrown to the ground as James charged Jackson. A gun went off. The sound reminded Susan of an unpleasant fact she had overlooked; she rolled herself up like a hedgehog, arms over her head. But the impulse was only momentary. She didn't want to miss what was happening. She opened her eyes and rolled aside as a foot thudded onto the ground near her nose. The fight didn't last long. James needed some assistance from Peter in disposing of Jackson, but Alex knocked Gordon flat, and Ewen landed a magnificent blow on Campbell's jaw while the latter was groping for his pistol. Ewen *was* shouting, "Sons of the hounds . . ." Susan unrolled herself and sat up as the laird of Glen Ealachan came charging up, still brandishing his sword.

James ducked as the weapon whistled over his head.

"You bloody old maniac," he shouted at his sire. "Whose side are you on?"

The laird fell off his horse. The animal gave him a

contemptuous look before turning away to crop the grass.

"Jamie," the laird wheezed, leaning on his sword, which promptly bent. The laird sagged to his knees. James grabbed him by the collar and pulled him up.

"You never can do anything right," he snarled, his face inches from his father's. "Can't you do anything without turning it into a rotten farce?"

"Fine thinks I get for saving you," his father retorted, between gasps.

The Erskines were themselves again. Susan turned away and left them to it. Ewen and Peter had disappeared, leaving the others on guard over the recumbent prisoners. From the dark pit below a series of echoing blows resounded. A battalion of policemen was advancing in close order; they appeared somewhat uncertain as to what they were going to do when they reached the scene of action. A jeep bounced across the grass and stopped. From it stepped a tall, gray-haired man dressed in shabby tweeds, carrying a stick. He bowed to Susan, who was the only one looking at him; the Erskines were still shouting at each other, and the archaeologists were busy tying up the prisoners.

"We've not met," he said pleasantly. "But I believe I know who you are."

"You have the advantage of me," said Susan, in her best manner.

James broke off in the midst of a complicated description of his father's mental condition.

"He's the Hereditary High Constable. I told you I'd rung him."

"Ah, ye say that, do ye, ye wretch," screamed his father. "Good morning to ye, Lindsay," he added, nodding at the newcomer.

"How did you get here so fast?" Susan asked, accepting the hand the dignified gentleman extended.

"I was visiting a friend not far from here," answered

the High Constable. "The call was passed on to me there, so naturally I came straightaway. We all met on the road."

"That was lucky for us," Susan said. "Are you—I mean, are we under arrest or anything?"

"Now there never was much reason to suspect you of Tammas's death, was there? If you hadn't let this irresponsible young man rush you away so hurriedly, we'd have settled the matter in no time."

"Hmm," said Susan.

"Oh, I assure you, we're quite competent, young lady. The threads have been coming together. Miss Ellen Glascow, who reached a local police officer earlier this morning, was somewhat incoherent, but she admitted being involved in some sort of harmless student prank that had gone wrong. However, if we had not received Tammas's last message—"

"Message?" James broke off his tirade and turned.

"Oh, no," Susan said slowly. "Don't tell me all this was un—"

"Unnecessary?" Lord Lindsay smiled in a kindly fashion. "I'm afraid so, my dear. If you had only trusted us. . . ." He contemplated James's unkempt state and shook his head. "My dear boy, you look like one of Scott's less fortunate heroes. What a time you must have had! All for naught, I'm afraid. Tammas was once a canny lawyer. He left a letter to be delivered to me in case of his death, and he named Professor Campbell as the man to investigate should he meet with violence. I confess that my first reaction was incredulous; the professor is quite a respectable citizen. But investigation indicated that his recent financial transactions have been somewhat questionable. University funds. . . . We also learned that he had been seen in the company of a certain person who is wanted for illicit antiquities dealing in several countries. So, you see . . ."

"I see," said Susan.

"However, all's well that ends well," said Lindsay originally. "At least I trust it is ending well; young Erskine's message was garbled a bit in transmission, I fancy. Some fool in my office actually understood him to mention the Stone of Scone." He chuckled.

James, who had been looking crestfallen, drew himself up.

"You mean you don't know what the plot is all about? Tammas didn't explain it in his letter?"

"No. He merely named Campbell."

"Ah," said James. A smile spread over his abused countenance. "Lord Lindsay, we have a little surprise for you."

A hail from below ground interrupted him. It echoed eerily up into the air and was followed by Ewen and Peter. They moved slowly under the weight of a large chest bound with rusty metal. Under the fascinated eyes of the onlookers they deposited their burden on the ground.

"We haven't opened it yet," Ewen said, breathing quickly. "Who are you?" he added, looking at Lord Lindsay.

The latter drew himself up. "I, young man, am—"

"Never mind." Ewen dismissed him with a wave of his hand. "You open it, Erskine. If anyone has the right, you do."

James snatched the sword from his father's hand and inserted the blade into the crack between box and lid. The ancient lock was rusted; it gave at the first pressure and James threw the lid back.

At first Susan felt a sagging of disappointment. The box was filled with rusty, blackened scraps of metal without any discernible form. Then a spark winked darkly; a quick, brilliant blaze of light caught the light.

"Silver," Ewen said in an awed voice. "It was preferred over gold in the eighth and ninth centuries." He picked a small loose object out of the box. It shone crimson in his calloused palm.

"A ruby," Susan whispered. "Cut cabochon. They didn't know about faceting gem stones then."

"Probably a carbuncle," Ewen said. "Like the Black Prince's 'ruby.'"

"What is this?" Lord Lindsay was shaken from his aplomb. He dropped to his impeccably tailored knees and stared as eagerly as the others, while a babble of voices tried to explain things to him. Finally the gist of it penetrated.

"Good God," he exclaimed. "So that's what all the fuss was about. No wonder! Boys, you've done a splendid job. Whether this is part of the ancient regalia or simply some old Viking's treasure trove, you've earned a considerable reward. The Crown must pay the finder the full value, you know."

"The Crown," Ewen said. "Yes. It belongs to the Crown."

"It can't be Viking treasure," Peter said. "The Vikings were considerably later. All the indications—"

A universal howl drowned him out. Ewen stood up, leaving the others to investigate the chest. His eyes met those of James.

"And was that all there was in the crypt?" James asked in a low voice.

"Isn't that enough?" Ewen grinned through a mask of stone powder.

"Nothing else," James said. It was not a question.

"Nothing," said Ewen. "Only a lot of . . . stones."

From the laird of Glen Ealachan, who had followed the exchange interestedly, came a choking gurgle.

"Dad," James said warningly.

"What. Oh. Aye, aye, aye, it's fine laddies ye are, all o' ye." He choked again.

Susan shook her head. Men, she thought.

"I do think we ought to get James home," she said

to his father. "Can't you see he's just about ready to drop?"

"I am not!"

"Well, I am," said Susan tactfully. Lord Lindsay turned from his contemplation of the treasure.

"Yes, do run along, all of you. I'll take charge of matters here. By Jove, I am anxious to see the site of our splendid discovery! The most thrilling since Tutankhamen, I shouldn't wonder."

The new conspirators exchanged glances of alarm.

"It's frightfully unsafe, sir," Ewen began. "We took our lives in our hands down there; whole place is about to collapse."

"Give us a few days to shore it up," Peter added. "We couldn't possibly risk you down there, sir."

"And," said the laird, in a voice that brooked no argument, "ye'll have to come along and hear the bairns' evidence, Lindsay. The tale they'll have to tell! I've a bottle or two I've been saving for a special occasion. . . ."

"Very well," Lord Lindsay said. "I expect you're right about the excavation, boys; you're the experts, aren't you. I'll leave it to you, then. Of course I'll just take the chest of jewels along with me."

"Certainly, sir!"

"Very good of you, sir!"

"Come back tomorrow, sir," Peter added. "We'll have it all ready for you by then."

Lord Lindsay nodded graciously at them and turned away. Two husky constables picked up the chest and followed him toward the jeep.

Never had Susan experienced a silence so fraught with emotion as the one that followed Lord Lindsay's departure. The air fairly vibrated with drama; but none of the participants seemed able to find appropriate words.

"Well!" James said finally.

"Well," remarked Ewen.

"Thanks," said James.

"Oh." Ewen shrugged.

"Er—need any help?"

A slow transfiguring smile illuminated Ewen's face.

"We'll let you know," he said significantly.

"Yes," James said gloomily. "I expect you will. And I expect I'll be fool enough to—"

The speech ended in a gasp as the laird caught him in a mighty embrace.

"Jamie, Jamie! My son . . . my ain true son after all, a true Scot, true to the great traditions of his house! Och, the gift ye've gi'en Scotland this day. . . . I canna speak for greeting, tears of joy they are, that I should live to see this glorious moment—"

"I should live to see the day when you can't speak," James grunted, trying to free himself.

"Is this old—er—gent related to you?" Ewen inquired. "If so, try to shut him up before he gives the whole show away."

"I'll shut him up," James promised. "Dad. Dad! I spent the whole fifty pounds. And I owe—another hundred, at a guess."

The laird's beaming face slowly congealed.

"A hundred—"

"A new bike for the doctors," James said. "And the dress you—er—borrowed, Susan, we'll have to replace it. You seem to be frightfully hard on clothes. What else have we smashed along the way? That can't be all. . . . Oh, there's that cat of Gordon's. Splendid animal, excellent taste. I think we'll have to adopt it."

The laird took a deep quivering breath and rose to new heights of nobility.

"Dinna heed the siller," he said. "Naught is too guid for the gallant laddie that saved the—"

"Get him out of here," muttered Ewen, with an apprehensive glance at the policemen littering the landscape.

James looked at his father.

"You aren't planning to ride that poor horse all the way back to the castle, are you?"

"I could hardly do that," said his father self-righteously. "The puir beastie belongs tae one o' the crofters here. I found him innocently grazing a piece back. Jamie, I sometimes think your wits are lacking, lad. Did ye suppose I rode the creature all the way? The car's doon by the inn."

Susan began to laugh. The laird beamed at her.

"Och, it's a great ceilidh we'll have, you and I. All the auld songs, eh? What a day to celebrate! The first o' mony great days for bonnie Scotland—and the bonnie new lady o' Glen Ealachan! Mairi is making braw plans for the wedding. 'Twas only yesternicht she saw ye—the second sight, ye ken—coming doon the grand staircase in my auld grannie's wedding gown. The whiskey . . . the pipes . . . the loyal crofters . . ."

"Wait a minute," Susan gasped. "I'm not—Jamie isn't—"

James reached out a long, bare, dirty, bandaged arm and pulled her to his side.

"If you think we're going to live in that abandoned wreck of a castle you're daft," he remarked to his father, in the shout that was the normal Erskine conversational tone. "A nice flat in Edinburgh, that's the ticket."

"That's what's wrong with this generation," replied his father. "No respect for the traditions, the history. . . . Susan is different. She'll take you in hand, my lad. She understands these things. A wee lassie like Susan—"

James gagged audibly.

"Wee lassie! You get worse every day. Just when I think you have reached the absolute heights of frightfulness, you surpass yourself. And if you think I'm going to allow Susan to live anywhere near you, where you can contaminate her with your nonsensical ideas. . . .''

"She'll not need any teaching from me," bellowed his father. "She's a true Scot, a bonnie lassie. . . ." A sudden thought seemed to strike him. "By the bye," he said. "What is your name, my dear? MacDougal? Fraser? MacDonald?"

Susan drew herself up to her full five feet two inches.

"My name," she said proudly, "is Jezovnik."

James's arm tightened. Susan could feel him shaking with laughter. For a moment, the laird looked taken aback. Then a grin spread across his wrinkled face.

"Aye, weel, whisht," he said. "Nae doot there's a MacDonald somewhere i' the background."

"There is good reason to believe . . . that the true Stone, of very different quality from the shapeless lump of red sandstone hallowed for so long by later royal posteriors, never actually left Scotland, having been secreted away by the Abbott of Scone before Edward could lay hands on it."

Nigel Tranter, *Land of the Scots*.

BESTSELLING BOOKS FROM TOR

☐ 53103-5	SHADE OF THE TREE by Piers Anthony	$3.95
☐ 53104-3		Canada $4.95
☐ 53206-6	VOYAGERS II: THE ALIEN WITHIN by Ben Bova	$3.50
☐ 53207-4		Canada $4.50
☐ 53257-0	SPEAKER FOR THE DEAD by Orson Scott Card	$3.95
☐ 53258-9		Canada $4.95
☐ 53147-7	DRINK THE FIRE FROM THE FLAMES by Scott Baker	$3.95
☐ 53148-5		Canada $4.95
☐ 53396-8	THE MASTER by Louise Cooper	$3.50
☐ 54721-7	FLIGHT IN YIKTOR by Andre Norton	$2.95
☐ 54722-5		Canada $3.95
☐ 51662-1	THE HUNGRY MOON by Ramsey Campbell	$4.50
☐ 51663-X		Canada $5.95
☐ 51778-4	NIGHTFALL by John Farris	$3.95
☐ 51779-2		Canada $4.95
☐ 51848-9	THE PET by Charles L. Grant	$3.95
☐ 51849-7		Canada $4.95
☐ 50159-4	THE MILLION DOLLAR WOUND by Max Allan Collins	$3.95
☐ 50160-8		Canada $4.95
☐ 50152-7	TRUE CRIME by Max Allan Collins	$3.95
☐ 50153-5		Canada $4.95
☐ 50461-5	ONE OF US IS WRONG by Samuel Holt	$3.95
☐ 50462-3		Canada $4.95

Buy them at your local bookstore or use this handy coupon:
Clip and mail this page with your order.

Publishers Book and Audio Mailing Service
P.O. Box 120159, Staten Island, NY 10312-0004

Please send me the book(s) I have checked above. I am enclosing $_____
(please add $1.25 for the first book, and $.25 for each additional book to
cover postage and handling. Send check or money order only—no CODs.)

Name _____

Address _____

City _____ State/Zip _____

Please allow six weeks for delivery. Prices subject to change without notice.

MORE BESTSELLERS FROM TOR

THE BEST IN FANTASY

THE BEST IN HORROR

☐	51572-2	AMERICAN GOTHIC by Robert Bloch	$3.95
☐	51573-0		Canada $4.95
☐	51662-1	THE HUNGRY MOON by Ramsey Campbell	$4.50
☐	51663-X		Canada $5.95
☐	51778-4	NIGHTFALL by John Farris	$3.95
☐	51779-2		Canada $4.95
☐	51848-9	THE PET by Charles L. Grant	$3.95
☐	51849-7		Canada $4.95
☐	51872-1	SCRYER by Linda Crockett Gray	$3.95
☐	51873-0		Canada $4.95
☐	52007-6	DARK SEEKER by K.W. Jeter	$3.95
☐	52008-4		Canada $4.95
☐	52102-1	SPECTRE by Stephen Laws	$3.95
☐	52185-4	NIGHT WARRIORS by Graham Masterton	$3.95
☐	52186-2		Canada $4.95
☐	52417-9	STICKMAN by Seth Pfefferle	$3.95
☐	52418-7		Canada $4.95
☐	52510-8	BRUJO by William Relling, Jr.	$3.95
☐	52511-6		Canada $4.95
☐	52566-3	SONG OF KALI by Dan Simmons	$3.95
☐	52567-1		Canada $4.95
☐	51550-1	CATMAGIC by Whitley Strieber	$4.95
☐	51551-X		Canada $5.95

Buy them at your local bookstore or use this handy coupon:
Clip and mail this page with your order.

Publishers Book and Audio Mailing Service
P.O. Box 120159, Staten Island, NY 10312-0004

Please send me the book(s) I have checked above. I am enclosing $_____
(please add $1.25 for the first book, and $.25 for each additional book to
cover postage and handling. Send check or money order only — no CODs.)

Name _____

Address _____

City _____ State/Zip _____

Please allow six weeks for delivery. Prices subject to change without notice.

THE BEST IN SCIENCE FICTION

THE BEST IN SUSPENSE